Once Upon a Midwinter's Kiss

The Gardner Girls Series

A Novel by Fenna Edgewood

1

Flourish Art by Emmie Norfolk and Gordon Johnson (GDJ)

Special Thanks to: <u>Made Me Blush Books</u>

Lyrics included are from "The Death of the Hart Royal," a traditional English folk song found in the archives of Somerset folk song collector Ruth Tongue. Special thanks to Terri Windling for featuring the song on her blog.

http://www.fennaedgewood.com

Books by Fenna Edgewood

The Gardner Girls Series

Masks of Desire (The Gardner Girls' Parents' Story)

Mistakes Not to Make When Avoiding a Rake (Claire's Story)

To All the Earls I've Loved Before (Gwen's Story)

The Seafaring Lady's Guide to Love (Rosalind's Story)

Once Upon a Midwinter's Kiss (Gracie's Story)

The Gardner Girls' Extended Christmas Epilogue (Caroline & John's Story – Available to Newsletter Subscribers)

Must Love Scandal Series

How to Get Away with Marriage (Hugh's Story)

The Duke Report (Cherry's Story)

A Duke for All Seasons (Lance's Story)

The Bluestocking Beds Her Bride (Fleur & Julia's Story)

Fenna's Newsletter

Get the latest book updates, opportunities for ARCs (advance reader copies), giveaways, special promotions, sneak peeks, and other bookish treats, including a FREE special extended epilogue for the Gardner Girls series coming in late 2021, exclusively for subscribers.

www.fennaedgewood.com

Dedication

This one is for all of my ARC readers.

I am so very grateful for your time and effort. Thank you for not getting bored with my stories! (At least, not yet.) It is only October as I write this, but in the spirit of Gracie's story, I hope you have a very merry Christmas.

Prologue

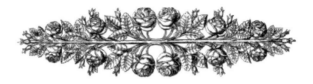

The child would live but the father would die.

But his boy would live.

Live, live, live, and go on.

The sand was wet and cool against the man's cheek. He could feel the waves lapping against his feet as he lay on the beach in the shallows.

He should get away from the water, away from the rising tide.

But he could not seem to move his body.

He would rest a while.

Soon someone would come.

The boy had run for help.

At first, the child, too, had lain as if dead on the sand and the father had feared the worst.

All of that sacrifice, only to have his boy die anyhow.

Well, it would still have been worth doing no matter what the outcome.

But then there had come the sounds of coughing and retching, and when the father had managed to open one eye, it was to see the small boy standing over him.

The child leaned down, kissed his cool cheek with his warm little mouth, and then with a choked sob, was gone.

He had run to get help. He was a good boy. A dear, brave lad. So much like his mother.

Time passed.

His mind repeated the moments in the water over and over as if in a living dream.

The terror, oh, the utter terror, of seeing the child go under, of thinking him lost.

He could not save his wife, but he had saved his boy. He had done that much.

A shadow stood over him, blocking the sun's warmth.

He struggled to open his eyes and with relief saw the familiar cloak and boots.

Would they not turn him over? Get him to a house? A warm fire? What were they waiting for, he wanted to cry?

But he had no strength left in him to complain or to protest. He could only be grateful that help had come.

Then, incredibly, he felt himself being pulled across the sand.

But not towards the grassy bluff nor towards the keep or village.

No, he was being dragged slowly back into the sea. Back towards death.

The water began to come up over his face and he sputtered.

His body wished to live, while his mind had already accepted its fate.

He felt a calmness. The sea was to take him after all.

At least it would end. This terrible pain in his heart would be put to rest.

But then he recalled his boy and his heart broke a second time.

The child had been saved, yes, but only for now. The wolf was on his doorstep.

How long would it be before his child joined him in these dark depths?

The water rushed over him and darkness fell.

Chapter 1

What country, friends, is this?

— Twelfth Night

November 28, 1827

Gracie was cold and wet and weary. Moreover, she was fairly certain the trickling of wetness down her face was not just snow but blood.

Yet she was not so weary as to not recognize a castle when she saw one.

If she were to guess, she would estimate she had been walking for almost three hours.

The snow had kept pace with her, soaking her to the bone. Now her arms were wrapped around herself in a futile attempt at keeping warm as she looked up in amazement at the vast stone fortress that lay in front of her.

It loomed out of the winter night, shadowy and forbidding—a motte-and-bailey castle on a grand scale, high on the top of an broad craggy hill.

The stone walls towered upwards, ancient and medieval, and stretched so far back into the darkness that Gracie could not see where they ended. There seemed room enough within those walls to enclose an entire village.

Soaring above the ramparts were the tops of higher structures—rounded guard towers, what looked like the stone steeple of a chapel, and looming over them all, a great square keep.

From where she was standing, Gracie could see two large circular towers flanking a huge arched gate house, from which had been drawn up a heavy portcullis gate. It was towards this that Gracie slowly maneuvered, uphill, in wet footwear and sodden clothes, slipping and tripping her way up the snow-covered crag until she reached the top and stood before the arch, breathless and uncertain.

If the portcullis had been lowered, she might have frozen to death that night. But whether by chance or custom, it had been left half-open.

She ducked beneath the latticed grate, then felt her head spin as she stood upright.

Inside the moated walls, all was quiet and still under the snowfall.

A number of small huts and buildings were within the walls of the bailey. Gracie saw a large stable, what looked like a blacksmith's workshop, and now that she was inside the walls, she could see there was indeed a small chapel with a high, narrow steeple.

Ahead of her lay the keep, with a wide wooden ramp leading up to a set of heavy-looking doors. Light streamed from small windows that dotted the first floor of the keep, and larger ones on the two storeys above.

As she walked up the ramp, her weariness nearly overcame her and she stumbled forward, righting herself just before she could come down hard on the slick wood slats.

She stood in the dark a moment, trembling. When the light-headedness had faded a little, she moved forward again, stepping more carefully.

She reached the doors, pushed a hand tentatively against one, and it moved very slightly beneath her touch.

She put more weight into it and this time, opened a gap large enough she could squeeze through.

As soon as she slipped inside the great stone hall, she felt a welcome wave of warmth.

A fire was lit towards the end of the hall and braziers burned along the walls. A large iron chandelier hung overhead, filled with lit candles. In front of her was a narrow staircase with shallow stone steps, twisting up into the second storey.

Inundated by the warmth and the light, Gracie closed her eyes. That was a mistake, for her body seemed to take it as permission to succumb to exhaustion.

Head-spinning and vision a blur, she fell forward onto the floor.

She crumpled like a petticoat and lay there, stunned.

She was not swooning, she told herself. She never swooned.

She had merely intentionally collapsed on the floor until she had regained sufficient energy to return to a standing position.

And then a warm hand touched her brow and from that point, her mind flitted in and out of awareness. Later, some parts of the night would be clear as day, while others merely a haze.

"The boy is soaked to the bone," a worried female voice announced from somewhere near Gracie's ear. "We must get him upstairs and into a bed."

"Might not get a chance, my girl," Gracie heard an older man's voice mutter. He sounded gruff but kind, and reminded Gracie of the Gardners' old groom, Arthur. "Not if *he* has anything to say about it."

"Hush now," the woman whispered, anxiously.

"What is this?" A second man's voice barked, harsh and commanding. "Who lies there? Get them up. Get them out of the keep."

"Would you not like to know who it is first, sir, before you turn them out into the storm?" The woman asked, her tone deceptively mild.

"We do not take in travelers, Mrs. Lennox, as you well know. Nor do we offer shelter to vagrants. He may have broken in to steal—or worse, murder us all in our beds," the cold male voice responded.

"He's a scrawny lad. Doesn't seem much of a threat to me. He can't steal much lying on the floor now, can he?" The older man observed. "Don't see how it's much of a plot to open a door and fall down."

"Ah, and this is why you are not paid to think, Mr. Lennox," the second man snapped, haughtily. "That is my task. Prince-wood's safety is my responsibility, and I say get them gone."

"Where would you have us put him?" The man called Mr. Lennox asked, sounding exasperated. "Should we lay him outside the walls to die in the snow?"

"I do not care where you put him," the other man replied. "As long as he is outside of the keep."

"We'll simply have to haul him back in again in the morning, you know. To prepare him for burial, that is. Unless you'd like to leave him there to rot and have flowers sprouting from his bones by springtime," Mr. Lennox said, sounding danger-ously, cheerfully cocky.

"Here comes the true master of the house, Cam," the woman murmured. "We'll see what he has to say about it now, won't we, you arrogant old fool."

"What have we here, Mrs. Lennox?"

The voice was young, male, and sounded aristocratic. In contrast to the other man's cold imperiousness, the young man's tone was warm and curious.

"A stranger seeking shelter from the cold, my lord," Mrs. Lennox said, loudly. "The poor lad is injured as well. There is blood on his head, you see, here and..."

"Warburton wants us to toss him outside the walls," Mr. Lennox spoke up helpfully. "Suppose I'll go and fetch Jasper to help me carry the poor sod..."

"Very well, Mrs. Lennox. That is quite enough. Carry him to the stables," the older man interrupted curtly, evidently sensing his position was about to weaken.

"The stables?" Mrs. Lennox exclaimed, clearly dissatisfied. "But I..."

"Mrs. Lennox, we have plenty of rooms to spare, do we not?" The young man interjected, quickly. "If you would be so kind, Mr. Lennox, as to carry our guest upstairs. Perhaps the Blue Room, Mrs. Lennox?"

He was softspoken, yet firm.

There was a strange and sensual quality to his voice which sent a chill running through Gracie—as if she had sipped from a goblet of hot wine or spicy cider. A glowing rush of warmth and light.

She gave a little moan and struggled to open her eyes, curious to see the new speaker.

Instead, she was blinded for her efforts—the glare of light too much. She closed them again quickly. At least she had been able to open them. She was not dead, then. Though she could hardly feel her extremities.

"Tsk, tsk, the poor lad's fingers are nigh blue with cold," Mrs. Lennox fretted. "Come now, Cam, pick him up. I'll go and have the room prepared."

Gracie felt a hand touch her head gently, then a light breeze as the woman rose and walked away.

"Would you like my assistance, Mr. Lennox?" The young man asked, politely. "Or shall I fetch Jasper?"

"Oh, no, sir. Thank you, sir," Mr. Lennox replied. Gracie felt a strong male arm sliding beneath her knees. "I'll manage. Not so old as that yet."

"Of course not, Mr. Lennox," the young man said. There was a smile in his voice. "You're as strong as an ox and likely to live a hundred years or more."

Gracie was in Mr. Lennox's arms now, her weight against his chest. She felt the rumble as he laughed appreciatively.

"Aye, a hundred years. Poor Paulina wouldn't know what to do with me for another fifty," he guffawed.

"Do you think he will be all right, Cam?" the young man asked, worriedly. His concern made him sound more youthful. "He looks so pale."

"There's life in him yet. Mrs. Lennox will have him hearty and hale in no time," Mr. Lennox said, confidently.

"And then he'll be around to slit our throats in the night," the man they had called Warburton proclaimed. "Princewood has had enough bloodshed. We must keep strange folk out and protect our own."

"Protect our own," Mr. Lennox muttered to himself, beginning to tread up the stairs. "That's rich, coming from him, it is. And what did he do to keep our lord and lady alive?"

Gracie wished she could make her eyes stay open—or even find her tongue to thank him for his kindness, but she was too groggy.

She listened to the voices like something from out of a dream, unable to participate in the scene and fearing she would not recall any of it come morning.

"We will have to take our chances this time, Warburton," the young man was saying, down below. "We have a duty to the stranger as well as to our own people. I cannot in good conscience turn him away, especially on a night like this."

The voices were fading the further Mr. Lennox went up the stairs.

He shifted her a little in his arms.

"Light for a lad," he observed to himself. "Though you look no older than our Jasper."

Finally, there was the sound of a door being pushed open.

"Here you are, Mrs. Lennox," the good-natured man announced. "Your package has arrived."

"Thank you kindly, Mr. Lennox. Please place the package on the bed," Mrs. Lennox answered, sounding amused. "He's a fine-looking lad, isn't he?" She leaned over the bed to push some hair from Gracie's face, and frowned. "Here now," she said. "His cap can come off. It's soaking wet and not doing him much good, poor thing."

The cap was removed.

There was silence for a moment.

"Oh, my," Mrs. Lennox said.

"You can say that again, love," Mr. Lennox agreed. "What now?"

"Now nothing," the older woman said, firmly. "Boy or girl, they needed a bed and some warmth."

Mr. Lennox chortled. "They'd have been out in the cold before you or I could say naught about it if that sly dog had known he was a she."

"True enough," Mrs. Lennox mused. "It seems one of that silly old man's aims to keep all young women away from our master. So, better that they don't find out. Yet."

"Yet?" Mr. Lennox said, raising his brows. "You make it sound as if the lad... I mean, the lass... will be with us some time."

"Perhaps she shall," Mrs. Lennox said. "We could certainly use a fine girl about the place."

"Oh, ho, ho," Mr. Lennox crowed. "I see. It's like that, is it?"

"Oh, shush now," Mrs. Lennox hissed. "Don't pretend you don't agree with me. That young lady—and I use the term lightly—isn't fit to... Well, you know very well what she isn't fit for."

"She doesn't fit our lord. Doesn't suit him at all," Mr. Lennox concurred. "But no one has asked us for our opinions."

"Aye, but they should have," Mrs. Lennox said, her eyes flashing. "Haven't we known him longer than anyone? We were both there when he was born. We were there as he was raised. We knew his mother and his father both. And what's more, we care for him more than either of those... those...Oh, pish posh."

"Lost your words again, Paulina?" Mr. Lennox asked, cheerily. "The rooster and the cold fish are what I like to call 'em in my own head."

"I'll not resort to insults, thank you very much," Mrs. Lennox huffed. "She's a lady, I suppose. Though I don't like her much, she's a lady nevertheless. Aye, she's cold and standoffish, but perhaps there is good in her...somewhere. Regardless, the young lady's not the right match for our lord."

"Is this one a lady?" Mr. Lennox asked, curiously. "What do you make of her, Paulina?"

Mrs. Lennox moved back to the bed. "She's not dressed like one with these rough boy's clothes. I wonder why she has put them on."

"Mayhap she's running away from something. Or someone. Mayhap she is a murderer like Warburton said," Mr. Lennox said, gruesomely optimistic.

"Nonsense," Mrs. Lennox announced. "She's a harmless girl and a pretty one now that she's turning from blue to pink again. She's been gently reared, I'll wager it. She'll have her own clothes some place. Nicely made ones, too, I'm sure."

"Skinny little thing," Mr. Lennox said, doubtfully. "Sure she's not a boy? Though boy or girl, there is something rather pixie-like about her. Perhaps she's a changeling left by the fairies. Rather old for that though, I suppose."

"She's a girl, I tell you, and that's all there is to it. Now listen here, Mr. Lennox," his wife said, suddenly. "Not a peep to anyone about this young sir being a miss. Not yet."

"What's that? Why not?" Mr. Lennox demanded.

"Just listen now, Cam. Let the master figure it out for himself. It's none of our business when he does or doesn't," she advised.

"If he doesn't?" Mr. Lennox asked.

"He's not a fool," she said. "But it will give her some time."

"Time without that one breathing down her neck? Or time for you to pull loose that thread you've had your eye on? Oh, don't scoff at me, Paulina. I've seen the look on your face more than once. Can't say I don't wonder the same. The years go by and soon it will be too late to try to mend what is broken at all," Mr. Lennox said, with a sigh.

There was a silence.

"Very well, love. I'll play along. Nothing to lose, I suppose," he said, softly.

"And everything to gain," Mrs. Lennox said, softly, smoothing Gracie's hair again. "Sleep well, my dear. Rest now. And when you rise, I hope you're the maiden we wish you to be, for all our sakes."

Chapter 2

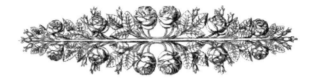

I'll say as they say, and persevere so,

And in this mist at all adventures go.

— The Comedy of Errors

Eight Hours Earlier

The day had started off well enough, with little to indicate that it would conclude with Gracie lying on a castle floor, dressed as a boy, after a terrifying attack in the woods in the midst of a blizzard.

In hindsight, however, perhaps her luck had begun to fail that very morning when Matilda, her chaperone, had come down with a cold and had to be left behind at the inn.

The chatterbox of a cook had come along with Gracie from Orchard Hill, officially as a chaperone, but in fact to see her sister who worked in the Crawfords' house.

As for the Crawfords themselves, Gracie had begun regretting her decision to accept their invitation to visit them in Scotland for a few weeks at Christmastime almost as soon as she and Matilda stepped into the coach.

It had soon become abundantly clear that Matilda was much more eager for the visit than Gracie.

As long-time friends of her mother, Caroline Gardner, there was nothing untoward about the family receiving such an invitation.

But when the invitation was pointedly directed to Gracie, with a separate, shorter letter addressed explicitly to her from John Crawford, everyone had known what it really meant.

And what it meant was impending doom.

Or, marriage.

However, one wished to view it.

To Gracie they were now one and the same.

She had spent the last three days wishing she had never accepted the infernal invitation, had never met John Crawford when she was a little girl and he a little boy, and had never left Orchard Hill.

Back home, her three sisters, mother, and all their extended families—brothers in law, nephews, nieces—would be gathering together. There would be feasting, dancing, games, and other boisterous fun.

And Gracie would miss it all.

All because she had fallen prey to a young man's flattering attentions and fooled herself into believing she might be able to reciprocate his interest.

But as hour after hour passed in the coach, the more certain Gracie was that she could not. John was her friend and nothing more. What had happened between them two years ago had been a mistake and one she immensely regretted.

She had only just turned eighteen-years-old and was certainly not ready for marriage, a family, or the words which sent a chill through her veins—"settling down."

In fact, Gracie was not sure she ever really wanted to *settle down*. Or that she was fit for marriage. To anyone.

But now John had gotten it into his head that he and Gracie were all but betrothed.

When the truth was that Gracie would make him a terrible wife.

Furthermore, if John Crawford were to find out that Gracie had spent a not inconsiderable portion of her young life working as a cabin boy—dressing in boy's clothes, living unchaperoned amongst sailors, engaging in the most menial of labour and hardly bathing for weeks on end—it would tarnish his view of her even more.

He was likely to recoil in revulsion at the idea of a young lady of his acquaintance having crossed such boundaries—and worse, of having enjoyed doing so.

For the truth was that Gracie felt just as much herself when she was playing a boy as she did when playing a girl.

Playing was all it was, either way, really.

She was still her very own self underneath it all, wasn't she?

But that was a minority viewpoint, to say the least.

An insecure young man puffed up with burgeoning masculinity would not find the idea of taking a wife who thought little of engaging in such defiant playacting.

Nor would Gracie wish to be married to such a young man, when it came down to it. Insular and unadventurous, content to live the life his parents had lived before him.

And so, really, when the coach was attacked on the third day, as they traveled through Northumberland, Gracie was quite ready for the interruption.

Which was tragically ironic in hindsight.

Gracie had spent the morning in the coach alone. The only other person there was the coach driver, a young man who looked not much older than herself.

They had briefly paused for a midday meal. If all went according to the same schedule as the days before, then in another hour or so, they would stop again to allow the driver a break and her, the sole passenger now, a chance to take some air.

But rather than going according to schedule, three things happened in quick succession.

A heavy snowfall began, bringing an early twilight to the forest.

The coach was attacked.

And Gracie saw the white stag.

She had been gazing out at the forest, and envying the trees. Trees had no need for marriage or attachments. They did not have to concern themselves with being male or female. They simply *were*.

Primordial. Mysterious. With lifespans of hundreds of years.

An especially large and gnarled oak caught her attention and she looked at it with interest. Its trunk was immense, wider than the carriage in which she sat by far.

What marvels had trees such as this one witnessed through their long lives? Monarchs rising and falling. Wars fought, men killed, their blood spilled to water those archaic roots. Love trysts consummated on the mossy carpet between the ridged trunks.

How unfathomable centuries were when one was a mere eighteen years old.

The woodland they were passing through was vast and its perennial occupants ancient. Some of the trees must have been centuries, if not thousands, of years old. Gracie spotted ash, rowan, oak, and yew. Their boughs stretched out above the road, meeting in the middle to form a high arched ceiling under which the coach rolled.

While it was only midday, the dense growth of the forest blocked out much of the dim winter light.

Now a heavy snow had begun to fall.

The branches of the trees were swiftly weighed down with white, thickening the canopy overhead.

With a start, Gracie realized that if the snow continued, the journey could stretch.

What should have been two more days of travel in fair weather could become seven on snowy roads. Matilda would be waiting for the Crawfords' carriage to return for her in a few days and losing her mind with impatience and boredom.

The coach had already begun to slow its pace, no doubt hindered by the snow.

And then it suddenly stopped.

For a moment, Gracie sat patiently waiting. But when they did not begin to move again, she opened the window and peered out.

The falling snow distorted her view, the large white flakes coming down heavy and thick.

Gracie did not see the driver. Perhaps the carriage had gotten stuck and he had stepped down to try to free it.

All was quiet. Unnaturally so.

"Driver! Are you there?" Gracie called out, feeling rather foolish to still be sitting inside. "Shall I step out and help?"

There was no answer.

"Fiddlesticks," she muttered, and reached over to open the door.

And then she heard the driver scream.

The sound seemed to go on forever.

She froze in place, her hand still poised upon the door.

As suddenly as it had begun, it stopped. There was not another.

Gracie clenched her jaw. It had been a cry of pain. The driver was injured. She must go to him and help as best she could, not sit like a frightened rabbit in a hutch.

It was an admirable plan until she heard the horses beginning to panic.

They were snorting and stamping and squealing.

The carriage began to rock back and forth as they reared and pulled, trying to break free from their harness.

The coach was rolling forward and backwards, and it was all Gracie could do to keep from falling off the bench.

And then the horses succeeded. Their panic had made them powerful and the shafts must have broken.

She heard the pounding sound of hoofs and then things happened very quickly.

The coach was rocking and rolling as the horses left it behind. At first, slowly; then faster.

There was no ditch to speak of to break its path. It was rolling off the road, straight into the trees.

And then it hit them. Hard. The carriage shook with the force of the collision, and began to tip.

Gracie slid from one side of the bench to the other, slamming shoulder-first into the coach wall with a cry of pain.

For the next few moments, the entire world was upside down.

Her head smashed into the carriage roof.

It was an old coach, cushioned with a luxurious faded velvet in the interior, including a soft padded roof. If it were not for that, she might have broken her neck.

As it was, she felt a painful wrench and closed her eyes from the sharp pain.

She fell back heavily, hitting her forehead against the carriage door, as the coach finished its inevitable descent onto its side and then moved no more.

Time passed.

Slowly Gracie put a hand to her forehead. When she drew it away there was red on her fingertips.

She lay still. Just a few more minutes to get her bearings.

Then she thought of the driver. Was he still out there somewhere? Had the carriage rolled right over him?

She forced herself up, standing on the door. It was fortunate she was tall and fairly strong, for to get out of the carriage she realized she would have to clamber up through the opposite door which was now above her head.

She jumped. Once, twice. She pushed it open, then grabbed hold of the frame and pulled herself up.

The exterior of the coach was slippery with snow. As she came out the hole, she began to slide, face forward. Her arms reached out in panic as she tried to brace herself, but it was no use and she fell unceremoniously into snow-covered grass and brambles.

The stars were out, she saw, looking up through the tree branches as she lay on her back.

She felt dizzy and ill. She closed her eyes.

Slowly the cold and the wet began to claim her attention more than the pain, and she became uncomfortably aware that she was laying in the muck, soaking wet, and freezing cold as the snow continued to fall on and around her.

When she opened her eyes and lifted her chin a little, she could see she was already coated in snow—like a statue in a garden, lifeless and still.

But she was not lifeless.

Merely soaking wet, and...

She struggled to her feet and looked about.

She was quite alone.

The coach lay on its side, sadly desolate. She did not see the coachman's body beneath, thank heavens.

Items had been flung or fallen from the coach as it crashed, including her valise which was now crushed beneath one wheel.

She stepped towards it, hoping to perhaps pull some dry item of clothing out from underneath, but it was no good. The valise was wedged beneath the heavy wooden frame, along with other items the coach must have been delivering—small brown-papered parcels, a canvas bag which perhaps belonged to the driver.

The driver! Where could he be?

Gracie lurched to her feet and walked slowly around the carriage.

Her heart sank as she saw drops of blood in the snow, on the driver's seat. She followed the blood back up and onto the road where the carriage had first come to a stop.

There was a great deal more of it there.

The trail of red ran into the woods.

Perhaps the driver had been injured but managed to flee into the forest.

Or perhaps he had been dragged.

There were scuff marks along with the blood, like the rut made when pulling something heavy.

Gracie stood there, peering into the dark trees, shivering, and feeling more terrified than she had ever been in her life.

In the end, she decided she was a coward—for she found that no matter how much she urged herself to step forward and follow the trail, her body would simply not obey, no matter how awful she might feel for the poor young man.

She rubbed her arms, feeling the soaked thin muslin.

This would not do. She could not stay here. Would not stay here.

But it was also incredibly daunting to consider the prospect of continuing along the road in a blizzard to seek aid and shelter, with the wind picking up, sending icy blades cutting through her damp dress with every gust.

She could shelter in the carriage overnight and wait until someone passed by. But the thought of spending the night alone in the dark in the middle of these woods was decidedly unpleasant.

The was the sound of a snapping tree branch.

It came from the direction the driver had gone.

Filled with hope, she shouted before she could think, calling loudly for the driver. Perhaps the poor man had stumbled off the road but was now making his way back. He would be cold, injured, and disoriented.

But there was no reply to her calls nor did anyone emerge.

That did not mean that no one was there, however.

Gracie stood frozen, in the dark, staring into the trees. Which was hopeless for from the road, she could see nothing but blackness. The moon and the stars were out, reflecting off the snow, lighting the road and the coach and herself...but doing nothing for the space beyond where the trees closed in.

Someone could be standing there now, watching her.

Another twig snapped. This one closer still.

She felt very certain it was not the driver.

Moreover, she was afraid she was going to scream. Very undignified and unbecoming a bold Englishwoman, but she did not think she would be able to help it.

Something was coming out of the woods and she could not see it.

This was why humans had invented fire. Oh, her kingdom for a flaming torch!

And then the stag appeared.

It came from the opposite side of the road and for a moment Gracie wondered if she were dreaming for the stag was a pure white.

It was immense. In the moonlight, its coat glowed like alabaster-marble, gleaming wet with melted snow. The hart's dark brown eyes were wide, proud, and unblinking. Upon its head sprouted branch-like antlers, wild and beautiful, far more magnificent than any human-made crown could ever be.

The creature came towards her slowly, claiming her attention and distracting her from her terror.

When it was no more than a stone's throw away, it stopped, staring down at her.

It was otherworldly and towered above her. And so, perhaps at another time, Gracie might have been unnerved. Even afraid.

But right now, all she felt was awe mixed with a strange thankfulness.

Another twig snapped on the other side of the road. It sounded as if it were further away this time. Gracie did not even turn her head.

Whatever it was, whatever malignant thing had lurked there, the white hart was as opposite to it as light from dark. Pure and radiant and protective.

It watched her silently, curious and wise, regal and strong, and Gracie felt an urge to cry.

She was not alone. A creature pure and bright had come to her aid, gracing her with its presence.

She took a step towards it, hesitantly. Then another.

The white stag was lowering its head, and for an instant she believed it might actually allow her to touch it.

Then an owl hooted loudly from a nearby tree, and quick as a flash, the stag turned heel and bolted back into the forest in the direction it had come.

She was alone again.

Yet somehow, less alone than before.

It was time to leave. She had received one miraculous reprieve. There would not be another.

A gust of wind blew across the road, sweeping snow against her skirt and reminding her of her discomfort.

She would look just once more, she decided, in case she had missed something. Anything that might protect her from the bitter cold.

She walked around the coach slowly, and this time, looked more carefully at the toppled driver's seat.

There was a compartment next to the bench, stuffed with what looked like rags.

She gave them a tug.

Her hopes were realized. The driver had used the compartment to stash away an extra set of clothes.

There was a hat, a pair of trousers, a homespun shirt. And most precious of all, a coat. Not as thick as Gracie would have liked, but mostly dry, and with pockets.

She ducked behind the coach and began to change.

Chapter 3

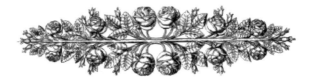

Who ever loved that loved not at first sight?

— As You Like It

"Do not even think of opening that door, Jasper," Linden said.

The young man he was addressing turned guiltily to face him.

Jasper Lennox was a dark-haired young man with a face as impish as a pixie's and a penchant for mirth. Around Princewood, such levity was a rare thing.

"The boy needs to rest, Jasper," Linden said, firmly. "Not to mention his privacy."

"Yes, but..." Jasper began.

"But nothing. I'm not leaving you alone in this corridor so you'd best just walk along with me. I'm headed to the stables. Perhaps you'd like to come along for a ride?" Linden suggested.

Despite their differences in position, Jasper was his closest friend. His only friend, really.

"Yes—but—" Jasper said again, drawing out the words. "You can't tell me you aren't curious about him. A young man wanders into a castle on a dark snowy night and collapses. It's like the start of a fairy tale."

Linden rolled his eyes. "And will this fairy tale end with the young man falling into your arms?"

Jasper elbowed him hard, but was grinning. "Perhaps. I cannot say for certain until I have seen his face now, can I? He might have warts. Or be missing ten teeth."

"Ten? What if he was only missing two?" Linden inquired.

"Then I would seriously consider him," Jasper replied, before cackling with laughter.

Linden raised his eyebrows. "And what about Peter in the village? Won't he be heartbroken if you take up with someone else?"

Jasper frowned. "I am not sure how much Peter would care. It might not bother him as much as you fear." He looked at Linden. "My mother tells me that Warburton wished to throw the stranger out in the snow to die. Is it really true?"

"That is... a little exaggerated," Linden replied, evenly. "Warburton is overly-cautious. His immediate thought was our safety—" He caught Jasper's expression. "What?"

"You flatter him, Linden," Jasper said, dryly. "When you credit Warburton with thinking of the good of anyone but himself."

It was Linden's turn to frown. "He can be difficult to get along with, I know. But he has been the steward here for many years. He means well. Furthermore..."

"Yes, yes," Jasper interrupted. "He knew your parents. He was your father's most loyal friend. Your parents trusted him and so do you. He saved your life. You are engaged to his daughter. I know the speech."

"Well, it is all true," Linden said, quietly.

"You are doing him a service by marrying that harpy of a girl," Jasper scolded. "Not the other way around, you know, Linden. Pretty or not, no one else would take her off his hands with such a temperament."

They were nearing the castle doors. They pushed through them and stepped out into the sunlight. It was a crisp winter morning. The storm had let up hours before, and now the snow was already beginning to melt under the sun's rays.

As they tramped through the courtyard, Linden tried to form the best response. He knew Jasper and Fleur disliked one another.

"Fleur," he said, finally. "Has many fine qualities."

He tried to ignore the snorting sounds Jasper was making.

"I have known her from childhood," he continued, ignoring him. "My parents approved of the match. This was one of their last wishes for me. And I will honor that." He sighed.

"You might have some pity for the girl, Jasper. I do not think she wishes to marry *me*."

Jasper chortled. "Who wouldn't want to marry you? You've the disposition of a saint, are as handsome as a devil—though where that expression came from, I really don't know. Aren't devils and demons supposed to be hideous creatures? Oh, yes, and you possess a castle, a village, and most of Princewood forest, while Fleur has no dowry to speak of and could sour a pitcher of milk with a single glance. Have I forgotten anything?"

He had forgotten love, Linden almost said. But he held his tongue. He knew it would be taken as a complaint, and so he would not mention it for he knew how Jasper would react.

Jasper would say a marriage without love or passion was a ridiculous way to go through life and that Linden most certainly did not love Fleur, nor she him, nor were they even remotely attracted to one another, and so they were bound to make one another miserable for so long as they both should live.

Then Linden would argue that he did *love* Fleur—which was true. At least, he was fairly certain he did. He cared for her welfare. She was like a sister to him.

A very crochety, slightly-frightening younger sister.

After they wed, she would become more. Their feelings for one another would kindle with time.

He had to believe that.

He had to believe that when Warburton reminded him over and over again that this match was one of the things his parents had believed would guarantee his happiness, that his parents had known something which he did not.

He would trust them, then, and marry the girl they had chosen for him.

No matter what.

They had reached the stables.

"Will you ride through the village?" Jasper asked. "Perhaps we might even visit the tavern?"

Linden's face hardened. "I do not think that would be a good idea."

"Oh, Linden," Jasper said, softly. "You cannot hide forever."

"I am not hiding," Linden said, looking down. "But I cannot pretend I enjoy spending time in the village amongst people who look at me only with fear and hatred in their eyes."

"They don't hate you," Jasper insisted. "They don't. Some are afraid, that is true. But you could change that. Years and years of exaggerations and rumors that were never put to rest. That is all it is. If you desired, if you tried...."

"Let us get to the horses, shall we?" Linden interrupted, trying to keep his tone light but wishing to change the subject.

Jasper stood indecisively for a moment. "On second thought, if you would not mind, I believe I'll walk into the village." He saw Linden's smile. "Yes, yes. I'll visit Peter."

Peter Carson was the village schoolmaster, a quiet but capable young man who was well-liked by his young pupils.

"You are fond of him," Linden said. "He is good for you."

"Yes, well," Jasper muttered. "His parents would probably not agree with you about that."

Linden shrugged. "He is a grown man. Who he chooses to spend time with is his own business." He hesitated. "You are...cautious though, Jasper? There are some who..."

"Yes, yes, I know," Jasper said, with resignation. "There are some who would not take kindly to two men stepping out together. We are discreet. Well, relatively," he reflected. "There was this one time in the stables during the summer when..."

"Spare me the details, I beg you," Linden pleaded, blushing a little.

He was happy for his friend's happiness. But Jasper's stories of passion also served to remind him that he had never experienced anything close to what his friend described—and quite possibly never would.

Gracie woke with a splitting headache and a growling stomach.

The last time she had felt similarly was after a May Day festival two years back when she had ingested too much elderberry wine and become very silly...and very foolish. That was not a mistake she wished to make again.

The events of the previous night came flooding back as she pushed herself upright and tried to clear her head.

Her arduous trek through the snow.

Sighting the castle in the dark, like something from another time.

Pushing open the door.

And then...warmth and people.

But before that. The coach accident in the forest.

No, do the poor driver justice and call it what it was—an attack.

Though by what or whom, she still did not know. In the light of day, however, it seemed obvious it could not have been mere bandits. Highwaymen preferred to leave their victims where they found them. They certainly did not drag them off into the woods, leaving valuables behind or good horses to run off.

Gracie's heart beat faster as she remembered the white stag, mighty and majestic.

She had not imagined it. The creature had been real, though admittedly seemed supernatural. The stag's antlers should not have been there at all, for one. Harts grew their antlers through summer, only to have them drop off as winter neared, regrowing them in the spring—a regenerative cycle of death and birth. But perhaps the white stag was exempt from the laws of nature which bound its fellow creatures.

Gracie recalled a story her father had read to her as a child. A young hunter spotted a white hart and chased it through the forest, only to become hopelessly lost within its brambling paths. Deeper and deeper the hunter went, following the hart, until the young man reached the very heart of the woods and encountered...

What was it he had encountered?

Gracie wracked her brain but could not recall how the story had ended. She had loved the tale, and yet strangely could not remember if the ending had been a happy or a sad one. Had the hart led the hunter to good or ill?

With a sigh, she pushed down the coverlet and began to take stock of her surroundings.

She was in a bed. A very comfortable bed with heavy dark crimson and gold curtains drawn around her to keep the warmth inside. As she sat up and poked her head out, she could feel the chill in the room. There had been a fire in the hearth but it had gone out and a maid had not yet come to rebuild it.

From the position of the sunlight on the wall it looked to be about mid-morning. She had slept much later than usual.

She slid out of the bed, landing lightly on the stone floor.

The bedchamber may have been medieval but it was surprisingly cozy. Tapestries hung along the two largest walls and braided mats covered the floor, helping to keep warm air in and drafts out.

There was a window at the back of the room beside the bed. Not an arrow-slit kind like Gracie had always imagined all castles to have, but an arched, leaded window with glass panes. The castle was hundreds of years old but evidently some effort had been made to modernize it.

Peering out, Gracie could see that she was high up in the castle. Perhaps a second or third floor.

Down below, servants in the courtyard were going about their daily routines. There were a few small children running around as well. She spotted fenced in areas holding chickens and goats.

The blizzard had ended as quickly as it had begun. Only a few clean white patches of snow remained. The sun was out and the day seemed mild.

None of this was particularly surprising. But there was one thing she had missed at first.

As she looked beyond the courtyard, up and over the battlements, she caught her breath—for past the castle was broad blue sea.

She had come through the forest and had expected to see it surrounding the castle on all sides.

But beyond the courtyard to the east were sandy beaches in both directions and crystalline waters.

Gracie's heart leapt with excitement at being near the ocean again. She had been landlocked for years. Now, the sight of the white capped waves and sea birds flying over the waters was enough to fill her with anticipation.

Being on a ship had been the closest thing to pure happiness she had ever experienced.

But being near the sea was the next best thing to being on a ship.

She wanted to be down there, walking along that beach. It would be cold closer to the water. She would need to be properly dressed.

Gracie touched a hand to her head. There was a lump on her forehead and bits of dried blood came away. The wound still throbbed with pain, but she had rested as much as she could. She was not about to lie in bed all day.

She tried to remember how she had been injured. First, in the carriage as it rolled.

Unluckily, she had also slipped and fallen in the forest, hitting her head against a tree, the second injury right on top of the first bump.

It might have been much worse. She had been stunned from the fall. If she had not forced herself up and out of the snow, she might not be alive now.

But she was. Though she did not know where precisely.

Who had she to thank for her accommodations?

Furthermore, where were her clothes?

She was wearing the long homespun men's shirt she had arrived in, though someone had pulled her trousers off and taken away the coat and hat she had been wearing.

It was odd to think of being touched by a stranger, but then, her clothing had been completely soaked through. They had been doing her a kindness.

There was a trunk at the foot of the bed and items laying on top. She stepped over to inspect them. Clean, dry clothing.

A shirt, trousers, stockings, and a cap, as well as a thick woolen cloak with a hood.

Men's clothing.

There was no way someone could have undressed her last night and come away believing she was truly a boy.

She put her hand up to her head again. Yes, her long mousy brown hair was still there and hung in a tight braid down her back. A strong indication that she was female.

And yet she had been left male clothes.

Perhaps there was a no extra women's clothing to spare right now. Perhaps these were the only clothes that her hosts had which would fit her.

She was rather thin and lanky after all. Nor did she have the womanly curves her three sisters had aplenty.

It had been almost four years since she had last purposely dressed as a boy. Last night did not count, for it had been a matter of necessity not a mindful decision.

She looked down at her chest. Well, it would not be altogether hard to pass for a boy even now.

She would not even need to bind her breasts, for she had none. Or none to speak of. For a while she had expected them, but as the years went by, she had given up believing her flat chest would ever change. Eventually, she simply embraced their absence. Breasts could be cumbersome. Heavy and frustrating when one wished to do something like run across a field or climb a tree.

Not that a young lady was supposed to be doing either of those things.

But Gracie had never been particularly good at doing what was expected. It ran in her family—and she feared she might have inherited the stubborn streak in double-measure. Certainly, her three older sisters thought so.

Her stomach growled again, reminding her that it was empty and she scanned the rest of the room.

A plate of food had been left on a little table near the door. It was cold now, but Gracie rushed towards it. The simple slices of buttered bread and preserves with a small pot of cold tea were heavenly after nearly a day's fast.

Once she had devoured everything that had been left, she dressed quickly, twisting her braid up and under the cap and pinning it in place. Then, for good measure, she pinned the cap to the braid. It would not do to have it fly off in the wind.

Once she had met her hosts she could see about different clothing, but she did not wish to make immediate demands of the kind people who had cared for her thus far.

Besides, it was freeing to be in trousers once again. She could not pretend it was not a somewhat welcome change to return to her old persona—the boy named Grayson.

Stepping into the corner, she noted a maid stepping out of a room nearby and quickly asked her for guidance to the main hall.

So far, so good. The maid had not looked askance at her.

Gracie had pitched her voice lower, but not as deep as she could have. It would have been arduous to have to continue that way for long; she was not sure her vocal cords were up to it. Besides, she might pass for a lad of sixteen or seventeen but certainly no older. And some young men retained relatively high voices.

When she reached the hall, the vast vaulted space was empty.

She took the steps quickly, but then ground to a stop at the bottom to stare upwards.

A huge mural took up nearly an entire wall of the hall.

It depicted a white hart—exactly like the one she had seen in the forest.

The stag was in profile and stood in a meadow with trees to each side. It had been painted mid-stride, running through the field.

The image was striking.

Even more so because behind the racing stag, followed a slavering pack of grey wolves, their sharp teeth bared as they came after their prey.

Gracie was transfixed. Would the wolves catch the hart? Who had painted such a thing? She had never seen its like.

One thing was clearly—she could not have been the only one to have seen a white stag in these woods.

"Incredible, is it not?" A man's voice said from behind her.

Startled, she turned to see the speaker.

A man of perhaps sixty or so stood there. He was of average-height, with a stocky build and grey hair, shot through with a few leftover strands of reddish-gold.

The man was smiling. Yet Gracie found the expression unsettling. The rest of his features seemed to belie his sincerity. His eyes were cold and flinty, and there was a tightness to his face.

"Indeed, it is magnificent," she murmured, wondering how quickly she could escape to the outdoors.

"Are you feeling rested after your travels last night?" he inquired. "We do not often have lost young... gentlemen showing up on our doorstep in these parts."

Gracie understood he was not questioning her masculinity—merely her quality.

Nevertheless, she crossed her arms over her chest self-consciously. As she was holding the cloak folded over one arm, it covered nicely.

"No, around these parts, everyone knows everyone else," he continued. "It can grow rather tedious, to tell you the truth. But perhaps you know of what I speak. Do you hail from London, sir...? Or other parts?"

"Grayson. Grayson Gardner." Something close to the truth would be best, she decided. "And yes, I grew up in the country, near a small village. In fact, I was traveling from there to visit some family friends but the coach I was in was waylaid."

"Waylaid?" the man interrupted, frowning. "What do you mean?"

"We were attacked in the forest," she said, bluntly. "By whom, I do not know."

An odd expression passed over Warburton's face. Then it cleared and he looked only concerned, as anyone might. "You do not know?"

"I did not see what happened exactly. I was inside the carriage when the attack occurred. The horses became spooked. They broke free and ran off. The carriage rolled and then tipped. I bashed my head, as you can see. When I managed to make my way out, my driver was gone. But there was blood in the snow. A great deal of it." She took a deep breath. "I was too frightened to search for him. And so, I left."

"Or he deserted you, one might say," Warburton suggested, his voice cold. "Injured or not, he ran off and abandoned his duties. He is probably miles away by now."

Gracie frowned. "I do not see his duty being to remain in a dangerous place or to protect me. He was not a soldier. And besides," she added, scuffing a foot on the floor. "I am a grown man. I can take care of myself."

She could take care of herself as a woman, too. But she was not about to say that.

"He was injured," Gracie said, a little defensively. "There was blood in the snow. No, I cannot blame him if he did run away."

"How terrible it must have been for you," the man said, with a sober shake of his head.

"Terrible, yes, but there must be something I might do now that I am here," Gracie said, wondering if he was the one she must petition. "We must send a search party back to see if the driver is there. Surely this was not the first time something like this happened so close to Princewood."

Warburton appeared offended. "I do not know what kind of lawlessness goes on where you are from, Mr. Gardner. But here, it is an uncommon thing. You are quite a way off the north road now. You must have strayed when you wandered in the snow. In these parts, travelers may not be common, but certainly we do not accost them."

He shook his head. "No, it sounds to me as if your carriage had an accident. Perhaps the driver was injured when it rolled. You say you did not see what happened? How do you know he was not hurt when the horses broke away? He must have felt a fool for letting them escape. Of course, he must have known he would be punished most severely when he returned without them."

Gracie felt a flush of embarrassment. He was looking at her so doubtfully that she began to second guess what she had seen.

He could be right. About the driver.

Certainly, he was correct about the road. As she walked through the snowy night, the path had become almost impossible to see and at least twice Gracie had come to a split where she had been unable to tell which was the main road and which was a new path.

"I am glad to hear I have arrived in such a safe place," she said, forcing a smile. "May I inquire as to where precisely I am?"

The man raised his eyebrows, as if surprised she did not already know. "You have reached the lands of the Chevalier family. A minor barony in the greater scheme of the peerage, but in these parts, they have been an influential and powerful family for hundreds of years. Since the time of the Norman kings."

"A barony," Gracie said. "That sounds rather medieval."

"In point of fact, the feudal baronies were done away with many years ago," the man agreed. "However, the Chevaliers retain the title of baron and all this land remains theirs, including much of the forest through which you traveled last night. If you hoped for entertainment, you will be disappointed, I am afraid. There is little society here. We are a backwater of the first order. Decades might pass with little changing here for the village or its people." His lip turned up in a sneer, as if he did not care for either.

"Although," he continued, looking past Gracie and up at the mural, with a grave expression. "There have been changes of a kind, I suppose. The Chevalier line is not what it once was. They have dwindled. Become almost extinct."

"How sad," Gracie murmured. "And it is the Chevaliers who I have to thank for their hospitality, I take it?"

"Not Chevaliers plural," the man said, smiling as if what she had said had pleased him. "Singular. There is only one Chevalier left, sadly. He has out lived his closest kin. His lordship, Linden Chevalier. I serve him as steward, but as his father's second cousin am also next in line to the—" He spoke so pompously that Gracie almost expected him to say 'throne.' "—barony."

The last Chevalier. Gracie pictured an ancient man, white-haired and frail.

"I see. I must thank his lordship for his kindness then..." Gracie started.

"Ah, there you are!" A woman's voice interrupted, carrying loudly from one side of the hall to the other.

A petite woman with her curly grey hair under a white cap hurried up.

"I wondered where you had wandered off to," she said, a little breathlessly, coming up to Gracie. "You were in no condition for introductions yesterday, young sir—" She emphasized the last word, and Gracie gave a slight nod.

As if she were in any danger of forgetting her disguise.

Mrs. Lennox knew very well that Gracie was no he.

What was this game she was playing then? And why did she wish for Gracie to continue playing it with her?

"I am Mrs. Lennox, the housekeeper," the woman went on. Gracie suspected she was much more than simply that. "And I see you have already met Sir Guy Warburton, Princewood's steward."

Gracie repeated her own introduction, then briefly restated what she had told Warburton moments before.

"But I believe Mr. Gardner may have misconstrued things," Sir Guy declared authoritatively, as she reached the end. "It sounds to me like a case of an inexperienced driver causing an accident and recklessly losing his mounts. You are very lucky, sir, that the accident was not a much worse one, especially as your coachman abandoned you without even seeing if you were injured."

Gracie opened her mouth to stubbornly insist that the driver must have been more injured than she was, but Mrs. Lennox spoke first.

"Of course, we imagined something of the sort must have befallen you," Mrs. Lennox said, her voice full of sincere concern. "But if you truly think a man may be injured so close to us, then perhaps Sir Guy will take it upon himself to look into this matter."

Warburton's response was to frown at Mrs. Lennox. "Of course, I shall undertake an investigation if I believe it has merit *and* if Lord Chevalier instructs me to. As of yet, he has not."

"Of course," Mrs. Lennox said. Gracie saw that her jaw had clenched a little. Evidently these two only tolerated one another. "Well, my young lad, you must be desperate for some fresh air after being cooped up all morning. You must go out. Walk the grounds. I see you've found the cloak I left you. The village lies on the north side of the castle courtyard, opposite from which you came last night. Perhaps you will run into my Jasper when you go. He stepped out an hour or so ago to visit some friends."

Mrs. Lennox seemed to want Gracie out of the castle and she was not of a mind to argue. A walk was very appealing, though she was not interested in seeing the village but rather the shore.

"Thank you, Mrs. Lennox, I believe I shall," Gracie said, politely. "I must also thank you for the cloak and the clothes. My own must have been soaked through last night. I only hope they are serviceable still for when I depart."

Mrs. Lennox waved a hand. "No need to concern yourself with them, my dear. They are being washed for you, but you are more than welcome to my Jasper's clothes. You are of a size with him, only a little more..." She bit her lip.

"Slender?" Gracie provided, smiling impishly. "Yes, I have been told I am rather a skinny fellow. No meat on these bones."

Warburton was still scowling behind Mrs. Lennox's back. At least Gracie's conversation with him would be cut short. She could not say she was disappointed.

"Good day to you both." As she walked away, she glanced back and noticed how swiftly Mrs. Lennox and Warburton had gone in opposite directions across the great hall.

No love lost between those two.

This time, when Gracie passed through the doors of the keep, she was much more aware of her surroundings. Stepping out onto the stone ramp and into the winter sunlight, she turned back to look up at the high tower behind her and marveled.

She had slept in a castle last night. How many people could say the same?

It was no *Witch of the Waves*, of course, but Princewood was impressive in its own right.

Walking down into the bailey courtyard, people were going about their daily tasks. A woman was feeding chickens in a pen. Two men were bent over a table outside of what looked to be a smithy. Two young maids were walking side-by-side carrying heavy-looking buckets of milk or water to the kitchen building, which was connected to the keep by a covered stone passage, chattering away as they went.

Gracie walked slowly. Now that she was outdoors, under the full light of the sun, her head was beginning to pulsate with pain again.

Yet she did not wish to return to the keep without having had a true glimpse of the sea.

"Whoa, watch out there, lad," a man cautioned, and Gracie looked down quickly to see that in her distracted state she had nearly tripped over a pile horse tack set outside of the stable doors.

The man who had spoken sat on a stool nearby mending a bridle. The sun was striking his silver-hair and reflecting off his weathered-browned face.

"Head in the clouds, boy?" He asked, smiling good-naturedly up at her.

"Yes," Gracie said, returning the smile. "Thank you for the warning."

"You don't look as if you need another bump," the man said, gesturing to the lump on Gracie's forehead. "'Suppose you're the young fellow who came in out of the storm last night?"

"I am," Gracie said. "I am very grateful for your hospitality."

The man quirked his mouth. "Ah, it's not I who is master here. Only the stablemaster, that is. But you are welcome just the same."

"Have you worked at the castle long?" Gracie asked, curiously. "I understand there is a village close by."

"Close by?" the man said, laughing. "I should say so. It is just through those gates." He pointed past Gracie to the north wall where she could see a second gate house with a drawn portcullis. "The village of Princewood. The castle, the forest, the village—they all share the same name. We have a church, a shop, a tailor—well, he shares the shop, not to mention a tavern. You can't have a village without a pub." He grinned.

"It sounds a regular high street," Gracie observed, smiling. "Though I am not sure how you keep the three Princewoods straight."

"Ah, but it's tradition," the man said. "I've been stablemaster at the castle, oh, twenty years or more now. One of the few who stayed on, after..." He shook his head.

"After?" Gracie prompted.

The man sighed. "After a great tragedy, lad. It split us in two, and not just here." He gestured to his chest. "The castle and the village—in the past, they were almost one and the same. But now, there are those in the village who won't set foot within these walls."

"Why on earth not?" Gracie asked, in surprise.

"Some nonsense about the master of the place being evil." He waved a hand. "That and a lot of hearsay and tales that some people take as God's honest truth." He stood up and looking about the courtyard, seemed to brighten. "But those folk you see about you—working hard and happy to be doing so, they had the common sense to take work where it's offered and have fared well. Stupid to be frightened away from decent work with decent pay by nasty tales told by gossips about a little boy."

"A little boy?" Gracie asked, puzzled.

"But before that," the man continued, missing her question. "Ah, but this was a bustling place. Always a festival or a dance or some sort of activity happening when the last baron and his lady were alive." He shook his head and looked back down at the bridle in his hands. "Well, I've dawdled enough, lad. There's more work to be done. Name is Jock Robertson if you ever need anything."

Jock stood up from the stool, hung the mended bridle over his shoulder, and then, with a friendly nod at Gracie, disappeared into the stable.

Gracie looked up at the ramparts as she walked towards the north gate. The walls of the outer bailey must have been at least two metres thick. Built to withstand invasion, by land or by sea. There must be a magnificent view of the forest and the sea from the top.

She passed by the kitchen block, through the portcullis gate, and immediately saw the little seaside village stretching out before her. There was indeed a small high street, and perhaps twenty or thirty small huts, houses, and other small buildings. The tavern was easily spotted by the white sign hanging from a post outside—The White Hart, of course.

She walked along the main road, looking for the best way down to the sea, and soon spotted a well-worn path beside the tavern leading to the beach.

As she turned off onto the path, someone came walking quickly around the back of the building and collided with her.

It was a young woman, carrying a basket. Two small children followed behind her, poking one another energetically with sticks.

"Pardon me," Gracie said, apologetically, stepping back to allow them to pass first.

They were all looking at her so curiously that she quickly added, "I was just coming down from the castle and looking for a path to the sea. I saw this trail and it seemed the best one to follow." She trailed off as she saw the queer expression on the woman's face.

"The castle?" the woman said, stepping back. "You're staying at the keep?"

"Yes, I am. They put me up last night when the coach I was travelling in was attacked on the road," Gracie said, beginning to feel awkward. "Well, good day to you." She stepped into the grass to skirt around them.

"Wait," the woman said, suddenly, clutching at Gracie's cloak. She lowered her voice and hissed. "I wouldn't stay at that place any longer if I was you, lad. There's evil there. The master's a cruel man, not right in the head. None of us goes up there, except those that's getting paid for the trouble."

After speaking with the man outside the stable, Gracie was prepared to dismiss most of what the woman said as rubbish, but the comments did pique her curiosity.

"I see," she said, calmly. "Well, thank you. I shall consider that, certainly."

She walked on, without looking back, her long cloak trailing through the tall sea grass.

When she reached the sandy shore, she paused, drinking in the sea air and thinking of what the woman had said.

There was no doubt Princewood was an odd place. There was all of this talk of the castle's master and yet she had not even laid eyes on the man. How could an elderly baron elicit such fear?

If the friendliness of Mrs. Lennox was any indication, then the castle certainly did not seem a foreboding place.

She shrugged to herself and began to walk closer towards the water. What did it matter? She would be on her way soon.

Surely there would be some method of transportation for hire in the village. If worse came to worse, she would send a letter to the Crawfords and they would arrange something.

She had a little money on her that had been in the reticule she had stuffed in her dress pocket.

It was good to be near the sea again.

The smell of the salty water and sound of the waves crashing against the beach were pleasant to her senses after being away from the ocean for so long.

She walked along the damp sand, appreciating the view of the castle from afar. It was a massive structure. One could easily imagine knights of old defending it from the ramparts. Shooting through those arrow slits and repelling invaders from sea.

A wave of dizziness passed over her as her head pulsated again with pain. Perhaps Mrs. Lennox would not mind too much if she were to rest at the castle another night or two. Truly, she did not think she could manage being bumped along in a coach again so soon.

She was standing there, with her arms crossed over her chest, her cloak pulled tightly around her, when she heard a whistling.

Looking over at a cluster of rocks, she saw a young man she had not noticed at first. He had stripped off his coat and was laying stretched out on a large, flat rock, evidently enjoying the warmth of the sun.

"You must be the stranger," he said, smiling languidly at her from under a mop of curling black hair.

There was something so friendly and easy about his face that Gracie could not help smiling back.

He jumped to his feet and came towards her.

"The mysterious stranger," he said. "Pleased to meet you. I'm Jasper."

"Oh!" Gracie said. "Mrs. Lennox's son."

"The one and the same," Jasper replied.

He had shot her an odd look when she first spoke and was now looking her up and down carefully—not in a lascivious manner, but with a strange thoroughness.

"And as for yourself? Are you a prince or a duke? An earl or a baron?" he asked. "Mister…?"

"Grayson Gardner of no title whatsoever, a mere mister from the miniscule village of Beauford," Gracie quipped, grinning. "I am sorry to disappoint."

Jasper laughed. His laughter was a beautiful peal, like bells ringing.

"You have not. Well, perhaps, a little," he said, truthfully. "We do not get many handsome strangers turning up on our doorstep, in such an out of the way place as this. And so, we must take what we can get."

He shot her a wink that was almost flirtatious.

"So, everyone tells me. And yet my coach cannot have been the first to be waylaid in these woods," Gracie said.

She thought again of the trail of blood leading from the coach and into the woods.

Warburton had downplayed her experience, but Mrs. Lennox had seemed to share her concern for the driver. Perhaps Gracie could speak with her about sending someone back to search tomorrow.

Jasper frowned and put a piece of grass between his teeth. "Perhaps not, but if so, the victims have not turned up here. If they had, I can assure you I would remember."

He eyed her up and down again. "I say, are those mine?"

Gracie glanced down at her costume. "I believe your mother said they were, yes."

"Well, we are of the same size," he said, grinning. There was something about the way he hung on that last word which made Gracie blush even more deeply.

"Aha, an untested youth, I see," Jasper smirked. "A green boy."

He walked all around her. "A very pretty boy," he observed, as if talking to himself. "I suppose my mother knew very well you were a girl when she gave them to you."

Gracie's jaw dropped.

"I am that obvious then?" she said, ruefully. "I have not done this in quite a while."

"You've done it before?" Jasper looked impressed.

"When I was much younger," Gracie said.

"Let me guess," Jasper said, a finger to his chin. "You ran away to sea."

"How did you know?" Gracie said, only a little astonished.

"It is a common story, is it not?" Jasper's eyes twinkled mischievously.

"Well, your secret is safe with me," he said, bending over to pluck a piece of sea grass and put it between his lips. "Though I have no inkling as to her reasons for the charade, my mother is no fool. The clothes suit you. Keep them."

He shot her a dangerous grin. "Besides, it will be much more fun this way. Now, what did that idiot Warburton have to say about you?"

"About my being at the castle?" Gracie replied. "I spoke with Sir Warburton, but only briefly. He did not complain about my presence." Though he had not exactly been welcoming either.

"And yet last night, he wished to heave you out into the snow," Jasper said, cheerily. "No Christian charity from Warburton. Oh, no, sir."

"Did he?" Gracie said. "He was fairly cordial when I encountered him."

Jasper rolled his eyes. "Well, count yourself fortunate then. He considers himself the true master of Princewood. Why Linden has allowed that man to remain for so long..." He threw up his hands.

"Linden?" Gracie inquired.

Then she remembered the name Warburton had dropped. Linden Chevalier.

"The baron," Jasper explained. "The heir to Princewood."

"Ah, yes," Gracie said. "I believe Sir Warburton said something about Lord Chevalier being the last of his line. He must be a very old man, I suppose. Is he quite frail?"

"Frail?" Jasper said, looking amused. "Old?"

"Yes, is he not old?" Gracie said, hesitantly. "I received the impression he was quite an old man..."

Jasper hooted. "He is hardly a year older than I am."

"Oh!" That changed Gracie's impressions immensely. There was a blank in her mind now, where she had filled in a picture of an old, dignified baron on the verge of death. She was not sure what to put in its place.

Jasper wore a wry expression. "I take it Warburton gave you the impression that Linden was a feeble, old man?"

"Well, he did not say it in so many words," Gracie admitted. "He simply made it sound as if the baron was..."

"Decrepit? Yes, I see," Jasper said, scowling. "It fits in with what Warburton really thinks of Linden. He sees him as weak and frail and easy to control."

"And is he?" Gracie asked.

"No," Jasper said, shortly. "Warburton underestimates him. It is Warburton who is reluctant to give up the reigns, though it is high time he did. But Warburton is not the only one to denigrate our baron. As I've told Linden, a hundred times or more, if he does not..."

They were interrupted by the sound of hoofbeats.

Gracie turned around to see a black stallion cantering towards them with a cloaked rider on its back.

When it neared, the rider slid down and strode towards them.

"Speak of the devil," Jasper said, cheerfully. "Here is my lordship now."

The rider pushed back the hood of his cloak and Gracie's breath caught in her chest.

This.

Him.

The man before her was not what she had expected.

Lord Linden Chevalier was far from decrepit.

Rather, he was the most striking figure of manhood Gracie had ever seen.

Indeed, it would not be far-fetched to say he resembled a prince stepping off the pages of a fairy story.

He was neither burly nor broad. His figure was long and lithe, yet there was no question he was virile and strong. There was a kind of coiled power to him, and he moved with a fluid grace.

Gracie suddenly understood why Jasper believed this young man might be underestimated.

He moved with a controlled restraint, which might be mistaken for shyness. But to Gracie, all that she could see was a perfect masculine balance. Everything about him was at once hard and soft at the same time—but flawlessly so—from the angles of his jaw to the planes of his high cheekbones, to those green eyes, at once kind yet strong as steel, and framed by ridiculously long, dusky brown lashes.

His hair was a dark gold and worn long enough to reach his chin. It had been pulled back into a tight queue for riding and bound with a leather strip, but the wind had pulled it loose and now it flew around his face. Perhaps on another man, the style might have been unflattering. But on Linden Chevalier it only added something more alluring to his presence, and as he lifted a black-gloved hand to push it back, the set of his jaw and twist of his mouth made him look sharp and wicked.

Oh, that mouth!

Gracie's first thought was that it was unfair a man should have such a sinfully beautiful mouth.

Her next was that it was made for seduction and unspeakable delights.

And her third was that it was made for despair—for despair was what she could not help but feel as she stared at this young man, who seemed a strange and uncanny reflection of herself. Not only a more perfect specimen of manhood than she could ever pretend to be in her feigned garb, but a man who reflected her very soul back to her without even seeming to realize it, more herself than she was, yet in the way that fire complimented frost, or the ocean reflected the stars.

Such stupid, ridiculous romantic thoughts filled her head until she realized she had been standing there, speechless and staring for who knew how long, while Jasper looked on with an amused expression and as Linden Chevalier stared back at her, his expression veiled.

And yet even then, when she should have been embarrassed, when she should have glanced away, even then she could not help looking a moment longer—at the sliver of bare flesh she saw exposed at his throat, where his shirt had come open and loose while riding, exposing a delicate bronze patch of satin.

She felt herself leaning forward, and sucked in a breath to steady herself, then wished she had not, for immediately the fresh, sweaty, sun-soaked scent of him filled her nostrils, fueling the mad urge to reach out a fingertip and graze that trian-gle of skin, a desire of such intensity she could hardly breathe or move.

She blinked rapidly and felt her eyes moistening, the pin-pricks of tears in the corner of each one, as if her mind had already realized what her heart had not—that this other-worldly demigod was utterly inaccessible to her, enticing yet forbidding, and so curse him for being all that she had never known she so desperately wanted until she saw it.

And she had never wanted anything as badly as she wanted Linden Chevalier.

Chapter 4

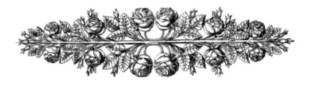

Love looks not with the eyes, but with the mind,

And therefore is winged Cupid painted blind.

— A Midsummer Night's Dream

The boy was skinny and pale and completely confounding.

There should have been nothing to warrant a second glance. He was just another young man, much like Jasper or Linden himself.

Yet the intensity of the youth's gaze upon him was disarming, as if the boy were seeing through him, through to a part of Linden that he had never seen himself.

He felt laid bare, stripped, and at the same time, moved by the naked distress he saw in the young man's eyes.

Jasper coughed awkwardly and touched the boy on the arm.

The moment was broken.

Immediately, the young stranger stepped back, stood straighter, and seemed to come out of a trance.

"This is your mysterious guest, Linden," Jasper said, his voice light. "Perhaps he'll tell you his name himself." He turned to look at the young man expectantly, a half-smile on his face.

There was uncomfortable silence as they waited for the boy to speak.

And waited.

Finally, the stranger's lips parted. He licked them carefully—a little pink tongue darting out to moisten soft, pink rose petals.

Linden blushed at the thought, and then hoped Jasper had not noticed the blush.

But, then, Jasper noticed just about bloody everything.

"Grayson," the youth muttered, his voice so low that Linden could hardly catch the syllables.

Jasper had not removed his arm, Linden noticed. He had kept a grip on the stranger's elbow as if he required continued support.

And perhaps he did, Linden realized, as he saw the young man's pale complexion and the bloody, bruised spot on his forehead.

"Well, Grayson, you are looking rather peaky," Jasper observed. "I think we'd best get you back to the castle and your comfortable bed."

"Yes..." The young man agreed, his voice a husk of a whisper.

He staggered.

"Catch him," Jasper commanded sharply, as the young man began to pitch forward, and Linden obeyed, reaching out to steady the youth who quickly became deadweight as he lifted him into his arms.

"I suppose you'd best take him home," Jasper said, surprisingly chipper.

He took the slender boy from Linden's arms and stepped back as his friend mounted, then passed the injured youth up.

The young man's head fell against Linden's chest. He was soft and warm and very light. Linden looked down at the boy's face, his rosy lips the only color there.

"Light as a bird, isn't he? Yet there's something about him, isn't there?" Jasper remarked, with an uncanny instinct, and Linden looked down at his friend as guiltily as a child caught stealing cookies.

"He's a pretty youth," Jasper said, casually. "That is all I meant." Then he shrugged and grinned. "He is no Peter, of course."

Linden opened his mouth, then closed it again. There were a hundred different replies he might give, including disagreement, but he could not form a single one into a sentence.

He felt as unsettled as a sailor on a stormy sea, uneasy without being able to pinpoint the source of the feeling.

So, he simply nodded, and turned the horse back along the beach in the direction from whence he had come.

It was a quiet ride. He kept the horse to a slow, steady trod, not wishing to jostle the young man more than necessary.

The beach was deserted, especially this long stretch away from the village. The keep was always to his right, the massive stone fortress so familiar to his vision it was unworthy of note. Ahead in the distance and around the bend in the beach, lay the place where the forest encroached upon the sand.

Princewood Forest. Vast and dark, beautiful but deadly.

As this boy had nearly found out. He would have to make further inquiries about what exactly had taken place. Warburton had been dismissive when he had suggested it. As far as the old steward was concerned, Princewood was only of interest if it was for felling trees or some other source of income. He had been remarkably blasé about the attack.

But then, as Jasper had rightly noted, Warburton was rather... well, insular, in who he cared for and about.

He cared for himself. He cared for his daughter, Fleur.

As for Linden himself? As a child, he had looked upon Warburton as a father figure and assumed what he felt was love. But these days, he was not certain what exactly he felt for Sir Guy or indeed Sir Guy for him. The man had been one of the few constants in the castle since the death of his parents so many years before and Linden would always be grateful for his steadfast presence.

Linden was ever-conscious of the weight of the boy against his chest. His warmth. His slow breathing. As Jasper had said, he was light as a bird.

Unable to help it, he stole a glance.

Yes, he admitted, Jasper was right about that as well. The boy was uniquely pretty. One might call him scrawny—or delicate, if trying to be more complimentary. He was freckled with a fair complexion, a wide mouth with lips just the right amount of fullness, and a pointed chin that suggested a stubborn personality.

What color was his hair? The cap covered most of it. Linden had the strange urge to pull it off and satisfy his curiosity. He resisted.

Of course, none of this explained the feelings this strange lad was provoking within him.

The urge to protect, to safekeep. The urge to wrap the boy in his arms and sweep his cloak around them both.

Linden swallowed hard and raised his chin, determined to keep his eyes ahead.

He had never felt anything like this for Fleur.

He had never felt anything like this for anyone.

When they drew up before the castle a quarter of an hour later, the boy had still not roused.

Linden had seen a child fall once, when he was younger. A little girl had been climbing a tree and slipped on a branch. She had a bump on her head and her family made much fuss over her, but in a few hours, she was up and playing again.

But the next morning, she would not wake. And later that afternoon, she died.

All from a tumble.

A stable hand stepped up to take hold of his mount while Linden slid down from the saddle, still grasping the boy in his arms.

He heaved the youth up, cradling him as he walked up and into the keep, pushing open one of the oak doors with a shoulder and stepping into the shadowy cavernous space.

"Oh, there you are. Father has been looking for you."

He looked over and saw a girl slouched in a high-backed armchair beside the huge stone hearth. Her head was resting on her hand as she stared into the flames, her expression one of deep boredom.

"Thank you, Fleur," he said, quietly, continuing towards the stairs. "I will find him shortly."

"Who is that?" The girl asked, sounding faintly interested. She had turned away from the fire and was looking suspiciously at the bundle in Linden's arms.

"The boy who came in from the storm last night," Linden explained. "He was wounded and he pressed himself too hard today while out walking. It is a good thing Jasper and I were there when he collapsed."

She turned her head back to the fire. A soft grunting sound was the only indication she had heard him.

He started walking up the steps, then paused. "Are you well today, Fleur?" he asked, tentatively, looking down at her.

She was a very pretty girl. He knew this, objectively, as one might admire a lovely flower. Her hair was a reddish-gold like her father's had been, and it fell long and loose around her shoulders for she rarely permitted it to be put up, in spite it being unfashionable.

Her mouth was full and sultry. She had a willowy, curving figure and Linden had heard it remarked upon more than enough times to know most men found it lush and appealing.

She was pretty, he told himself, again. He did not know why she had never sparked anything in him besides confusion—and perhaps a measure of pity, for as long as he had known her, she had always seemed unhappy.

It was the same with girls from the village. They were afraid of him, of course—they all were. But once, on a night where there had been a festival in the village, he had come across a group of young women while walking on the beach. A bold one had come up to him and before he had known what she was going to do, stole a kiss—then ran away shrieking, back to her friends.

They had probably dared her.

Steal a kiss from the beastly boy. Steal a kiss and then run before he chases after you with his... Well, what was he said to have now? Besides a murderous heart. That part of the story never seemed to change.

Still, the kiss had elicited a reaction of a kind. The girl had been attractive. Her lips had been sweet. Linden had been so surprised at the touch—and then shocked again when he was so quickly and easily aroused by it.

He had stormed away from them, of course. What else could he do? Their laughter was only a cover for their fear.

Still, even if only that were true with Fleur. It would be better than feeling nothing at all towards her.

As it was, he could not imagine their wedding night being anything but a disaster.

He knew she had no wish to wed him. Indeed, some times he believed her feelings for him tended more towards hate than love or even liking.

But she would do what she was told, because doing what her father wanted her to do was the only thing Fleur could be counted on to do uncomplainingly.

"I am fine," she said, crisply, scowling at the flames without looking back up at him again.

She did not ask how he fared or express any concern for the young man.

Mrs. Lennox was in the hall talking to a maid when Linden reached the landing on the way to their guest's room.

"My goodness," she exclaimed, coming towards him quickly. "What has happened?"

"Hopefully only a setback," Linden said. "But his head wound may be worse than we realized. He pitched forward while talking to Jasper and I down on the beach, and I've brought him back. Should we call a surgeon?"

"A surgeon to look at the young lad..." Mrs. Lennox repeated, looking at the young man with something like dismay.

She seemed of two minds, but soon nodded firmly. "Yes, a surgeon would be best. Here, bring him in. Lay him on the bed. I'll see to him now, Linden. You go and have Cam fetch the surgeon from the village."

"It was good of you to bring him back," she added, quickly, before he had stepped back out into the hall. She touched his arm gently. "You are a good lad. You always are."

It was not the done thing—a housekeeper calling a baron by his Christian name.

He knew this. He did not care.

There were few people on this earth who Linden truly, deeply loved. Mrs. Lennox was one of the few, as was Jasper. And Cam, for that matter.

He was not certain there was anyone else he could add to that list.

He hesitated and stole a look past Mrs. Lennox to the boy on the bed.

"Will he be all right, do you think, Mrs. Lennox?" he asked, quietly. "I should hate to think of a lad losing his life in our woods, after all..." He stopped suddenly.

"I know, my dear," she said, softly, patting his arm again. "Put your mind at ease. Likely all they need is rest." She shook her head, ruefully. "I was foolish to encourage them to step out for some fresh air. I will take good care of them now. You can be sure of that. I'll sit with them a spell and wait for the surgeon."

He nodded, feeling oddly reluctant to leave. But he did so, pulling the door shut behind him.

Chapter 5

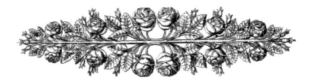

How many goodly creatures are there here!

How beauteous mankind is! O brave new world,

That has such people in 't!

— The Tempest

When Gracie woke, her lips were parched.

Her eyes felt tight and gritty. She rubbed a hand across them.

She was back in bed. Back in the castle.

The curtains around her bed had been pulled back. Leaning on her side, she could see through the window, out into the winter twilight. It was snowing again. Soft flakes falling against a deep blue sky. The stars would soon be out.

There was a squeaking sound and Gracie looked across the room to see a little maid hopping up from where she had been sitting in a wooden chair, sewing. She stared at Gracie a moment, wide-eyed and frozen like a rabbit. Then she curtsied, sprang towards the door and pulling it open tossed back over her shoulder, "I'll tell Mrs. Lennox that you're up."

Gracie leaned back against the pillows. She felt disoriented and her body ached from lying in bed so long.

But her head was not hurting as badly as it had been when...

When she had swooned like a fool and fallen... Fallen where?

She closed her eyes and groaned. Fallen at the feet of the master of this castle.

She groaned again. He thought her a boy.

She had gawked at him, fallen on him...and he had seen a skinny boy who could not even stand on his own two feet or answer a simple question.

And when he found out she was not a boy at all? Well, then he would simply think her a lunatic. It was one thing to dress as a boy out of necessity but to continue the pretence...

Why did it even matter? Why was she obsessing over a man she had only just met?

She was not ready to acknowledge the reason. It was too preposterous to *be* acknowledged.

She must have hit her head very hard indeed to be behaving like one of those daft girls from a gothic novel. Tumbling head over heels into...

"Oh, my dear, you're awake again, are you?" Mrs. Lennox bustled into the room, making straight for the bed where she put a cool hand against Gracie's forehead.

She reminded Gracie of her mother. Of her mother and a kindly hen. "How is your head? The surgeon came while you were sleeping, but there was little he could do. He will be back in the morning to see you again." She bit her lip and looked at Gracie indecisively.

Gracie was aghast. A surgeon? Had he examined her? What must be think! How many other strangers had been in the room with her while she slept?

"He did no more than look at your head," Mrs. Lennox quickly added, as if knowing her thoughts.

"And he thinks I am a boy as well, I suppose?" Gracie said, grimly, deciding to get straight to the point. "I do feel better, thank you. But Mrs. Lennox, there has been a mistake."

Mrs. Lennox smiled slightly and put a hand out to touch Gracie's cap.

She carefully pulled out the pins that held it in place and lifted it up, letting Gracie's coiled braid spill down and onto her shoulder.

"I know you are a young lady, my dear," Mrs. Lennox said, softly. "And a pretty one, too."

"Thank you," Gracie said, automatically, though she knew it was not true. "Although that is not true. I probably make a better boy."

She sounded sorry for herself and hated it. But it was the truth.

She was freckled and scrawny and thus had easily passed for a boy in the first place. She had no delusions about her appearance.

But it made her encounter with Linden Chevalier all the more painful. He had shone like a golden star, while she remained a plain lump of coal.

Mrs. Lennox was smiling at her in that semi-condescending way that older people had when they looked at those younger than themselves.

"Is it such a terrible thing? To be able to shift between? I must say, when I was a girl, I sometimes dreamed of putting on a pair of my brother's trousers and going off and seeing the world," Mrs. Lennox confessed.

Gracie started. "You did?"

"Of course, I did. I am sure many girls do," the older woman said. "And now that I see you—" She touched Gracie's hair again, almost in wonderment. "—I believe I might have done just that. It is a marvel how little of one another we are truly able to see. You look at me and see a matronly woman, a housekeeper. The surgeon looked at you and had no doubt you were a boy. No doubt at all."

"We see one another as clothing," Gracie said, with understanding. "At least, at first."

"Perhaps a little more than that, but certainly not the whole," Mrs. Lennox said. "How often does one truly look beyond the surface?" She shook her head. "In my experience, not very often."

"I did what you dreamed of..." Gracie said, slowly. She was not sure how much she should say. But why bother holding back? "I put on trousers and I went to sea. As a cabin boy."

Mrs. Lennox did not look appalled or horrified, but then Gracie had not expected her to. Rather, she looked impressed, as her son had been.

"Did you now? On a ship?" She said, admiringly. "And how did it go for you? I cannot imagine a place with more men, all crammed in together like sardines."

"Yes," Gracie agreed, remembering the smells of the ship, the cramped spaces. "But it was beautiful, too. And I was happy. I did not feel out of place. I felt as if I..."

"Belonged?" Mrs. Lennox suggested, watching her.

"Yes," Gracie said. "Although I didn't. Not really. And eventually, the captain found out and a few of the crew. They were good to me, and didn't tell all of the men. They let me remain cabin boy until we reached London again. But it was different after that. They treated me differently, and so then, of course, the crew did as well."

"Yes, I can imagine so," Mrs. Lennox said. "Still, what an incredible adventure."

"It was. Being here, close to the sea again... Well, it makes me miss ship life. Coming home was hard. I do not think I real-

ized until now how much I've missed it. And how confined
I have felt ever since." The words were pouring out. Why oh
why was she telling a complete stranger all of this? She had
not even confessed these feelings to her own family.

"I knew you were a bonny, brave one," Mrs. Lennox declared.
"Now, I suppose you are wondering about the clothes."

Gracie nodded.

"Where do you come from, Miss Gardner?" Mrs. Lennox
asked, watching her keenly. "Is your family gentry?"

Gracie furrowed her brow. "I do not know what that has to
do with anything, but yes, I suppose. Of a sort. Though we
were not particularly well-off when I was growing up. We
lived humbly, near a small village much like this one. My
mother's mother was a baron's daughter. My sister is married
to a duke."

"A duke?" Mrs. Lennox looked impressed. "I thought so," she
said, looking pleased. "Even in boy's clothes, you had that
look about you."

"Why does it matter?" Gracie asked, puzzled. "What about
the clothes?"

"Very well, but first—" Mrs. Lennox rose and went to the
door, where she pulled a bell concealed behind a wall tapestry. "I think some refreshments. At least, bread and tea?
Could you manage that?"

"I could manage a great deal more," Gracie said, wriggling cheerfully in anticipation of hot food and drink.

"Very well," Mrs. Lennox said, smiling. A maid appeared at the door and Mrs. Lennox conveyed instructions, then sat down beside Gracie's bed again. "I've asked her to bring up some of our Cook's beef pie along with the tea and bread."

"Perfect," Gracie said, trying not to salivate in anticipation.

"But I won't be put off," she added, eying Mrs. Lennox suspiciously. "Pray, continue."

The older woman sat down beside the bed again.

"Well, I suppose it was a test of sorts," Mrs. Lennox said, slowly. "Unfair of me, I know. But then, you played your part so well. Not that I thought you would come to any harm. I certainly wouldn't have sent you out if I had known you would..."

"Swoon at the feet of Lord Chevalier," Gracie finished, covering her face with her hands.

"Oh, so you remember Linden, do you?" Mrs. Lennox sounded amused.

Gracie peeked through her fingers. "How could anyone forget him?" she grumbled.

Mrs. Lennox looked pleased. "He is a handsome lad. And more importantly, honorable and kind-hearted, too."

"Of course, he is," Gracie said, dully. "He probably has the temperament of an angel and the courage of a lion. It is only a wonder he does not ride a white horse rather than a black and have a herald carrying his banner before him. And where was his shield today?"

"He does rather remind one of the knights of old," Mrs. Lennox agreed. "I suppose Jasper would have been his squire, had we lived a century or two ago."

"It feels as if you still do live a century or two ago," Gracie said, looking about pointedly. "I half believe I have traveled back in time."

"Perchance not back in time, but for a purpose," Mrs. Lennox said, quietly.

"What do you mean?" Gracie asked. "

"Do you believe in fate?" Mrs. Lennox asked. Apparently, a quick look at Gracie's face was all she needed. "No? I am not sure I do either. But still, I believe you are here for a reason. It cannot be chance. Not after what you saw."

"And what am I supposed to have seen?" Gracie asked, bewildered.

"The white hart, of course," Mrs. Lennox said. "You did see it? In the forest?"

Gracie felt as if her mouth were agape. It most likely was. "How did you know?"

Mrs. Lennox looked at her shrewdly. "It doesn't matter."

"Doesn't it?" Gracie narrowed her eyes. "I call that very odd. Very odd indeed."

"The hart is a symbol here," Mrs. Lennox said, softly. "A very old, very powerful one. Few have actually seen one. Those who have are said to be under its protection—all their lives."

"I see, and let me guess, you have a second sight and can see who has been marked by the white stag of the woods," Gracie muttered, rolling her eyes.

She knew it was disrespectful, but it was also frustrating to see Mrs. Lennox knew more than she was sharing.

Besides, all of this superstitious talk was nonsense, of course. It was the nineteenth century, for heaven's sake, not the Dark Ages.

"Marked, yes, in a sense," Mrs. Lennox said, not put off in the slightest by Gracie's reaction.

"As what?" Gracie demanded.

"A catalyst." Mrs. Lennox put her hands in her lap and sat quietly as Gracie absorbed this.

"A cata-what?"

"A catalyst. A spark. Whatever one wishes to call it. Something is coming to a head," Mrs. Lennox. "And your presence here. In boy's garb." She set her mouth stubbornly. "You are a part of it all. That much is clear. You need not believe in any of this, but let me ask you something. Would you help Linden Chevalier if you could? If it meant his life? Would you help him?"

Gracie sat as if struck dumb. The way Mrs. Lennox was looking at her—as if she already knew the answer. As if she knew so much.

It was unnerving.

Though not as unnerving as seeing Linden Chevalier on the beach that day had been.

"Yes," Gracie whispered, finally. She felt a fool, but it was the truth.

"Then you must stay," Mrs. Lennox said, swiftly. She clasped Gracie's hand. "Stay and heal. Stay and learn. Stay and listen. That is all I am asking."

"Listen to what?" Gracie exclaimed, impatiently. "Learn what? Why must I do so dressed-up as a boy?"

"Call it a hunch," Mrs. Lenox said, pursing her lips and ignoring the other questions. "Have you heard any of the tales of this castle, Miss Gardner? Do you know what took place here fifteen years ago?"

Gracie shook her head slowly. "I spoke with a man outside the stable today. Jock Robertson. He said people from the village are afraid of the baron. And then, in the village later, a woman told me I should not stay at the keep."

"Nonsense, you are certainly as safe here as you would be in the village," Mrs. Lennox waved a hand dismissively.

Gracie noticed that she did not say either were particularly safe places to be.

"Ignorance and stupidity. But at the heart of it, all too genuine fear."

"Fear of what?" Gracie asked.

"Fear of him. Fear of the lord of this castle. Even though he was only a boy when it happened. They marked him as a monster, as if he deserved such a thing. As if he were responsible for any of it. When he was just a child and had already been so terribly punished, so terribly hurt." Mrs. Lennox shook her head irritably. "They treat him as if he were a beast. Not the master who protects them, provides for them, feeds them when harvests are bad, maintains a school for their children, ensures there is a capable surgeon in the village. They are blind to all that he does."

"But I do not understand," Gracie said. "What happened fifteen years ago?"

Mrs. Lennox looked at her in silence a moment. "I will tell you, if you stay. But not yet."

She rose from her seat. "It is late now. You should rest. I will have more clean clothes brought to your room, and breakfast in the morning. We should send a note to your family as well, telling them where you are."

And to the Crawfords, Gracie thought. And to poor Matilda. Well, Gracie could send her funds. She could either go on to the Crawfords or back to Orchard Hill, as she chose.

"Boy's clothes, I suppose?" Gracie said, wryly.

"Of course," Mrs. Lennox said, with a bold wink. "Every good spy needs her disguise."

And then she closed the door.

Gracie looked at the wood panel long after it had closed.

A spy?

Was that what she was now?

A spy for a housekeeper?

What on earth had she just agreed to?

At least there was one good thing coming from all of this—it did not seem likely she would see John Crawford this Christmas season after all.

And that did make her feel lighter.

Chapter 6

And to be merry best

becomes you; for, out of question, you were

born in a merry hour.

— Much Ado About Nothing

"You should host a festival," Jasper announced. "A winter festival. With juggling."

"Juggling?"

"Yes, juggling. And perhaps a puppet show. For the children, you know. And skating, of course. And then dancing..."

"Dancing?"

"Yes, dancing. Reels and country dances, of course. Or if you wish to make it more formal, you might go all out and host a ball. With the village invited, of course. Throw open the doors. Let people see inside the castle."

"Inside the castle?"

"Yes, let them dance in the great hall. And fireworks. There should be fireworks at the end. A spectacular display. We could summon a fire-master from London. Or perhaps Edinburgh."

"Fireworks. Edinburgh."

"You know, you do not have to repeat everything I say. It makes you seem rather... Well, how shall I put this kindly... Dim. Very dim. A dolt, in fact. Decidedly dunce-like."

"Ah, I see. You wish me to open the castle coffers so that you may make merry and believe the best way to encourage this is by insulting my intelligence repeatedly," Linden said.

"Well, you make it rather easy..." Jasper grinned. "But it is an excellent idea, is it not?"

"Not. Decidedly not," Linden said, grimly. "Moreover, Warburton would be very much opposed."

"Then we simply must do it!" Jasper clapped his hands together. "Why, that is the best reason of all! We could call it the Warburton Winter Festival and he could be a kind of...special performer."

"Performer?" Linden raised his eyebrows. "Have you ever seen Warburton perform anything in your life?"

"He performs the part of the cantankerous old fool very nicely," Jasper said, pleasantly.

"Jasper..." Linden glared at his friend in exasperation. "He is a loyal, faithful man, no matter how frustrating you may find him."

"Very well, no performance by Warburton. Simply a winter festival. Come now, you know it is a good idea."

"I know nothing of the sort," Linden exclaimed. "All that I know is you have been nattering on about it nonstop for what feels like months."

"Minutes. Not months. And I plan to continue. I will not stop, you know," Jasper said. "Look at me, Linden. Look deep into my eyes."

"Yes, they're very nice."

"No, I mean see the intensity there. The determination. The sheer resolve." Jasper slammed his hands palm down on the table dramatically. "I tell you now, I shall not rest until the winter festival has been held."

"Do you know how idiotic you sound?" Linden said. "Dramatizing about the necessity of a carnival as if you were Henry V giving the St. Crispin's Day speech?"

Jasper's eyes lit up dangerously. "Ah! An excellent speech. Should there be a Shakespeare play, too, do you think? We could hold auditions. A Midsummer Night's Dream, perhaps?"

"And you would play Puck, of course," Linden muttered.

"Warburton could be Bottom. And you, of course, could play Oberon," Jasper offered, generously. "Or Theseus, if you don't want many lines." He frowned. "I cannot see Fleur as Titania, can you?"

"No, I cannot." Linden rolled his eyes.

"We could hold it on St. Nicholas Day. You could have a sack full of gifts for the children," Jasper mused. "Or perhaps a week-long festival would be better…"

"I'm going," Linden announced, rising to his feet. They had been sitting in the solar on the second floor, which adjoined Linden's bed chamber. The bed chamber that had once been his parents.

The solar was a comfortable space—much smaller than the great hall, and more importantly, more private. Linden had long lost count of the winter days spent in the solar with Jasper, reading and smoking and talking.

Today, there had been a little too much talking.

"Oh, yes? Going for a walk? Perhaps I'll tag along," Jasper said, brightly.

"Oh, wonderful. I cannot wait to hear more of your plans," Linden said, sardonically.

"Truly?" Jasper said, his eyes widening. "I knew you'd come round…"

"No," Linden snapped. "Not really. Jasper—" He took a deep breath. "—they all hate me. There is nothing I can do about it. You know this. I must simply make the best of it."

"Nothing you can do about it? Or nothing you *will* do about it?" Jasper set his jaw stubbornly. "There is quite a difference you know. And have you thought about the future? About your children?"

Linden stared.

"Yes, your children. I'd say there's a fifty-fifty chance you'll eventually have some if you go along with this foolhardy marriage to Fleur. Will you simply accept that they will be shunned as their father is? Will you let them suffer the same fate as well? Outcasts of their own people? Always uncomfortable in the place they should most belong? All because of a misunderstanding that you could have cleared up before they were born?"

Linden gritted his teeth. "I should hardly call believing I murdered my own parents a mere misunderstanding, Jasper."

"But it is a lie. And you are misunderstood," Jasper insisted. "It is a lie that you have never made an effort to clear up. Nor has Warburton for that matter. Perhaps that is why I detest him so much."

"He has tried! You know he has tried. He did all that he could at the time—and more. He brought back your family to the castle, let your mother care for me," Linden reminded.

"Brought us back!" Jasper scoffed. "As if my parents would have stayed away. As if my mother would have done anything less than what she did. Warburton did not bring them back. He merely permitted them to stay. Reluctantly at that, I might add."

Linden closed his eyes. "We must simply accept that we have different versions of events," he said, slowly.

"You know I care for you, like a brother," Jasper said, softly. "I am only trying to help."

"I know that," Linden said. And he did. "I feel the same. But..."

"What are you so afraid of, Linden? You are the strongest person I know—except for this," Jasper said.

"I must go," Linden said, abruptly. "I have tarried too long this morning as it is."

"Where are you heading?" Jasper said, following him out into the hall.

"To see our guest," Linden said. "To find out what happened to him in our woods that night. And then to do something about it."

He started down the curving flight of steps towards the second floor. Jasper followed.

"And will Warburton be meeting you there?" Jasper asked, innocently.

"No," Linden said, tersely. "I will handle this on my own."

When Gracie woke that morning, all she could think about was the coach driver.

Despite Sir Warburton's having convinced himself that she had been in a simple carriage accident at the hands of a reckless driver, he had failed to fully convince Gracie.

She could not stop thinking about the deep, bloodied marks in the snow.

It had been more than a full day since she had left the place where the coach had crashed.

Yes, she had been injured, but she had been well enough to hold conversations, to eat, to walk—albeit only for a time; and she had not been particularly clear-headed throughout.

Nevertheless. She should have done more. She should have immediately demanded a search party be sent out.

Now it would be too late. The driver might have frozen to death, injured, alone in the woods.

She was stupid. Stupid and reckless and self-centered.

Self-centered? Yes, because from the moment she set eyes on the castle's master she had lost all good sense and could think of little else. Even last night's conversation with Mrs. Lennox. What she had agreed to was madness. She was bewitched.

There was a knock at the door.

"Come," she called. She was sitting in a chair between the fire and the window, with her legs up and her chin resting on her knees. At least her brooding would be cut short.

"Mister Gardner?"

Blast! It was him.

Lord Linden Chevalier poked his head around the edge of the door. Even as a disembodied head, he could take Gracie's breath away.

"Yes?" she breathed. She cleared her throat. "Yes, what is it?"

He came in and shut the door behind him.

Of course, he would. There was no need for a chaperone with just two men in the room.

Gracie bit her lip to keep from laughing. It was all too ridiculous. She was heading towards an embarrassing outburst if she did not keep herself in check.

"How are you feeling today?" Lord Chevalier asked, solicitously, hovering by the door with his hands clasped behind his back.

"Much better," she said, cautiously. "Was there something you wished to speak with me about?"

He came further into the room and took a chair across from her.

He was only a few feet away now. She could see the fine shape of his lips, the gleam of his hair. It was back in a queue. She wondered why he wore it so long. But she rather liked it. It made him look a little like a pirate. A very regal, very beautiful pirate.

"Firstly, I wished to make sure you understand that you are very welcome to stay at Princewood as long as you need to," he said, courteously. "You are my guest. If there is anything you require, please let me know. I wish for you to be comfortable."

He seemed fidgety. Why? Gracie would not flatter herself that she could be the cause.

"Thank you," she said. "You have all been very kind."

Especially Mrs. Lennox.

And incredibly mysterious and cryptic. Also, Mrs. Lennox.

"Secondly, I wondered if you might recount to me what happened to you on the road," he suggested. "If it will not trouble you to do so."

Gads, was he always this mannerly? Even when speaking to other men? She felt as if he were walking on eggshells around her.

"Of course," she said, quickly. "In fact, I am exceedingly glad that you have asked, for I have just been sitting here feeling terribly guilty about leaving the coach without knowing what had become of the poor driver."

"What happened to him precisely?" Lord Chevalier said, leaning forward.

He was so close. If she were to lean forward as well, their faces would nearly be touching. He had a lovely forehead, with a distinct widow's peak. She had never seen a fair-haired man with a pointed brow.

There was a cleft in his chin, she noticed today, and his jaw was square. Yet the hardness of those features was so impeccably balanced by those full beautiful lips.

Any woman on earth would be happy to have those lips.

He was prettier than she was, Gracie thought. Oddly, this did not bother her.

But it did hurt to look at him. He was so beautiful and so very far out of reach.

"Mr. Gardner?"

She jumped. "Yes, of course." She wrapped her arms more tightly around her knees, determined not to move a muscle closer towards this entrancing man even though part of her longed to throw herself at him. And since when had Gracie ever, *ever* wished to do such a stupid, humiliating thing?

In any case, it was not his fault he looked this way, she thought, with a sigh.

She lifted up her head and met his eyes carefully.

"The coach was passing through the woods when it came to a stop. I heard the driver scream. Then the horses began to panic and rear. They broke free of the harness and bolted. The carriage rolled backwards, crashed into the trees, and turned over." She touched her forehead. "That was how I got this. Well, that and another tumble in the snow as I walked."

He looked displeased as he heard of her injury.

"Well, when I managed to clamber out of the carriage, I found myself alone. The driver had disappeared. But there was blood. In the snow. On the driver's seat. A trail of blood leading into the woods."

"He walked away? Into the woods?" Lord Chevalier said, slowly.

"Or..." Gracie swallowed. "This may sound difficult to believe, but... Well, there was a rut in the snow with the blood. Like the track of a body being... pulled along."

And then there were the noises she had heard, as if someone were coming back. But not the driver. No, she would swear it had not been the driver.

Next the white stag had appeared.

But worried that the story might seem too far-fetched—as it had to Warburton, Gracie decided to mention neither of those things.

"I was wondering..." She started, tentatively. "I mean, is there any chance you would consider sending someone to see if the driver is still there? He might be horribly injured and alone." She shook her head. "Though why he did not stay with the coach..."

"Yes, that is very strange," he agreed.

"I could even go with them. Show them where it happened. Oh, of course, the coach will still be there," she remembered. Along with her crushed valise and clothing. Now wouldn't that complicate things if the wrong person found them. "But still, I am strong enough. I could go along. Or even alone. If you would lend me a horse, I feel certain I..."

"I will send someone," he interjected. His tone was gentle. "Do not distress yourself, Mr. Gardner—"

"Grayson," Gracie interrupted. "Call me Grayson. Please. Everyone else does."

He looked faintly surprised, then smiled. "Very well. Grayson. Then you must call me Linden."

"Linden," she said, feeling a rush of heat as she said his name. "Very well."

"I am sending Cam, Mrs. Lennox's husband, to search the area where the accident took place. He is an excellent tracker. If the driver is anywhere in the vicinity, Cam will find him, you may rest assured."

Gracie breathed a sigh of relief. "Thank you. Thank you so much. It is only... When I think that I have been resting in a comfortable bed, in a warm place, while he might... Well, thank you."

"You are very welcome," Linden said. "But please know that I do this not for you particularly, but because if there is danger, my people deserve to know. The men hunt in these woods, the children play there, the women gather berries and herbs. It is as much a part of their lives as..."

"Breathing?" Gracie suggested, smiling slightly.

His people. They were not in Scotland, but he played the part of laird so very well.

Once again, she could not help but feel she had stepped into another time. Mrs. Lennox had cast Jasper as her lord's squire, but Gracie was quite willing to play the role. To carry his banner, polish his sword, sit at his feet.

How debasing. How utterly pathetic. How very far gone.

"Yes," he agreed. "And so, if there is something to dread, I must find it out."

"May I go with Cam?" She asked, quickly.

He hesitated. "I do not think that would be wise. Mrs. Lennox tells me that the surgeon advised you to rest so that your head may heal."

"Rest," Gracie groaned, putting her head on her knees again. "I have rested all night and all morning. Can one's head ache from doing sheer nothing?"

"If you are feeling so very confined," Linden said, with amusement. "Perhaps Mrs. Lennox might not object if you had a little fresh air. Perhaps you might wish to go riding with me. Only a short ride, along the beach. At a very sedate pace, of course."

Gracie brightened. "Yes. Oh, yes, please."

She cringed at her own eagerness. To get out of the room. To have her time with him extended. Oh, anything for that.

"I should love it," she declared. "Shall we go now?"

Chapter 7

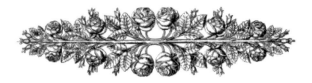

She loved me for the dangers I had passed,

And I loved her that she did pity them

— Othello

Grayson was looking at him with the eagerness of a young puppy. Linden half-expected the boy to begin running circles around his feet.

Why had he suggested the ride? There were other things he should be doing. Looking over the accounts, for one. Or accompanying Cam.

But he could not recant now. He had made the offer and would stand by it.

Besides, he admitted to himself, with a little disquiet—he enjoyed Mr. Gardner's company. The boy had a youthful energy and charm. A keen enthusiasm. Had Linden ever been this way? Not that he was so very old now at five-and-twenty, but he could not remember ever being so... well, lively.

Grayson and Jasper were sure to get along, he thought, his heart sinking just a little. Why should that bother him? Of course, they should. They were two of a kind.

Not that Mr. Gardner was necessarily of the same persuasion. But perhaps he was.

And if so?

Linden stood up abruptly, his chair tilting and nearly falling over. He steadied it without thinking.

"Very well. Meet me down at the stables in twenty minutes. I'll have the horses readied," he said, before striding from the room.

It was another crisp and sunny winter day. The kind where one might put on a cloak and then immediately have to strip it off again.

Linden made sure to bring a few extra items for the boy, stowed in a small saddle bag, in case Mr. Gardner proved overconfident from the sunshine.

Sure enough, Grayson came down in only a light cap, with his cloak over his arm, in only a thin coat. Short leather boots and fingerless mittens seemed to be his only acknowledgement that it was, indeed, winter.

"You'll freeze," Linden said, mildly, looking at the boy. "I should put the cloak on before you ride if I were you."

"Truly? I feel only the heat of summer." Grayson lifted his face up to the sun, smiling, his eyes closed. The picture of perfect bliss, Linden thought, with a pang in his heart.

The boy was gangly and coltish, all sharp points and bones. A playful spattering of freckles across his nose and cheeks mixed with those pretty wide lips and delicate cheek bones made Linden think of an elf. He was not precisely hand-some. His features were not perfect. But he was so spirited that it made him quite incandescent.

He could not help contemplating other things which might cause Mr. Gardner to wear a similarly blissful expression.

Linden coughed. "The cloak," he said, again, pointing. He tried to smile, to sound less parental.

"Oh, very well, then, my lord," Grayson said, with a pouty grin. "I am your humble servant."

He bowed with a beautiful flourish and Linden felt his face color.

"Shall we go?" He said quickly, turning away.

He had had the groom ready Lucy for Mr. Gardner to ride. She was a pretty roan with a calm temperament. He suspect-ed Grayson would prefer a more challenging mount, but he was not about to let the boy be thrown on his watch. Mrs. Lennox would have his head. Speaking of which, he was cer-tain she would not approve of Mr. Gardner riding today at all.

"We will only go a short way," he began, turning his mount, to see Grayson poised and waiting on Lucy.

"Very well," the boy said, cheerfully, and without letting him finish, took Lucy at a trot through the courtyard towards the south gate.

"Wait, you do not even know where..." Linden began to call, but it was no use. With a sigh, he followed.

Once they were through, Linden took the lead, directing them on a well-worn path down to the shoreline.

They rode in silence for a time, enjoying the fine day. Gulls cawed overhead. Small waves foamed against the sand.

Linden almost missed it when the boy brought his horse to a standstill. He galloped the short distance back to where Grayson sat astride, looking back at the castle.

"It is so beautiful here," the boy said, softly. "How do you stand it? A castle and the sea."

The sun was shining off the sandy strands of hair that peeked out from beneath the boy's cap.

"Your hair," he said, stupidly.

The boy whipped around to face him, touching his head self-consciously. "What about it?"

"I...hadn't noticed. The color." God, he was babbling like a fool. "I like it."

"Oh, I see," the boy said, looking more relaxed. "I like yours as well. You wear it unfashionably long, but it suits you."

Now it was Linden's turn to touch his hair self-consciously. "I never think about it."

"No, you wouldn't," he thought he heard the boy mumble.

"I suspect you have pirate tendencies," Grayson said, more loudly. "Do you secretly harbor a desire to escape on a ship and roam the deep blue sea?"

"How did you guess?" Linden said, with a wink. Then he shook his head. "The truth is that I haven't been much further than the forest."

"Not really?" The boy looked shocked. "Well, it is a very large forest..."

"The second largest in England," Linden said, with pride. "For hundreds of years, kings and queens came to hunt in this wood."

"But to never leave here," the boy mused. "Never?"

"Have you ever traveled?" Linden asked, curiously.

"I have, in fact," the boy said, looking happily out at the sea. "I was a cabin boy." He grinned. "I ran off to sea."

"Did you truly?" Linden grinned back, feeling warm and pleasantly at ease.

"Yes, my mother was not happy. Fortunately for her, my older sister was on the ship with me…" The boy stopped a moment. "She wound up married to the owner of the vessel, in fact. It was a rather exciting journey. We were boarded by pirates at one point."

Linden raised his eyebrows. "Really? Did you fight them off with a saber?"

"No," the boy said, shaking his head, and smiling. "Nor a pistol. But I helped to deliver a baby."

"A baby was born during a pirate invasion?" Linden lips quirked. "I would not have thought midwifery a requirement for a cabin boy."

"Nor would I, but we do what we must," Grayson said, beaming. "I think you would love the sea. One feels so free."

"While trapped on a floating piece of wood?" Linden said, skeptically. "I am not sure I would feel freer there than here with the wind in my face, a horse beneath me, and all of this—" He gestured to the expanse around them. "—to explore at my will."

"Perhaps it was not merely the ship," Grayson said, slowly. "But the entire experience of stepping outside one's normal life and… well, being someone else."

The boy looked about him. "I feel rather as if I have done so again."

"I am glad you are here then, if being here makes you feel that way," Linden said impulsively.

The young man's eyes widened a little at that, and Linden shifted in his saddle awkwardly.

"Tell me more about you," the boy said, suddenly. "You say you have lived here all your life and never traveled. And yet..." He paused, biting his lip.

"Yes?" Linden prompted.

"Well, it is only..." The boy hedged. "I wonder if it might be rather isolating. The village..."

So, he already knew something of it, Linden understood. Someone had said something.

But the boy was still here. He was not frightened. He had not come reluctantly. He had not fled.

"What have you heard?" Linden demanded.

The boy met his eyes. "Only that you are the victim of false rumors. And that the people do not seem to truly know you at all," he said, frankly.

"That's very charitable," Linden said. "To both myself and the villagers. They think I am a murderous fiend. They hold me responsible for... Well, for my parents' deaths. And as for myself, I..."

He did not know how to say it. That he both loved and loathed his own people. That he wished to care for and protect them like his father had done before him, and his father before that. But also resented them for judging him so cruelly and for believing the worst so easily.

"It must be very hard," the boy said, softly. And then he pulled off his gloves and nudging his horse closer, reached over with one hand to grasp Linden's own.

Linden stared at it stupidly for a moment. The boy's small white one clutching his own gloved black.

Then he pulled free. The boy looked dismayed a moment, until he saw Linden tug his own gloves off.

He picked up Grayson's hand again in his own, feeling its soft smoothness. Its warmth and coolness.

He could not help it. He ran his thumb gently over the top, feeling the ridges of the boy's knuckles, the silky flat smoothness of the rest—no coarse hairs there, just soft even skin. He traced a slow circle and heard the boy gasp.

Immediately he let go.

The boy was clutching his hand to his chest, as if he had been scorched by a hot coal.

"I'm sorry," he said, quickly, hot with embarrassment. "I...do not know where that came from."

"Do not be," Grayson said, softly. "I do."

"You do?" Linden raised his eyebrows.

"You must feel so alone sometimes," the boy said, bluntly. Then he blushed. "I mean, I know Mrs. Lennox cares for you. And her son."

Was he alone? Linden stared.

He had Mrs. Lennox and Jasper. Warburton and loyal Cam.

Ostensibly, he had Fleur.

Yes, he was an engaged man. How could he truly be lonely?

But, of course, he was. He had been for as long as he could remember. Since the day it had happened.

"And," Grayson continued. "It must be very hard, to be treated so unfairly by the people you care for so very much. Of course, you must wish it was otherwise. That there was something you could do. If only there was."

Linden looked at the boy.

"Yes," he said, slowly. "If only."

What would the boy say if he knew Linden had never really tried?

Oh, he had protested that he had to Jasper. But the truth was that he had simply accepted it as his lot to play the scapegoat. Unfairly tried and found wanting. Punished for something he knew he had not done, but would always feel responsible for nonetheless.

The boy would think him a coward.

"There is to be a festival," Linden said, suddenly. "A winter festival. At the castle. I hope you will stay for it."

"A festival?" The boy's face lit up with delight. "How lovely."

"Yes, it was Jasper's idea," Linden confessed. Oh, how Jasper would laugh now if he could see him. "To try to foster good will between the village and... well, and between myself. I doubt it will do much good, but..."

"Of course, it will," Grayson exclaimed. "Bringing people together and letting them set aside their cares for a little while, and most of all, showing them your true self—showing them you are not the ogre they believe you to be. It is bound to do something. Especially at Christmas!"

"Not an ogre," Linden said, smiling a little. "What a strange aim."

The boy flashed him a broad, beautiful grin and he felt his heart quicken.

"What is it..." Grayson started, slowly. "What is it that they think you did precisely? May I ask?"

Best to get it out of the way quickly. No sugar-coating. No pretense.

"They believe I killed my family," he said, directly. "Fifteen years ago, my mother was found dead in the forest. She had been stabbed, too many times to count. And there I sat, beside her body, crying and covered in blood."

Grayson had clapped his hands over his mouth, his eyes wide with distress. "But you were a mere child," he whispered.

"Yes," Linden agreed. "And I had no knife. But I was the only one there. And what happened next did not precisely clear my name. My father and Warburton found us. Warburton took me back to the castle so my father might... have a moment, to say good-bye to my mother."

This was the part he hated, for he could not remember any of it.

"I suppose I was upset—" Probably a vast understatement for a ten-year-old boy whose mother had just been murdered. "—for I did not stay put. Instead, I am told I ran off, precisely where I should not have—just over there—" He pointed, far into the distance at the shoreline past the village. "—Where the current is incredibly strong. I went straight in, apparently. Warburton does not swim. Nor do most of the villagers. Cam does, but he and Jock had gone to carry my mother's body back. Mrs. Lennox and Jasper were away. They had gone to take care of Mrs. Lennox's mother who was ill. So neither of them were there for any of this—" And so the fact that they had returned and believed in Linden's innocence unquestionably meant more to him than he could ever express. He could never repay their kindness to him. "—So, Warburton ran to find my father again. He was a strong swimmer. He was just coming back to the castle. He had come directly from seeing my mother, and then had to run after me—" Linden heard his voice becoming hoarse.

"Stop," Grayson said, reaching out an arm. "Stop, please. You do not have to continue. Please."

"It is all right," Linden said, flatly. "I will finish. My father found me in the water and got me to shore. Somehow. I will never know how exactly, for I have little recollection of anything that happened that day. Only a strong feeling of horror and, well, sadness, of course."

"Of course," he heard Grayson murmur. The boy's face was stricken with distress.

"My father's body was never found," he finished. "But it is commonly accepted that I pulled him under, while somehow making it to shore myself. Perhaps I did not murder him as directly as I am supposed to have done with my mother, but..." He shrugged.

"How could they believe that?" Grayson cried. "How could they believe that about a child? How could anyone?"

Linden shrugged as if it did not matter, while knowing it very much did.

"It was a horrid day," he said, wearily. It had taken something out of him to retell the story. One would think he would be hardened to it by now, but there it was. "They had no one else to blame. I was there. That was enough."

"Now I understand why Mrs. Lennox..." The boy stopped.

"Yes?" he prompted.

"Never mind," Grayson said. "I was simply going to say I understand why Mrs. Lennox cares for you so much."

"Do you? I still do not. I do not deserve her care," he said, knowing how bitter and sorry for himself he probably sounded, and feeling angry at himself for it.

"You deserve it," Grayson shot back, hotly. "You most certainly deserve it—that and much more. You deserve to be loved. You deserve to be happy."

Linden looked at the boy—so fierce, so serious, so ready to do battle on his behalf. "Thank you," he said, finally. And he meant it.

They rode back to the castle quietly. The boy seemed tired and Linden promised to have a tray sent up to his room.

But all in all, it had been a good day. He found himself hoping that the boy would stay, even though part of him knew he was bound to regret it.

Chapter 8

Virtue is bold, and goodness never fearful.

— Measure for Measure

Mrs. Lennox was sitting by the fire, mending a pair of Jasper's trousers, when Cam entered, stamping snow from his boots.

"You are back already," she exclaimed, rising to help him remove his coat. "I was not sure whether to expect you tonight."

"Nothing appealing about spending the night in the forest on a snowy night," Cam grumbled.

Mrs. Lennox smiled. The able hunter and tracker was no stranger to roughing it, but it was good to have him back.

"What did you find?" she asked. She looked past him to the package he had carried in. "What is that?"

"That, if I'm not mistaken, is your young lady's belongings," Cam said. "Not doing her much good stuck under a broken carriage and I didn't think you'd want to chance anyone else coming across it."

"No, certainly not," Mrs. Lennox said, picking up the leather valise and trying to brush away some of the wetness. "Oh, dear, it is sadly crushed." She opened it and peered inside. "But clothes are meant to be washed. The water shan't have hurt most of her things."

"Not that she needs them right now," Cam remarked. "Unless this fool plan has changed. If one can call something so daft a plan at all."

"Cam Lennox," Mrs. Lennox said, threateningly, taking a step towards him. "You know as well as I do that Warburton would have that lass out in the snow before you or I could say fiddle-de-dee about it! With some stuff and nonsense about it being improper for Linden to host a single young woman or another similar kind of excuse."

"He certainly knows how to play upon the lad's sense of honor," Cam agreed.

"Indeed, he does. And to our poor lord's detriment. Just look at this engagement as proof! What matter that it is a mismatch bound for failure and will make Warburton's own daughter unhappy. He cares nothing for that," Mrs. Lennox complained. "He sees a chance to have his line inherit and he is taking it, bold as can be, all while claiming the lad's parents wished it so. And," she admitted, begrudgingly. "Perhaps they did. Though I find it difficult to believe when we heard no mention of any such thing when they were alive."

She shook her head. "I almost feel sorry for the girl at times. Cantankerous and standoffish she may be, but a poor motherless creature all the same. And how is she treated? As a pawn on her father's chess board."

"As our young guest is on yours?" Cam said, pointedly.

Mrs. Lennox pursed her lips. "I suppose one could say so. But my motives are at least less selfish than Warburton's."

"What precisely are your motives, my dear?" Cam asked, with deceptive innocence, sitting down by the fire and taking out a clay pipe.

"Linden's happiness, of course!" Mrs. Lennox puffed.

"Of course, of course," Cam murmured. "And how exactly is a girl dressed as a boy to bring that about?" There was a small smile playing about his lips.

Mrs. Lennox put her hands on her hips and glared. "Have a little faith, Cam. Give it time. He's already taken the young lad...lass... riding, I'll have you know. Just let him spend time with someone from beyond these castle walls. The young lady has traveled, you know. Let her open his eyes. Let him get a taste of what else is out there."

"You're matchmaking, my dear, and no good will come of it—especially going about it in this batty way, where poor Linden won't know what to make of the girl," Mr. Lennox said, firmly. "You're not thinking ahead, and that's a fact."

"Well, there's nothing for it now," Mrs. Lennox said, stubbornly. "What's done is done. Let it play out. And you know very well there is more to it than matchmaking. Let our guest be a new pair of eyes and ears at Princewood. Perhaps she will see something we have not. I want the truth, Cam. And so do you. Fifteen years we have been waiting for it—as has poor Linden. Things are coming to a head. I can feel it in my bones. Something is coming."

"Something good or bad?" her husband asked, his face turning serious.

She frowned at him. "Why? What do you know?" She narrowed her eyes. "What did you find out there besides the valise, Cam?"

"Ah! See, I was wondering when you would get around to asking that," he said, in a satisfied voice. Then he sobered and shook his head. "A bad business."

"What do you mean?" his wife said, impatience in her voice.

"I mean I found the young driver, but he was beyond assistance. Not more than fifty meters from where the coach rolled, in amongst the trees, half-hidden in leaves and snow at the bottom of a hill."

"He was dead then?" she said, sadly, sitting down across from him and resting her hands on the arms of the chair, her sewing forgotten on the floor.

"Dead and cold. By the time the girl showed up here, the driver would have long since passed. We may put her mind at rest about that. Now, Paulina. Brace yourself," he said, reluctantly, looking at his wife. "When we found Hester Chevalier, her body had been slashed and stabbed beyond counting. Well, it's happened again." Cam sighed. "I've brought the body back with me."

"My God," Mrs. Lennox said, softly. "I...was not expecting that."

"Nor was I," her husband replied. "My money was with Warburton. Losing a valuable team of horses would have been enough to make many lads run for the hills. But the lass was right. There was a trail of blood, just as she said. Someone dragged the body."

"Someone? Or some animal?" Mrs. Lennox said. "Those are two quite different things, Cam."

"Oh, to be sure," he said. "There are wolves in the forest. Though few and far between these days. But wolves would never drag their prey as far as this."

"What about a bear?" Mrs. Lennox suggested.

Cam brushed off the idea. "There haven't been bears in Princewood in... oh, more than a hundred years. Or in any forest in England, for that matter. No, a bear couldn't have done this."

"So, a person then?" his wife said, tentatively.

"Probably the same person who killed Hester Chevalier fifteen years ago," Cam said.

Mrs. Lennox stared at him.

"Well," she said, finally, in a faint voice. "It is one thing to believe something is brewing and another to find it fully cooked, as it were. But you cannot be certain of that, Cam."

"No," he agreed. "But what are the chances lightning would strike twice, Paulina?"

"With fifteen years in between? Surely there would have been something. All this time passing..."

"'Tis strange, surely," Cam said. "But would it not be stranger to think there were two murderers on the loose, both killing the same way?"

"A murderer," his wife murmured. "To hear it put like that..."

She looked up sharply. "But why are you sitting here like a lump then, Cam? Get up! Go and tell Linden what you have found. Go on now!"

She stood up, shakily. "Bringing a body back, saying a murderer is loose, and then sitting down by the fire. Really, Cam..."

"Calm yourself, my dear," her husband soothed. "He knows. What do you take me for? I went to him first of all, of course."

"Though I did not say I believed the coach driver to have been slain by the same person who killed his mother," Cam added, quickly. "He will have to work that out for himself, if he is of a mind to. If he broaches it, well... Then we shall talk."

"He is sure to," Mrs. Lennox said, slowly. "He is a clever lad. Clever man," she amended. "And then?"

"Then we shall have a hunt on our hands," Cam said, cheerfully. "We'll find the bastard and string him up."

"It is sure to be someone we know, Cam," his wife said, looking ill. "Someone from the village. It will not turn out to have been a stranger."

"A wolf in our midst," Cam growled. "For fifteen years. They have had fifteen years of undeserved peace."

"It is time Linden received some," his wife asserted.

"There is more, Paulina," her husband said, taking a puff from his pipe. "I've saved the strangest part for last. I met Paul Brown from Sicilborough on the road. Sit down and let me tell you what he told me."

Linden's mouth was set in a grim line as he walked the hall towards Grayson Gardner's room.

He did not relish the prospect of informing the young man that his instincts had been right and the coach driver had been found dead.

Nor did he relish explaining the gruesome condition of the body. Perhaps he would not. There was no need for the young man to know.

There was more besides.

Cam had heard that livestock from the village had gone missing, then been found days later—in much the same state as the coach driver.

Whoever had killed the driver had not been content with mere beasts and had turned to hunting men instead.

There had been no need for Cam to say what Linden had already known—that there was an uncomfortable similarity between current events and those fifteen years earlier.

And when the whole village learned of the coach driver's death?

For surely, they would, as Linden would have inquiries made and in the course of that, the matter would become public knowledge. Would the consensus be that the castle's master had turned murderous once more? Or would his people finally see that some other malevolent person was responsible now, just as they had been for his mother's death fifteen years earlier?

"Lord Chevalier! Linden! A word!"

He turned to see Sir Guy, huffing and puffing his way down the hall. The older knight had turned portlier as the years went by. His love of fine foods and wine, combined with a reluctance to ride or walk outside of the castle grounds, meant he became quite breathless merely from climbing up the stone steps from the great hall.

Linden waited patiently for the man to reach him.

"I have heard," Warburton panted, putting his hands on his knees and bending over to catch his breath. "That there is to be a carnival. *Inside* the keep."

From his horrified tone of voice, one might be forgiven for assuming the event was to be held in the nude.

"A festival," Linden corrected. "And yes, I have been considering the idea."

"The notion is bound to have come from Young Lennox," Warburton said, looking displeased. "A ridiculous suggestion. I am surprised you believe it to have any merit whatsoever."

"You are?" Linden said, mildly. "I admit I do not know why you find the idea so objectionable. Jasper thinks I should make more of an effort to establish an amiable relationship with my tenants. Is a day of merriment truly so terrible to consider?"

"Pshaw!" Warburton waved a hand and looked disgusted. "Nobility," he said, with the utmost pretension. "Have no need to grovel for the favor of peasants. If they dislike you, then they are ungrateful fools and so be it."

"Yes, well, that is how it has gone on for fifteen years, Warburton," Linden said. "Perhaps it is time for a change."

Warburton puffed out his chest. "A change from the way *I* have done things, you mean. It has not been easy, young man, overseeing all of this—" He swept out his hands. "—all alone, waiting patiently for the day when you might take on greater responsibility. Especially while taking on the duties and responsibilities of a father as well. Heavy is the head that wears the crown," he misquoted, pompously. "Very heavy."

"You have been very self-sacrificing and I am grateful to you," Linden said, patiently. "Of course, when I came of age four years ago, your duties were somewhat lightened. Now, no one is placing blame on you for the state of things. No one is to blame for a poor relationship between the castle and the village but myself. I have had years in which to try to change it. Jasper is proposing something which to you may seem a foolish endeavor." He sighed and ran a hand over his hair. "But truth be told, Warburton, I am ready to try just about anything. I find it difficult to believe my parents would wish for things to continue as they are. The people hate me. Mistrust me. Are frightened of me."

"Because they are idiots," Warburton said, dismissively. "Ignorant rustics. They persist in gossip and lies. All we can do is ignore it."

"I find I am reluctant to do that any longer," Linden said, quietly. "They are under my charge. I care for them and place some value upon their opinion of me. That will not change."

"Perhaps there is more to this than you are saying," Warburton said, suddenly, frowning. "Perhaps you desire more than to simply win over the villagers."

Linden raised his eyebrows. "Oh? And what is that?"

"There are pretty girls in the village," Warburton announced. "Perhaps one has turned your head. Perhaps you are regretting your promise. I will not have my Fleur slighted, I tell you, my lord. Not when you have given your word. I will not have her..." Warburton was red-faced, searching for a word. "Humiliated! Degraded! By your fancy girls parading around the castle, trying to win a lord."

"You are being ridiculous, Warburton," Linden said. He did not know whether he was more in danger of laughing or losing his temper.

"Am I?" Warburton cried, drops of spittle flying from his lips rather unpleasantly. "You say you desire to honor your parents wishes and marry my daughter, but when it comes down to it, will you truly fulfill your oath?"

"Of course, I will," Linden said, slowly, feeling his anger rising. "I have said so and I shall do so. There is no girl in the village." No point in mentioning that none would dare to look at him. "There is no one else. Fleur and I have had an understanding for years, and of course, I will marry her as I have promised to do."

Something stirred regretfully in him as he made this decree, but he pushed forward.

"Fleur's entire future rests upon this alliance. She would be devastated were you to break the engagement," Warburton griped, unwilling to let the matter go. "Absolutely heartbroken."

Linden doubted that, but he was not about to argue with Warburton about whether or not his daughter had a heart.

"Of course," he said, gently. "But I would never do that to her. I have known her since we were children. She is very dear to me."

That much he could say truthfully. Whatever he could or could not feel for Fleur, his desire to protect her was genuine.

"Now," he continued. "Please do not concern yourself with this festival idea anymore. If it does go ahead, the blame will be mine if it fails and you need take no part in it."

Warburton had his hand to his chin. "Perhaps I was too hasty," he said, consideringly. "Perhaps a festival is a perfect opportunity."

"Oh, yes?" Linden said, his heart sinking a little.

"Yes, perhaps your engagement to Fleur is exactly what might bring people together," Warburton said, slowly. "We could hold a ball—well, more of a simple country dance, as the village would not know what to make of anything so grand as a ball. But we could call it an engagement ball for you and Fleur. A spectacular celebration of the upcoming marriage of the lord and soon-to-be lady of Princewood."

"An interesting idea." Linden shifted impatiently. "Well, Jasper did say something about dancing," he admitted.

"Aha! He has the right of it," Warburton proclaimed, nodding his head. "Is he to be the master-of-ceremonies for this event? I shall go and seek him out now to inform him of your decision."

"Yes, I mean, no," Linden said, suppressing a groan. "Very well. Yes. You may do so. Thank you, Warburton."

Jasper was going to be thrilled at the idea of making Linden's engagement to Fleur the centerpiece of his winter festival. Linden could imagine the look of horror on his face all too easily.

Warburton was already scurrying back down the hall. "Excellent, excellent. I will offer him my assistance in any way I can," he called back, distractedly. "It will be an unforgettable event. Utterly unforgettable."

"Wonderful," Linden said, quietly, and mostly to himself.

He walked the last few paces to his guest's door and rapped.

When it opened almost instantly and Grayson stood before him, he was a little taken aback.

"What was all of that noise about just now?" Grayson said, sounding amused. "Were you in an altercation?"

"Of a sort, I suppose," Linden said, sighing. "May I come in?"

"Of course," the young man said, stepping back to allow him to pass.

Linden hesitated a second, the moved forward. He felt over-ly-aware of the precise moment in which his body brushed for the slightest instant against the young man's. There was a rush of heat and a jolt went through him at the connection, ever so brief.

"I have brought you some news," he said, hurriedly, crossing the room and seating himself in the same chair he had sat in the day before. "It is not very good news, I am afraid."

"About the coach? About the driver?" Grayson said, eagerly, coming to stand before him.

The boy's trousers brushed against Linden's knees; he was standing so close.

"Please, tell me," the young man urged.

"Cam found the driver's body," Linden said, quietly. "He had been dead for some time."

He watched as Grayson sank into the chair opposite.

"Truly? He is truly dead?" The boy looked sick.

"Yes. But there was nothing you could have done," Linden reassured him. "Cam says it must have been quick. He did not die of exposure but of—" He hesitated.

"Yes?" The boy prompted.

"But of his wounds," Linden finished, reluctantly.

"What sort of wounds?" Grayson asked, slowly. "What happened to him?"

"It is hard to say for certain," Linden hedged. "But there is no doubt he was killed deliberately. By another person, not an animal."

"Oh, God," Grayson breathed, his face looking white. "I was right there. I could have done something. Oh, why did they take the driver and not me? I might have done something. If only I had gotten out of the coach. If only I had tried."

"What are you saying?" Linden demanded. "And meet the same fate? There was nothing you could do, Grayson. Unless you had a pistol with you? A saber, perhaps? No? A dagger then?" When the boy shook his head, he continued, ruthlessly, "Then there was nothing you could have done. Whoever did this to the man was utterly brutal and violent. All you would probably have done was succeeded in provoking them to attack you as well."

"I think they meant to do so," the boy whispered, his face still ashen.

"What?" Linden said, sharply. "What do you mean?"

"I was standing in the middle of the road, trying to decide what to do," the boy said. "I heard sounds coming from the direction in which the driver had been... taken. Snapping twigs and breaking branches. The sound of something—someone—coming back through the forest."

"And what happened?" Linden said, feeling oddly frightened for the boy, although the time for fear was long gone.

"Something... scared them away," Grayson said, slowly.

He met Linden's eyes. "Perhaps you will not believe me, but it was a stag. It came out of the woods, on the opposite side."

"A stag?" Linden repeated. He could not imagine a stag being enough to frighten away a would-be murderer. But the boy had been lucky, that was the truth.

"A pure white stag," Grayson whispered. "It was indescribable. Like something from a tale."

"You saw the white stag?" Linden's eyes widened. "I have never heard of anyone seeing it. Well, not in a very long time." He hesitated. "My father used to tell me stories of the white hart. He claimed he saw it once, when he was a young boy."

"It saved me," Grayson said, his mind clearly still on the horror he had narrowly evaded. "From whatever was there. It saved me."

"It must have been terrifying," Linden said, softly, watching the boy's face. "But Grayson. There was nothing you could do to save the driver. Please, do not fool yourself into thinking otherwise."

Grayson nodded slowly, then sniffed and wiped the back of his hands across his eyes quickly.

Linden sighed. He was such a boy, he thought, looking at the guest. So young. He could not have been more than seventeen or eighteen years.

Before he could think it through, he found himself rising and going over to the young man's chair. Kneeling beside him, he put his arms around the lad and drew him close.

"There was nothing you could do," he said again, softly, murmuring against the boy's hair. "We will find who did this. I swear to you."

But as he spoke, he realized he had made a terrible mistake.

For as soon as he touched the young man, enveloped him in his arms, felt him shaking like a fragile leaf, he found he could not let him go again. His arms tightened. His heart pounded.

His mouth was so close to the boy's own that he could smell the scent of warm chocolate. There was a pot on the table nearby. He must have been sipping it when Linden knocked.

The fragrance was suddenly the most intoxicating and seductive thing Linden had ever smelled. He imagined languorously reaching his tongue out, ever so slowly, and parting the boy's lips, darting his own inside and tasting from the young man's own mouth.

Grayson was breathing more quickly, little shuddering breaths. Linden could feel the young man's frame beneath his hands. So slender he could feel the ribs under the boy's thin shirt.

The young man was clutching Linden's arm with both hands, his fingers digging in almost painfully.

Linden took a strange pleasure from the sensation.

Too much pleasure, in fact. He could feel himself stirring and started to panic.

What was this?

Everything was a tumult of feelings. He wanted to protect the boy, keep him clasped in his arms. But another, hidden part of him wanted to do more. Much more. Throw the boy onto the bed, unbutton his shirt, press his lips to his skin—everywhere, anywhere.

He let out a shaky breath and pushed away.

"Well, I wanted to tell you," he said, brusquely, walking directly to the door, with his head down. He would not meet the young man's gaze. Could not.

Everything he wanted would show plainly on his face.

And if the boy were to look at his trousers. Damn and blast. He felt his face flushing with heat.

"I will leave you now," he declared, feeling clumsy and graceless. He stepped out into the hall.

Gracie climbed into bed. Her limbs felt heavy and sated.

She slid beneath the sheets, her mind turning slowly, as languid as her body.

He had touched her, she thought, in amazement. He had touched her and he had not wanted to pull away.

She had not imagined it. She had not.

Something was happening. She did not know what it was exactly. It went beyond anything she knew.

It went beyond her clothing. Beyond boy or girl—and Gracie found it so easy to be both, neither, either.

What she did know, undeniably, unmistakably, was that there was a tether running between Linden and herself.

Invisible but strong, tugging them together regardless of anything they did.

She wanted him to touch her again, and she knew beyond a doubt that he would. He had to. He was under a powerful compulsion, just as much as she.

Beyond a shadow of a doubt, she knew that she already loved him.

It was mad to think let alone say aloud.

If anyone of her acquaintance had come to her with a similar claim, she would have laughed and then turned to talking them down from their foolishness.

But it was true.

From the moment she set eyes on Linden Chevalier, she had known it in her heart.

She loved him. She would always love him. And ultimately, she would do so whether he loved her in return or not.

And whether it was to be one-sided or not, she had accepted Mrs. Lennox's calling as soon as she knew it would help the man she loved in some way.

It did not matter if he did not love her back, she told herself again. And it never would.

She loved him and it was madness, but she could not stop.

And she knew that he felt something for her as well. Whether love or something else.

He felt it and she knew he was afraid.

When Cam was finished recounting the story, Mrs. Lennox sat looking into the fire for a long time.

"Well," she said, finally. "Now isn't that something."

"What now, my dear?" her husband said, watching her face.

"If there is even half a grain of truth to it," she said. "Then we must find it out."

"Aye, we are of like minds there," Cam said, with a firm nod. He stood up, put out his pipe, and yawned. "But for now, to bed."

He held out his hands to her and helped her up, then slipped an arm around her waist.

"Would it not be something, Cam?" she said, looking up at him, wistfully. "If it were to be true?"

"It would at that," he said, leaning town and kissing her gently. "It would at that."

"But first," he said, when he had finished kissing her thoroughly. "This blasted festival Jasper has conjured up. When that is through, then I'll go out to Sicilborough and we shall see what we shall see."

"Very well, Cam," his wife said, prettily, as submissive as a lamb. "Whatever you say, my love."

He swatted her on the bottom and she giggled like a girl, then took his hand and tugged him towards the bedroom.

Chapter 9

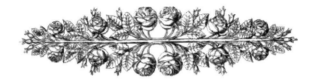

Love sought is good, but given unsought is better.

— Twelfth Night

It had been less than a day since Linden had, through his erstwhile spokesperson Sir Warburton, given his assent for the winter festival.

And it had taken less than a day for Jasper to throw the entire castle into a tumult of preparations.

A steady influx of villagers came like a long line of ants, trailing through the courtyard and into the kitchens and throughout the great hall, bearing all sorts of decorative items, baking samples, and proposals for festival events.

At first, people had come reluctantly—unwilling to step foot in the keep and risk being in the presence of its monstrous master.

But Jasper had anticipated this and prevailed. First, he physically escorted each person in, one by one. Linden had watched in amusement as Jasper gripped some tightly by the arm lest they attempt to escape.

When villager after villager left the castle in relatively the same condition in which they had entered, word must have begun to spread.

Linden could only imagine just what sort of word it had been.

Probably something along the lines of "There is no point in trying to argue with that Young Jasper Lennox so into the keep we must go."

At first, Linden had made himself scarce during all of this.

But slowly, he had stopped trying to avoid being in the great hall altogether. And, miracle of miracles, when he did put in an appearance, the villagers had not fled en masse but rather stole a few curious glances and then mostly ignored him.

A few remarkable souls had gone so far as to respectfully bob their heads.

To Linden, this was a vast improvement already.

It seemed as if Jasper might truly pull things off.

And now, there his friend sat at the center of it all—in the great hall, literally up on a dais, looking for all the world like the lord of minstrels, his feet hanging over the side of a chair, and a ridiculous-looking cap-and-bells on his head that he had dug up from a long-unopened chest somewhere in the castle. It had probably been used for a masquerade, held before Linden's time. Jasper preferred to believe he was being inspired by the spirit of an authentic medieval jester.

There was a loud din in the hall. A group of village women along with their children had just come in, all chattering together about the baking that would be needed and the booths they would set up.

One little girl had crossed over to the dais and was staring awestruck up at Jasper's hat, her little mouth agape.

It was rather adorable, Linden had to admit.

"Good day, dear child," Jasper called, waggling his fingers with a grin. "Step right up and see Jasper the Jester, Jasper the Magnificent, Jasper the..."

"The idiot?" Linden supplied, jumping up onto the dais and stepping up behind him.

"I was going to say 'Juggler,'" Jasper said with a frown. "Or perhaps firebreather. Can one learn how to breath fire in a week, do you suppose?"

"No," Linden said, exasperatedly. "Please do not try. You will only succeed in scorching your throat. Although," he amended. "It would be more peaceful that way. So perhaps you should give it a go after all."

"You are a terrible friend," Jasper said, sadly. "You never support my interests."

Linden rolled his eyes. "I am supporting your very large interest right now in spite of the inconvenience it has incurred."

"Inconvenience?" Jasper retorted. "Is that what you call having more than five people inside the keep at a time? Breathing life into these cold stone walls? An inconvenience, is it, to see people talking and smiling in the same room you are standing in? Hmm?" He smiled like a self-satisfied cat.

Linden sighed. "It is... nice."

Jasper raised his eyebrows.

"Very well, it is nice to see...people," Linden said.

"How very eloquent." Jasper rolled his eyes. "Yes, it is indeed *nice*. It will be good for you to have to converse with someone besides myself or my parents or Sir Curmudgeonly and his daughter. Not that she ever talks to you at all."

"Jasper," Linden said, warningly.

"And how goes the investigation into the murder in your forest?" Jasper said, blithely changing subjects.

"As it is your father who is the chief investigator, I would have thought you would be up to date on the matter," Linden said. "But it is not going well."

Jasper frowned. "I should not like any of the villagers to be murdered at the winter festival."

"Yes, that would rather put a damper on things, wouldn't it?" Linden said, drily.

He sighed and rubbed his temples. "I am not sure what else we can do. If no one will admit to seeing anything, hearing anything, or knowing anything then where do we go from there?"

"Have you sent word to the poor man's family at least?" Jasper inquired.

"Of course. Your father visited the inn the coach originated from and brought them the news of what had occurred. Not a pleasant task, I would imagine," Linden said.

"Well, perhaps it was simply animals, despite what my father thinks. A wild boar or some such thing," Jasper said, dismissively, returning to his usual level of cheer.

"There are no wild boars in Princewood..." Linden began to protest.

"Ah, look! Here comes Grayson," Jasper said, cutting him off and standing up to wave as the young man appeared at the top of the stairs.

Grayson stood, poised there a moment, then tucked a loose piece of sandy-colored hair into his cap, and started down.

"Yes, I've asked him to go riding with me," Linden said, watching Grayson cross over to them. The young man was smiling warmly at the village women and giving a friendly wave to the children as he traversed the hall.

Linden felt a stab of envy. It was so easy for Jasper. So easy for Grayson. Being around all of these people came naturally to them.

As it did not to Linden—at least, not yet. But he would try.

Though he could not imagine Fleur ever doing so.

Just as he thought of his intended, she appeared at the top of the steps, looking very pretty in a dark scarlet dress trimmed with gold ribbon.

That is, she looked very pretty until one's eyes reached her face. She was glowering like a gargoyle and looking searchingly around the hall.

When she spotted Linden, she hastened down the stairs and across the hall, reaching the pair just as Grayson did.

Linden tried to ignore the foreboding feeling he suddenly had.

"Oh, this should be interesting," Jasper said, sitting up in his seat and looking disturbingly gleeful. He rubbed his hands together. "Good day, Grayson."

"Good day, Jasper," Grayson said, giving them both a smile full of such charm and warmth that Linden could hardly look away. "Good day, Lord Chevalier."

"Linden, please," Linden reminded. "You are ready to go riding then?"

He looked past to where Fleur had stopped just behind the young man, out of his line of sight. Her arms were folded across her chest, and her chin jutted out sharply.

"Good day, Fleur," Jasper said, pleasantly. "Have you already met our guest?"

Grayson gave a little jump and turned around.

"Your guest?" Fleur said, not bothering to say good day.

"Well, Linden's guest," Jasper corrected. "But our guest in the sense that we are all so pleased that Grayson is here."

Grayson had moved away to stand a little closer to Jasper, which Linden thought was wise considering that Fleur was watching the young man from behind unfriendly narrowed eyes.

"Mister Grayson Gardner, meet Mistress Fleur Warburton," Jasper continued.

"Very pleased to meet you, Miss Warburton," Grayson said, his face slightly flushed.

"The same, I'm sure," Fleur said, looking the young man up and down before turning impatiently back to Linden.

"Linden, what is happening? Why are there so many people in the castle?" She put a hand to her head and scowled. "I was in the library reading and there was an incessant hammering and thumping outside in the courtyard. It made it quite impossible to continue."

"Oh, what were you reading?" Grayson blurted out, then just as quickly looked as if they wished they had stayed silent.

"A Vindication of the Rights of Woman," Fleur said, looking irritated by the interruption. "Have you read it?"

"Yes, actually, I have," Grayson exclaimed, perking up. "It is a favorite in our house."

"Really?" Fleur raised her eyebrows. "In a house full of boys...?"

"I have three sisters," Grayson said. "And I am sure a man can appreciate the sentiments put forth just as much as a woman."

Fleur sniffed. "I highly doubt that."

"Well, of course, a man cannot understand the female experience," Grayson rushed on.

Linden saw Jasper looking very amused.

"Indeed not," Fleur barked. "Now if you are quite finished, I should appreciate a reply from my fiancé..."

She so rarely called him this that Linden was surprised. Was Fleur actually displaying possessiveness? He doubted it. More likely she was simply trying to assert her position in the chain of things—ahead of Grayson's, of course.

"Oh, yes, of course, I am so sorry." Grayson's face flushed and he looked down at the stone floor in embarrassment. Then his head shot back up. "I beg your pardon. Did you say fiancé?"

"Yes," Fleur said, looking as if she were reaching the limits of her patience. "To Lord Linden Chevalier. Surely you have met him..."

"Of course, he has, Fleur," Linden said, deciding it was time to step in. "But Grayson—Mister Gardner, that is—has not had an opportunity to meet *you* before now, so it is understandable that he is confused."

"I did not know you had a fiancé," Grayson was mumbling. "My apologies."

"Yes, we must apologize for not having already introduced you to the lovely light of the castle, our diamond of the first woods, our paragon of perfection," Jasper said, brightly. "And Linden's intended. Our incomparable Fleur."

"Miss Warburton will do, thank you," Fleur snapped.

"Oh, of course, Miss Warbottom," Jasper said, speaking so quickly that Fleur looked as if she was not quite sure she had heard him correctly. She turned away, apparently deciding it was pointless to continue speaking to him.

"We are preparing to hold a winter festival, Fleur," Linden said, gently. "I had assumed your father informed you. My apologies, as it seems he did not. I am sorry your reading was interrupted."

"They are building a stage," Jasper said, helpfully. "Out in the courtyard."

"A stage?" Fleur seemed appalled. "For what?"

"Oh, for the performances, you know. Clowns, pantomimes, juggling, puppet shows. Whatever we can manage to put together," Jasper answered. "Shall I put you down for a performance? Pantomime perhaps?"

Linden shot Jasper a murderous glance. "There is also to be a dance, Fleur. Did your father truly not mention it?"

Fleur shook her head slowly, looking disconcerted.

"It is to be held in celebration of our engagement," Linden said, a little awkwardly.

Grayson had not said a word. He was standing silently behind Jasper, looking decidedly uncomfortable.

"In any case, perhaps we may speak more of this later, Fleur," Linden said, quickly. "We were just about to go riding."

"You and Jasper?" Fleur asked. She inclined her head towards Jasper's headgear and for a brief moment, Linden thought he saw the hint of a smile.

"Oh, this old thing?" Jasper touched his head as he caught her glance. "It wouldn't hold me back on a horse, I assure you. But no, Linden meant Mister Gardner."

"Mister Gardner," Fleur repeated, her eyes honing in on Grayson again. "Oh, really."

"Yes," Jasper said, quickly, bouncing to his feet and clapping his hands. "It is a lovely afternoon for a ride, is it not? Linden and Grayson, you should be off before it turns cloudy again."

"Yes, but I still do not..." Fleur began.

"Yes, Fleur, you feel slighted, but I assure you, I am excellent company," Jasper assured her, linking his arm through hers. "Why don't I show you some of the preparations for the festival? And then you and I can take a turn about in the courtyard..."

"Yes, but first I should just like to ask Linden about..." Fleur said, trying again.

"Oh, there will be plenty of time later," Jasper said, soothingly.

Fleur tried to pull her arm from his, but it was no use. She was swiftly dragged into the throng of chattering women.

"What are you doing, Jasper?" Fleur hissed. "Let go of me, at once!"

Jasper had tugged her all the way out of the great hall and down the corridor towards the kitchens before she had managed to dig in her heels so firmly that he could go no further.

"Fine," he said, releasing her. "I suppose this is far enough."

"Far enough from what?" Fleur said, frowning. "Honestly, Jasper, I don't know why Linden puts up with your nonsense. In any other household, you would be..." She stopped abruptly and looked away.

"What?" Jasper prompted. "Well? Say what you wished to say."

She lifted her head, chin jutting out sharply. "Very well. You would not have had free reign of a place like Princewood. Nor spent so much time in the company of its lord. It is... It's... unseemly. That's what it is. You are the child of servants, nothing more. Just because Linden sent you up to Cambridge and you received a gentleman's education, does not make you..." She broke off, and instead gave an imperious little sniff.

"A gentleman, I presume you were about to say?" Jasper looked amused. "And true, the education was wasted, I'm afraid. I was not cut out to be a clergyman or a lawyer. But unseemly? Really, Fleur? Did your father say so?"

"My father?" Fleur glared. "What does that have anything to do with it?"

"Oh, only that most of your worst opinions seem to come second-handed. But really, it is not as if there is a great pool of nobility in the vicinity for your beloved Linden to associate with," Jasper went on, sounding more exasperated than angry. "Would you have had him entirely friendless? Or are you suggesting he might have come to you for companionship?"

"I dislike your tone," Fleur said, her face sour. "Of course, he may have come to me..." She faltered.

"Lies," Jasper said, cheerfully. "All lies. I take him off your hands. I always have. You prefer your own company and your musty old books."

"That's not true... I..." She reddened.

"You prefer them," Jasper went on. "And that is very well. Although I do not see how they are much companionship. But do not pretend to jealousy. Oh, not because the sentiment does not suit you, but simply because it is completely implausible."

"Implausible?" Fleur snapped, crossing her arms. "Father says Linden has been stepping out to see some girl in the village. Is that also implausible?"

Jasper burst out laughing. "It certainly is." He looked at her and sighed. "But even if he was, would it really matter, Fleur? Are you really going to pretend that you care if he goes walking with some other young lady?"

She was silent.

"I don't care," she admitted, eventually, as if it were a revelation even to herself.

"I know," Jasper said, simply.

"Why don't I care, Jasper?" she asked. She looked at him, almost beseechingly, her eyes hollow.

"I don't know, Fleur," he said. "But you never have. That is why this marriage would be such a mistake. You must know that."

She lifted her chin. "Did Linden tell you to say that?"

"No," Jasper said, shaking his head. "Of course not. But it is plain to anyone who knows either of you..."

"You don't know me," she said, cutting him off. "None of you know me."

"Would you let us?" Jasper asked, very gently. "If we wanted to?"

Fleur became very white and very still.

"No," she said, finally. "Stay out of my way, Jasper Lennox."

Picking up her skirts, she ran down the corridor away from him.

Chapter 10

This thing of darkness I

Acknowledge mine.

— The Tempest

Fleur slipped down the spiral stone steps.

Princewood did not have a dungeon. Few English castles did.

But it did have an undercroft. A maze of cellars, some with fairly high vaulted ceilings and others cramped and close. All cold, wet, and dark.

Some of those which lay nearer the kitchen building were still used for storage. Many others lay beyond, empty and long forgotten.

At times, the undercroft was damper than others—such as at high tide, when the surging waters would fill a sewage tunnel that led out onto a nearby beach nearly to the ceiling.

One might easily walk through the tunnel, out and under the battlements, as easy as they pleased, with no one the wiser.

Fleur had done so, once or twice, but did not enjoy the claustrophobic feeling passing through the tunnel induced. A quick rush of water and into the eternal darkness she would go.

No, she preferred a more clandestine approach.

In her childhood, she had discovered the maze of secret corridors and narrow passages that lined the walls of the keep. Stealing away from countless governesses or a nagging father, she would slip behind a tapestry, push open a wooden panel, and be gone—down into the cellars or up onto the battlements overlooking the sea.

She would vanish like a ghost and be truly alone. Truly free.

It had taken her years to realize she was not as alone in the undercroft as she had thought.

The cellars beneath Princewood were not altogether devoid of inhabitants.

"Fleur? Is that you?"

A female voice hissed through the darkness, sending a shiver of anticipation and dread through Fleur as she walked closer to the source.

There was a pause.

"I know it is you," the woman said, again, sounding slightly disdainful this time. "I can tell from your steps."

Fleur stopped.

"Oh, come now. You have nothing to fear from me." Fleur could almost see the woman smile.

"That's not true," Fleur whispered.

"What was that?" the woman said, sharply. "Speak up."

Fleur stepped forward. "I said," she replied, slowly. "That is not true."

She held up the small, brass lantern she carried. The light inside sent flickering shadows dancing across the stone walls.

Hardly enough to see by, but enough for Fleur to make out the face of the woman sitting inside a small barred room.

"It was good of you to let me out," the woman said, from where she sat on a wooden bench along the back wall. "It had been so long. I had almost forgotten what the sun looked like."

"It was night," Fleur said, quietly. "There was no sun."

For a moment, the woman looked surprised. "So, it was. You are right. I had forgotten." She met Fleur's eyes through the barred window of the wooden door which held her captive. "Perhaps the next time then. Perhaps the next time it will be sunny."

Fleur rested her forehead against the wooden door. "There can be no next time, Mother."

"But of course, there must be. There has to be, Fleur. My darling, he cannot keep me chained and trapped down here forever," the woman said, her voice fervent but calm.

Fleur swallowed. "That is what I had thought as well. But I understand now."

The woman rose and reached the door so quickly that Fleur hardly had a chance to step back before a hand darted out from between the bars, reaching and grasping.

Fleur let out a little gasp, nearly dropping the lantern.

"What do you understand?" the woman in the cell hissed. "What can you possibly understand about it? He keeps me here because he hates me, Fleur. He has always hated me. He wants to keep us apart. He always has."

The voice became a croon. "But he cannot keep me from my darling, can he? You will always come for me. Always find me. You are a good daughter, Fleur. You let me out—and I came back, did I not?"

"You did," Fleur whispered, feeling sick at heart. "You did come back."

"There, you see?" The woman sounded satisfied. "I promised I would come back and I did. Even though you tricked me. Waiting there for me, with him. Putting me back in this miserable room again. Oh, you are cruel."

"What else could he do?" Fleur whispered. "After what you had done?"

"What I did? What I did was for you. For you both. To protect you. To keep you safe. It is always for you," the woman said, pressing her face to the bars. "And hasn't it worked out well? You are to marry the lord of the land, become his lady. All this shall be ours soon. You cannot tell me your father does not want that. I only seek to give you both what you most desire. And when he finally has it, he will stop this horrid abuse. He will take me back—as his true wife again. We will be a family once more, as we always should have been."

"I have never desired any of this," Fleur said, a hand to her stomach. She felt as if she would be ill. "None of this."

"Ungrateful girl," the woman said, but her voice was mild. "Here, let me out and we shall speak of this more. Let us walk on the beach, as we did that first night you found me. Was that not a lovely night?"

"It was," Fleur said, her voice breaking. "It was a lovely night."

"A lovely night. My lovely girl," the woman said, softly. "I will always protect my lovely girl."

"But Mother..." Fleur's voice caught in her throat. "You were not protecting me this time. The man you killed..."

There was silence on the other side of the door.

"Mother?" Fleur whispered.

"Go," the woman said, her voice turning sulky. "Go away. You are not here to let me out. Are you?"

"No," Fleur admitted.

"Then go!" The woman cried, her voice becoming a shout. "Go!"

And smothering a sob, Fleur did as she was bid.

Chapter 11

For where thou art, there is the world itself.

— Henry VI

"How is your head?" Linden asked, conversationally.

It had been a quiet ride so far. Too quiet.

Grayson had been aloof, hardly making eye contact.

Now that they had tethered their horses a short distance away in a grassy spot and were walking along the beach, Linden hoped that would change.

"Mostly recovered, I think," Grayson said, after a pause.

"The surgeon came a second time, Mrs. Lennox tells me?" Linden inquired, a little stiffly.

"Yes, thank you. He said things were healing nicely. Really, there was not much he could do."

"No further fainting spells?" Linden said, trying to tease some kind of reaction from his reticent companion.

"Gads, no," the boy exclaimed, blushing. "I am still terribly embarrassed about that. I am not prone to fainting spells, I assure you."

"Few young men are," Linden said, with amusement. "But you were injured. It was understandable."

"Yes, of course," Grayson mumbled, scuffing his feet in the sand as he walked.

Linden was searching for another way to fill the silence, when the young man spoke again.

"Have you been engaged to Miss Warburton long?" Grayson inquired, still keeping his eyes fixed ahead of them.

Linden did not particularly want to discuss Fleur.

He was not sure what he wanted, but it was not to be reminded that he was bound and tethered—much like the horses—and that it was not really by his own will at all.

Especially not while he walked alongside this young man who made his heart race so strangely, who made him feel more alive and excited than Fleur ever had.

He felt more seen by Grayson than he ever had by his betrothed.

Even as children, Fleur preferred her solitude.

They had rarely played together. She spent her time with books and when the village children tried to befriend her, she would send them scurrying with her harsh words. After too many times being rejected, he and Jasper had given up trying to include her in their games.

"A very long time," he said, finally. "It is less a formal arrangement than a longstanding agreement between our two families. My parents greatly desired the match."

He hesitated, then went on. "To tell you the truth, I do not remember them ever saying so to me, but Warburton told me of how eager they were for us to wed so many times throughout my childhood that it feels as if it were my own memory."

"So, you are not choosing your own bride at all?" Grayson said, sounding dismayed.

Linden frowned at their disapproving tone. "I have a choice, of course," he snapped. "And I have chosen to do what my parents wished."

He could hear the childish sullenness in his voice and he did not like it. Besides, how could he scold the young man when the truth was, he felt much the same way?

But it was a matter of honor. Not of personal choice.

Or personal happiness.

"Of course," Grayson murmured, not meeting his eye. "I am sorry."

Linden sighed. "No, I am sorry. But—" He tried to think of how to explain. "This is all I have left of them," he said, simply. "Perhaps that will not make sense. But if they wanted this for me, I feel compelled to honor that."

This time Grayson met his eyes. "I see. Yes, of course, you would," he said, softly. He extended a hand as if to touch Linden's arm, then withdrew it quickly as if thinking better of it. "That is very admirable. You are doing the honorable thing."

Perhaps it was honorable. But was it right?

Even if he took his own desires out of the equation, would this marriage ever bring Fleur any real happiness? That was the question Linden struggled with, though he could not admit this.

"Fleur and I are a strange match, I know," he confessed, as they walked along the damp sand. "Jasper points that out at every opportunity."

Grayson shot him another glance, and seemed about to say something.

When he did not, Linden wracked his brain for another topic of conversation.

The outing was proving less than comfortable, and yet oddly, he found himself desperate to extend their time together. He did not wish to return to the castle. To return to his duties.

Perhaps they were fumbling on together today, but being in Grayson's company still filled him with a mixture of excitement and contentment.

The young man was an enigma. And the desires he produced in Linden were equally enigmatic.

"What of you? What of your family? What do they desire for you?" he asked. "Who are they, for that matter? Do you have brothers? Sisters? Oh, yes, you told Fleur you had three sisters."

"Yes, they are all married now. I am the youngest," Grayson replied. "We do not live anywhere nearly so grand as this. But our family is warm, welcoming. I think I took for granted how happy a home I grew up in." He took a breath. "My father died when I was an infant, you know. I did not know him at all. But your loss—that is something very different. I cannot imagine losing both mother and father in one day, and so..."

He broke off as his foot caught in a tangle of seaweed and he began to trip. Before Linden could consider the wisdom of it, he had reached out a hand to steady the lad, gripping him by the arm.

And that was all it took.

The boy instinctively reached out his other hand to steady himself and it landed flat against Linden's chest.

There was a feeling of shock.

The awkwardness had dissipated. It was as if it never was.

In an instant, it had been replaced by something different.

Something no less uncomfortable—but Linden would trade away the way they had been walking and talking as if they were strangers in a heartbeat for this instead—this powerful current of connection as they stood there together.

Powerful—and beautiful, too.

There was a ringing in Linden's ears, a spinning sensation all around.

He took a deep breath and looked down at the young man.

"Thank you," Grayson said, a little breathlessly. "You make me feel quite short, you know."

"Do I?" Linden said, stupidly.

His mouth felt dry, his limbs stiff.

Looking into the young man's eyes was like having cold water thrown over him. There was such intense understanding in those eyes that it frightened him.

It was like looking at himself in a mirror—but a self full of sympathy. For an instant, he felt a deep longing to bare all—to tell Grayson just how hopeless and helpless and alone he had felt most of his life, and how much less alone he felt when they were together.

But once those walls were breached, there would be no going back.

They were less than two feet and an eternity apart.

Linden longed to close the gulf, knowing that once they returned to the castle again it was only bound to widen.

"I have never been so graceless as this in my life," Grayson said, giving a shaky laugh. "I promise you, I did not fall once when I climbed the rigging on the Witch of the Waves."

"I should imagine a cabin boy who swoons would not last long," Linden replied, hardly hearing his own words.

And then, "I feel lightheaded," he said, stupidly, and at the same time he spoke, he heard Grayson say, "I must tell you something."

He was lightheaded. It was the truth. He was a strong young man in the prime of his life. Yet here he was feeling as weak as a kitten.

He closed his eyes quickly, forcing himself to stop looking into that other pair belonging to this strange other half, struggling to break the spell.

"If you are lightheaded, the best thing to do," Grayson was saying. "Is to lie down and wait for it to pass. Here."

The boy tugged him over to sit on a patch of dry sand.

"Lay back," Grayson commanded, pulling on his shoulders gently, and Linden complied, his body unable to resist.

When he was laying on his back in the sand, the young man did the same.

The sun was high in the sky, warm and bright and blinding.

They lay there, in the sand for a few minutes, side-by-side, without touching—a finger's breadth apart. Linden knew if he were to open his hand just a little more, he would feel the boy's brushing against his own.

And then? Would he lace their hands together? Turn onto his side? Look into Grayson's eyes? At his lips? And then?

It was madness. Linden closed his eyes against the sun. It felt much hotter than November.

"It's strange, isn't it?" Grayson said, softly.

"What is?" Linden replied, his voice husky.

"This. This feeling." The words came out in whisper. "Do you feel it, too?"

Linden opened his mouth.

"No, wait, please. Do not answer that," Grayson begged.

Linden sensed him sitting up.

"I must tell you something," the boy said, urgently.

He had said the same thing before, Linden remembered.

But it was too late.

A horse was coming across the sand. Linden could feel the pounding of hoofs as it ran hard towards them, and he quickly sat up.

"It's Jasper," Grayson exclaimed, a hand to his eyes as he squinted in the sun, looking back down along the beach towards the castle.

Linden was on his feet in an instant. He would not meet Gracie's eyes.

"He's riding hard," is all he said.

"Yes," Gracie replied, faintly.

The spell was broken. The connection lost once more.

She had missed her chance, she knew, with sinking heart.

That had been the moment to tell him the truth. Now it was gone.

What would he say when he found out eventually, as he was sure to do?

She had no wish to betray Mrs. Lennox—nor did she blame her. But nor could she wait anymore, in this awful liminal state, betwixt and between.

Yes, it was true that Gracie had done something like this before.

But in a very different way. This was an entirely different disguise for an entirely different reason—and she did not wish to wear it any longer.

It was one thing to be someone else when one wanted to be, in order to further an aim, attain something she could not have done otherwise as a girl.

It was quite another to feel this low and nasty sense of deceit, to know that she was lying every moment she stepped out of her room—and to the one she wished more than anything else to protect and to see happy.

No matter what that entailed, she thought, grimly. If his happiness lay in marrying Fleur, so be it.

Where would she be when that happened? Her family would think her mad, but she knew she could not go home. She was trapped, she thought, helplessly. It was too late.

In her heart of hearts, she had sworn her allegiance to this man without a second thought and without him even knowing she had done so.

She would be standing at the back of the church as he said his vows to Fleur Warburton. She would smile until her face hurt.

Perhaps she could build a little hut at the edge of the village and spend the rest of her days there, waiting for a glimpse of Linden as he rode or walked...with Fleur? With their children?

Her heart clenched. She was a fool and she would not pity her own foolishness.

One foot in front of the other. That was all there was to it.

She lifted her chin and watched as Jasper reached them. He stopped but did not dismount.

"There has been an attack," he said, looking down at them both with a grim face. "It's Warburton."

Chapter 12

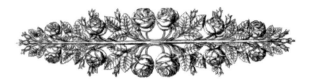

Lord, what fools these mortals be!

— A Midsummer Night's Dream

Sir Guy was nursing a lump the size of a goose egg on the back of his head.

"One would think a head injury was the latest fashion at this rate," Jasper grumbled, taking a seat by the window.

They were gathered in Linden's cabinet—a room in the castle he used as both office and study.

For such a small room, it was luxurious. In contrast to the stone walls of the great hall, here ornate oak wainscoting lined the room from floor to ceiling. The rich paneling had been added for warmth and decoration during the Tudor period. The hearth was a beautiful ivory marble and currently filled with a roaring fire.

Lush tapestries and Renaissance-era paintings covered the walls, lending the room a feeling of timeless decadence and reminding Gracie that Linden Chevalier's world was indeed a realm of unaccustomed lavish luxury.

Fleur stalked back and forth over the scarlet and green patterned carpet like a lean prowling cat, her arms folded over her chest, silent and glowering.

Now that they had met, Gracie found herself intrigued by the other young woman. Not simply because Fleur was Linden's intended, but because in another life Gracie suspected they might have been friends.

Fleur Warburton was, of course, caustic and off-putting. But she did not seem to wish to be otherwise, and Gracie could not help but admire this stubborn tenacity. Fleur was who she was—and who she was could not be more different from her father. They shared the same fair skin and reddish gold hair, but that was where the similarities ended. Warburton was all self-indulgence, where Fleur was all severe austerity. For all of his bluster and pomposity, Warburton seemed soft and weak. But his daughter had a fierceness to her that reminded Gracie of a Spartan soldier.

"Tell us again how this happened, Sir Guy," Linden was saying as Gracie turned her attention back to the room.

The old knight sat in a mahogany chair near the fire, holding a compress to the back of his head.

Linden stood over him, frowning a little.

Gracie knew without having to be told that something about the situation did not sit right with him. She felt it, too. There was something off here. As Warburton spoke, Gracie caught a mental whiff of barely contained secrets struggling to rise to the surface like steam from a pot of boiling water.

"I have already told Jasper," Warburton protested. "Leave an old man be."

"You did not tell me much," Jasper commented, from the other side of the room. "And you claimed you fell."

"Because that is what happened," Warburton protested, impatiently. "It was very simple. There is no cause for all of this fuss, I assure you. I was in the woods, I was walking, I slipped, and I fell."

"Backwards?" Jasper said, sardonically.

"I tripped...on a tree root," Warburton said, tersely, with a glare in Jasper's direction.

"You are not ordinarily one for long solitary walks," Linden observed.

"Or walking at all," Jasper muttered.

Fleur stopped her pacing. "Is this meant to be an interrogation? Are you calling my father a liar, Jasper Lennox?" she demanded, eyes flashing.

"No one is saying that, Fleur," Linden said, soothingly. "Perhaps you would kindly keep your witticisms to yourself, Jasper."

"Certainly," Jasper answered, with exaggerated politeness. "Do forgive me, Miss Warburton."

Linden looked back at Sir Guy. "Very well then. You were walking in the woods and you tripped on a root and fell so hard—backwards—that it resulted in a lump the size of an egg. And you were lying there quite some time—perhaps since early morning, for when Jasper happened across you, he claims you were near dead with cold."

"Preposterous! Near dead, indeed. Pfft! I was perfectly well," the old man puffed. "I should have found my way back to the castle in no time. Merely catching my breath after the fall."

Gracie did not have to look to know that Jasper was rolling his eyes.

"Ah, yes, there is nothing like a nice nap in the snow," Jasper quipped. "I suppose I should have left you where I found you then. It sounds as if you were doing quite well on your own."

"Jasper," Linden said, tiredly, putting up a hand. "Sir Guy, Fleur, you must know why we are so concerned. There has been a murder close to Princewood. The culprit has yet to be found. Walking in the woods alone—especially in the dim early hours—is not the safest pastime right now."

He hesitated. "Are you sure there is nothing else you wish to tell me, Sir Guy? You saw nothing of who hit you?"

"What hit me was a rock on the ground," Sir Guy insisted. He threw up his hands. "I am a doddering old fool who tripped on his own feet. There. Is that what Young Lennox would like me to admit? Very well. I admit it freely." He began to struggle to his feet. "Now if you will excuse me."

As Warburton spoke, Gracie glanced towards Linden.

He was already looking at her, she saw with a shock. His eyes lingering on her with something undefinable behind them.

Her heart caught in her chest. If she had to name what was there, she would call it desire. She knew, because she felt it, too.

He quickly looked away and she did the same.

"Perhaps we should postpone the festival," Linden said, quietly, before Warburton had reached the door.

Sir Guy stopped. "Do not do so on my account. I am nothing but eager to attend."

"It would not be for you," Linden said, his voice hard as granite. "It would be for the safety of my people."

Warburton reached the door and yanked it open. "Very well, do as you wish. You will anyhow, I'm sure," he snapped, before stepping into the hall.

Fleur moved towards the entrance, as if to follow.

"Fleur," Linden commanded. "A moment, if you please."

She paused.

"I think we can all acknowledge that it is strange behavior for your father to be roaming the woods on an early winter morning, can we not? Do you know of any reason why he would do so?" Linden said, carefully.

"No," Fleur said, shortly. "Is there anything else?"

"I merely wish to keep your father safe, you know. To keep you both safe," Linden said, quietly.

Gracie felt sorry for him. Was this how it was to be? Linden struggling to protect and care for a woman who seemed to chafe at simply being in his presence?

But she felt pity for Fleur as well. The girl seemed so alone and so determined to remain that way.

When Fleur had left the room, Gracie stood up quickly. "I believe I'll go to the library. Mrs. Lennox mentioned you have quite an extensive collection."

"That's probably where Fleur is heading," Jasper said, raising his eyebrows. "Do you really fancy a trip to the lioness's den?"

"I will do my best not to stir her ire," Gracie promised, and heard Jasper snort in response.

"Very well," Linden said, leaning against the wall by the fire. He sounded distracted.

"I agree with you, by the way, Jasper," Gracie said, as she reached the doorway and looked back. She shifted, uncomfortably, not sure how else to say it. "Sir Guy was not telling us what really happened."

"Perhaps Warburton is the murderer," Jasper joked, when Grayson was gone. "But I do not think he'd have the stomach for it. Nor the strength."

"Someone attacked him, on my land, near my people," Linden said, without turning around. "Whoever killed the coach driver is still out there. Warburton was frightened. There is something he is not saying. Did you notice?"

"The man is a scared rabbit who likes to roar as if he's a lion. He is probably always frightened," Jasper said, waving a hand dismissively.

"This is different," Linden insisted. "Why would he lie about what happened? Why would he not wish for us to find whoever did this to him?"

"Maybe it was Fleur," Jasper said, cheerfully. "She certainly has the right temperament. Perhaps she was just so fed up that she took a piece of wood and..."

"Not helpful, Jasper. Truly not helpful," Linden complained. "Perhaps your father will find something."

"I doubt it. There was snowfall this morning. Warburton was half-blanketed in it when I found him. If there were tracks, they would have been covered over—especially now that the snow has melted in the midday sun," Jasper said, sounding reluctant to disappoint his friend. "My father is good, though. Who knows, he could turn up something."

"This is intolerable," Linden muttered, rubbing his brow. "Surely there must be more we can do."

"Are you truly going to cancel the festival?" Jasper inquired.

"No," Linden said. "At least, not yet."

"Thank heavens for that," Jasper said, with exaggerated relief. "Well, then, what next? Should we gather the village? Have them go out in pairs and search the woods? We could make it a winter festival activity."

Linden ignored the flippant suggestion. "No, but I will have the castle and the grounds searched thoroughly, as well as the woods nearby. Even if there are no tracks, perhaps someone will find something."

"That seems rather extreme," Jasper observed. "Warburton was injured in the forest, not within the castle walls."

Linden turned to look at his friend. "Attacked. Not injured. I do not think you understand, Jasper."

"Oh, don't I?" Jasper said, quietly. "I understand that you believe whoever murdered your mother has come back after fifteen years to repeat history. But you must admit it sounds farfetched, Linden."

Linden set his jaw stubbornly. "Before my mother, nothing like that had ever happened—not in Princewood, nor anywhere within a hundred miles. Nor has it happened since. Your father said the driver's body reminded him of what happened to my mother. What is more likely? That a second murder who kills like the first has suddenly turned up out of nowhere?"

"Or?" Jasper shifted uncomfortably in his seat. "What is the other option? I do not like this one, but I suspect I will like the other even less."

"Or that the same murderer has been here all along, in our midst. Among us," Linden said. "Hiding. Waiting. Biding their time."

"In the castle you mean?" Jasper sounded horrified. "All right, that's enough of that."

He shivered. "I am not a rabbit, but you are making even this bold lad nervous. Are you sure you aren't laying it on rather thick, Linden?" Jasper's expression became uncomfortable. "Perhaps this is a case of wishing for something to be true."

"Wishing?" Linden snapped.

"Yes. I cannot imagine losing my parents—let alone having my mother's life stolen so horribly. Anyone in your place would long for justice, for answers. And as you have said, it has been fifteen long years. Perhaps you would like to believe that there is a pattern because you wish for there to be one," Jasper said, gently.

Linden was silent.

"I do not think so. But I will ponder what you have said," he replied, finally.

Jasper nodded and turned to go.

"And Jasper," Linden added. "You are a good friend."

Jasper grinned. "Oh, I know. Believe me, I know."

He winked and walked out.

This was rather a new situation, even for Gracie.

She had never tried to steal a private moment with a young lady while disguised as a young man before.

Common rules of propriety frowned upon the idea of following a single lady into a secluded area for a tête-à-tête.

But as Gracie was no true gentleman, she put that from her mind.

Fleur was already curled up in a chair in the furthest-most alcove with a gold-embossed red volume open in her hands.

"The Modern Prometheus," Gracie said, in delight, stepping into the alcove.

Fleur looked up with a frown. "Let me guess. You have read this one as well."

"Of course," Gracie replied. "I adore Frankenstein. If one can be said to adore a monster."

"The monster is not Frankenstein," Fleur said, disdainfully. "Frankenstein is the creature's maker."

"Isn't he?" Gracie said, tilting her head. "The one who made the monster may also be monstrous."

Fleur did not seem to have a ready retort for that. Instead, she stared at Gracie with suspicion—but also the first sign of interest.

"Shelley has had a sad life," Fleur said at last, and Gracie knew she was not speaking of Percy.

"She has," Gracie agreed. "Losing three young children, and then her husband besides. I cannot imagine."

"I can," Fleur said, her face souring again.

"Can you?" Gracie asked, gently. Determined not to be put off, she stepped into the alcove and took a seat across from Fleur, as if to show this.

"Well, not firsthand," Fleur admitted, watching her warily. "But my mother... She had three children before I was born. They all died. Then came my sister and I, twins. But only I lived past a month." Fleur's face twisted. "She was not right after that, my mother. She died before I could know her."

"I am so sorry," Gracie said, softly. "How terrible for her, and for you. For your father as well. No wonder he dotes on you so."

Fleur's head shot up. "Does he?" She gave a brittle laugh.

"That is how it seems," Gracie said. "Of course, I am sure you care for him very much as well."

"He is all I have," Fleur said.

Gracie noticed Fleur did not think to include Linden. Yet he would have been foremost in her mind were she in Fleur's place.

"You have Linden," Gracie reminded her, trying to tread carefully. "I am sure he cares for you dearly."

Fleur laughed, a little louder this time. "He cares for his honor. He does not care for me."

Gracie knew honor was part of it, so she could not dispute that. Nevertheless, she was a little shocked.

"I am sure he cares for you as well," she maintained. "You have known one another since you were children."

Fleur looked at Gracie. Her face was weary.

"Linden is *good*," Fleur said. "He does what he believes to be right. It has nothing to do with caring or not caring."

When Gracie made as if to protest, Fleur held up a hand. "Yes, he cares for me. As if I were one of his tenants. Someone he is responsible for. Someone he must care for. Can you not see the difference?"

"And do you care for him?" Gracie challenged, unable to help herself.

"Sometimes I wonder if I really know how to care for anyone," Fleur said, bluntly, with no hint of self-pity. "But I believe I do, yes."

Gracie's heart sank.

"In the same way I would for a brother," Fleur continued. "In a very chaste, very safe way." She gave a wry smile. "A very dull way."

"Linden is not dull," Gracie objected, perhaps too hotly.

"No, he is not," Fleur agreed. "He is strong and noble, fairly intelligent—" Gracie decided not to argue the point.

"—handsome as a prince in a story." She shrugged. "Yet I feel... nothing."

She met Gracie's eyes. "Why? Why do I feel nothing?"

"I... I do not know," Gracie said, falteringly.

"Have you ever been in love?" Fleur demanded, giving her that look of almost-interest again.

Gracie was flummoxed for a moment.

"I think so. Yes," she said, finally.

"And what does it feel like?" Fleur asked.

Gracie stared, uncertain of how to respond.

She decided to go with honesty.

"It changes you," she said. "Nothing is ever the same. You feel more alive when they are there. And you feel more real yourself, in their presence—" That was an irony, but also true. She swallowed. "You feel wild and burning, weak and brave at the same time, and you would do anything for them. Even if they never loved you in return at all."

"That sounds awful," Fleur said, wrinkling her nose in distaste.

Gracie gave a choked laugh.

"But even if they never do," she went on. "You don't mind. Because now that you've felt it, you know you've truly lived.

To live without ever experiencing the feeling—now that would be utterly tragic."

"You sound like a poet," Fleur said. It was not a compliment.

Gracie wanted to laugh again. But she wanted to cry, too. Because she knew what she said was true.

But even more true was what she had left out—that love hurt. It hurt so much that it had to be real. If she could love someone this much without being loved back and still find it exhilarating and impossible to stop, then it had to be real.

"I've never felt that way," Fleur said, softly. "I don't know if I would wish to. But I would like to feel... something. Other than what I feel now." That last was said very quietly.

"What do you feel now, Fleur?" Gracie said, leaning forward. "Is there something worrying you? Are you afraid of something?"

Fleur's expression changed so abruptly it was as if a shutter had been slammed closed. "What do you mean? Why do you say that? Why on earth should I be afraid?"

"I only meant..." Gracie started.

"Yes, well, don't," Fleur ordered, bitingly. "Will you be leaving? Or must I go?" She slammed her book shut, and made to rise.

"No, I'll go," Gracie said, hastily. "I'm sorry. I simply thought..."

"Don't. Don't think about me at all. I am fine. And I am most certainly not frightened." Fleur lifted her chin. "Not of anything."

"I see," Gracie said. "Well, if you should ever wish to talk."

"No, thank you," Fleur said, already re-opening her book. "Good day."

Gracie could not help but be impressed by the sheer imperiousness of Fleur's manner.

She would have made a wonderful queen.

Chapter 13

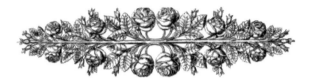

In thy face I see

The map of honour, truth, and loyalty.

— Henry VI

Fleur had lied, of course.

She was terrified.

What had her father done?

What had her mother done?

Ever since she had discovered her mother still lived—the happiest and simultaneously the worst moment of her life—she felt as if she had been asking herself those two questions unceasingly.

"We have to tell him," she whispered to herself, rehearsing. "We have to tell him now, Father."

She pushed open the door to her father's study. It was along the same corridor as Linden's, but thankfully she had not seen him.

Her father sat behind his desk, staring vacantly out the window where softly falling snow was beginning to melt and fog the pane.

She pushed the door closed behind her carefully.

"We have to tell him now, Father," she declared, keeping her voice level.

"Mmm," he said.

"Father?"

She crossed over to the desk and leaned over it to get his attention.

"Fleur," he said, sounding surprised.

He looked frail and old.

"Shall I walk you to your room?" she said, gently, feeling a stab of pity.

"No, no," he said, briskly, shaking his head as if to chase the fog away. "I must go out again to search the forest."

Fleur was aghast. "You cannot be serious."

Her father frowned. "Of course, of course, I must. She will turn up. You'll see. She'll come home. It will all be well. It will all be well, I promise you."

"I don't believe you," Fleur said, sharply, regretting her harsh tone but furious with his self-deception.

"Fleur?" Her father narrowed his eyes.

He did not look old or frail any longer. She took a step back.

"Father, she is gone. She is not coming back. And even if she does—" She licked her lips. "—We must tell Linden the truth. She has murdered someone. And it is our fault."

"My fault," she amended, hurriedly, as she saw him frowning. "I let her out that first time. I was stupid. So stupid. I know that."

He sighed. "She can be so lucid at times. So persuasive. So like she used to be."

"But she is not her old self, Father," Fleur said, carefully. "She never will be. Or even if she is, for a spell, she is..." She did not want to say the word. She did not want to say "monstrous" though the word was on her mind. Her mother was no Frankenstein's creature. She was not sure what she was. Only that somehow, after tragedy followed tragedy and abuse followed abuse, she had begun to delight in taking life.

In a way, Fleur would never blame her. She could not imagine the pain of losing a child, a baby, that one had brought into the world only to have weaken, sicken, and die. Nor did she think her parents' marriage had been a happy one. She suspected worse than this, but knew better than to inquire of either of them.

But she could refrain from blaming her mother, while refusing to condone her cruelty. She could not permit this to go on.

And she knew it would. Until she and her father did something to make it stop.

Her father was glaring at her as if he did not recognize her.

"We cannot tell him, Fleur," he said, vehemently. "Are you mad? He will never understand. Never. Never, ever."

"What is there to not understand?" Fleur exclaimed. "You did what any man in your place would have done. You tried to care for and protect your wife. It was a horrible accident. You did not know she was violent. You did not know what she would do. You cannot blame yourself for what happened to Linden's mother. Do not put that on your own head."

She drew a breath. "As for the coach driver. That poor young man. That is due to my wrongdoing, Father. Not yours. And I will tell Linden so myself."

Fleur had believed her mother when she told her that her father was holding her in captivity out of cruelty, for no good reason at all.

More the fool she.

She choked back a sob. But Linden would understand. To have found her mother—so close, after all that time believing her dead.

How could he fail to understand? She had been rash, yes. But he would forgive her.

As for that first horrible death—well, surely Linden would be grateful to finally know who had committed that terrible deed.

"He will throw us out," her father warned, his face clouded. "We have nowhere to go. They will hang your mother or put her in an asylum. They will hang me as well."

Fleur closed her eyes. "Perhaps she should hang," she said, quietly. "She has done terrible things. They cannot be undone. You know as well as I that she will never stop. She does not want to stop."

She frowned in confusion. "As for you, why would you hang?"

Her father's eyes darted back and forth shiftily. "I kept her from punishment. I hid her away. They will say I am as much to blame as she."

Fleur crossed over to a chair and sat down. Ever since Jasper had found her father in the woods and she had realized what had happened, she had not known a moment's rest.

"I do not know what will happen," she said, eventually. "But I will stand by you, Father. No matter what. And no matter what the punishment may be, for either of us, we must stop this before someone else is hurt. She is out there—right now. Think for a moment what harm she might do. She could hurt a child." She could hurt an entire family of children, Fleur thought to herself, with a shudder.

"She would never hurt a child," her father scoffed. "Never."

Fleur was appalled. How could he still be so sunk into denial? Even now?

"No? But she would kill a young man? A young mother?" Fleur asked, trying to bring him to his senses. "They have as much right to live as a child does. Who will she hurt next?"

She put her face in her hands. It was not a conversation anyone should ever have to have about a parent. The horror had weighed on her for weeks. Now it was omnipresent. She could not continue in this way.

"It is killing us, Father," she whispered. "Can't you see? We cannot go on living this way. In terror. With you as a perpetual jailer of your own wife."

Sir Guy looked angry rather than remorseful. "He will not understand. He will banish us both. We will have nothing."

"I would rather have nothing than go on this way," Fleur said, stubbornly.

"You will destroy us," her father roared. "Everything I have done for you. All I have worked for. It will all tumble down and be for naught."

Fleur looked at him in stunned silence.

"Perhaps it will be for the best," she said, as she turned to go. "For I have never wanted any of it anyways."

"Wait," her father ordered. "Stay. There is something you must   know."

Mrs. Lennox rose hopefully from her seat. "Did you find anything?"

"No tracks," Cam said, shortly, pulling his snow-soaked hat off and beginning to shrug out of his coat.

His wife came over to help him. "Well, there is tea and biscuits, and hot stew."

Her husband breathed a sigh of contentment.

"Linden summoned me while you were out," she said. "He will not let this go. He wishes to have the whole castle searched, as soon as it can be done. The grounds, the castle, and the woods around the keep and the village again."

"Indeed?" Cam raised his eyebrows.

"He does not believe Warburton. His trust in him is diminished." Mrs. Lennox pursed her lips. "I never thought a day would come when I'd feel sorry for Sir Guy. But I must admit, I do. He was once like a father to the lad, but Linden is a grown man now. He sees with a man's eyes, not a boy's. The sheen of admiration is gone. Warburton has not given an honest account. Linden will not forget that. Not when he believes it puts those under his care at risk."

"He is much like his father in that way," Cam agreed. "But search the keep itself? What does he think we shall find?"

Mrs. Lennox shrugged. "Perhaps nothing. But then, it is a vast place. Can even you or I say we know every nook or cranny? And whoever did this—to Warburton, to the young man. Well, they had to have come from somewhere." She twisted her apron in her hands. "Not that it is a very comfortable thought to think they may have come from here."

Cam shook his head. "I do not know what to make of any of it, and that's the God's honest truth. A murder and now an attack that Sir Guy says was not an attack in however many days. It's enough to make your skin crawl. Princewood is a quiet, peaceable place. The blood that was spilled—well, it was spilled long ago."

Mrs. Lennox crossed the cottage to where the tea kettle hung over the fire.

"Blood may fade with time, but it leaves behind stains," she said, quietly.

Chapter 14

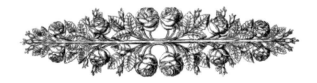

Nothing that is so, is so.

— Twelfth Night

December 6

Time had flown as it was wont to do, and the day of the festival had arrived.

As threatened, Jasper had timed the two-day festival to commence on St. Nicholas Day.

The day marked the beginning of almost two weeks in which the villagers would have a holiday break, enjoying a rest and taking advantage of the opportunity to stay home with their families.

Most of those independently employed in the village were fishermen. Cod was plentiful in nearby waters. Others worked at a small cotton mill that had been owned for many years by the Chevalier family, making textiles to be sent to Edinburgh to be sold in shops. During Christmas, the mill shut down, as did the village school.

The traditional air of subdued celebration which marked the Christmas season had, this year, become more of a roar as the entire village looked forward to enjoying shared merriment.

Many of the village folk had assisted Jasper in bringing his plans to fruition and were proud of their contributions and eager to show off the results.

A skating rink had been made in honor of the occasion, just outside the castle grounds. For the past few days, it had been a hub of activity for all the village children as well as some of their elders.

Linden could hear the pleasant shrieks of the young ones spinning and skating and falling from as far up in the keep as the solar.

Food and drink were to be in ample supply; some provided by the castle kitchen and some sold in small stalls set up by the villagers themselves in a kind of small market featuring sweets and baking and handiworks.

The castle coffers had been generously opened wider in order to fund the purchase of candy and small toys for all of the village children.

After a puppet show, musical performances, an archery competition, a skating competition, and an animal trick show, the day would culminate in a feast, with a large oxen roasted in the courtyard, a massive bonfire, and, Jasper promised, a performance from a trick horse rider who had journeyed specially from London and would ride about in a "ring of fire" (a coral lit by torches) in an unforgettable spectacle of wonder.

The second day of the festival would be more subdued. The day was to be mostly event-free. In the evening, the doors of the keep were to be flung wide open and there was to be a dance in the great hall—ostensibly in honor of Fleur and Linden's betrothal—followed by a fireworks display.

There had been no further attacks since the one on Warburton the week prior. Jasper had made Linden promise to put all thoughts of the recent troubles from his mind for one day.

But that was easier said than done. Particularly now that Linden knew what he knew.

The castle had been searched thoroughly, with Cam and Linden leading the search themselves tirelessly for four days.

In the end, what had been found left Linden greatly unsettled.

In the darkest recesses of the castle cellars, amidst the maze of storage rooms, centuries of forgotten clutter, and crumbling stone passages that threaded beneath the grounds, a gaol had been discovered.

What was shocking was not the existence of a barred room below the castle—for in the centuries past, prisoners had at times been held at Princewood for various reasons. Rather it was how recently the room seemed to have been occupied.

By the state of it, Cam would swear someone had lived within those four damp walls in a state of near total darkness until quite recently. There were signs that someone had tried to make the room a little more comfortable but failed. Books had been stolen and brought down from the keep's library, only to be ripped apart, their pages strewn about the cell like feathers. A straw mattress which might have offered comfort had been ripped up instead.

Who had been confined in the cell? Who had put them there? And where had they gone?

Further troubling was that recently, some food and articles of clothing had gone missing in the village. Mrs. Lennox had made subtle inquiries, but no one could say who had taken the items or why. It was rare for there to be thefts of any kind—and when a theft did occur, village chatter could usually be depended upon to bring the wrongdoer quickly to light.

Not in this case.

It troubled Linden to consider that until very recently Princewood had been the unwitting home of a mysterious prisoner—and that this unknown prisoner had now broken free, not only to pillage and steal from his people but to potentially do terrible harm.

The most troubling aspect of all of this was knowing, or at least strongly suspecting, the man who had been like a father to him in his youth and was to be his father-in-law could enlighten Linden on all of these matters if he so chose, but had instead committed to maintaining a dogged silence.

Despite Linden's misgivings, Jasper had argued that there was no reason to cancel the festival for they could not all go about hiding in their houses out of fear of the unknown. And so, Linden had allowed the event to go forward, praying he would not regret the decision.

In the midst of these weighty concerns, there was one small ray of light.

Grayson Gardner remained at Princewood.

The young man had written to his family and informed them of his injury, his recovery, and his plan to remain at Princewood for the time being.

Linden suspected Jasper's nagging and prodding had done much to achieve this. Indeed, Peter Carson, the village school teacher, had lately been urging Grayson to remain until the springtime and assist in the running of the school which had lately been blessed by a surplus of children but a shortage of instructors.

Few were willing to come teach at such an out of the way place. They were fortunate to have Peter, who had grown up in the village and returned after attending a grammar school in Edinburgh.

Grayson seemed to have received a fine education. The young man said he had been tutored at home by his mother and sisters.

But besides his book knowledge, the young man was more well-rounded than many a more educated youth, for he had seen at least a little something of the world outside of Princewood—and outside of England for that matter.

In a village like Princewood, for which Edinburgh was an exotic locale, that was saying something.

But it was not Grayson's education or the prospect of him teaching at the village school which brought Linden pleasure.

It was something more elusive.

He and Grayson had hardly said more than a few words to one another since their ride along the beach.

But even passing in the halls or seeing Grayson in the courtyard was enough to lighten Linden's heart.

The silence between them was a kind of sweet pain, a torturous absence which could have been remedied if Linden truly wished. But instead, he allowed it to extend, giving himself only the pleasure of awareness of the young man's presence. Hearing his voice. Seeing his face fleetingly once or twice a day.

Knowing he was there.

It was enough.

Linden could not help but acknowledge to himself that Fleur's presence in his life had never been such a comfort—and she had resided at Princewood almost all her life, since her mother had died in London and she had been brought across the country as an infant to reside with her father.

Never in Linden's life had he ever felt so utterly responsive to another person. So completely in their power, moved beyond measure by the hint of a smile, a glance, an accidental touch.

His only fear was that it would all disappear. That one morning Grayson would wake up and decide to go back from whence he came, out of Linden's life, leaving it somehow much more barren than it had been before he arrived.

"Marchpane?"

Something white and sticky was being dangled in front of his face. A pastry smelling of sweet almonds.

"Marchpane?" Jasper asked again, grinning. Linden had not noticed him come into the solar. "You aren't growing deaf at such a tender age, are you?"

"Hardly," Linden said, shortly, leaning against the wall of the solar and looking out the window at the skaters down below.

Grayson was one of them. Even from so high up, Linden could see the young man's rosy cheeks and beaming face as he sped back and forth across the frozen rink, pulling a train of small children behind him.

"Are you coming down or do you mean to spy on us from up here all day? That would rather defeat the purpose of the event, don't you think?" Jasper said, mildly, taking a large bite of the marzipan sweet and munching slowly.

Linden sighed. He never balked from going into the village or interacting with its inhabitants when duty required it. While the peoples' fear and suspicion were ever-present, he could at least count upon a measure of awestruck courtesy to help him muddle through.

But this was different. This was an occasion designated for pleasure, fun, and laughter. Two days for his tenants to let down their guard and put their cares aside.

Would Linden's presence inhibit that? Would they scowl and recoil as he walked amongst them?

He had to admit that part of him was reluctant to have Grayson potentially bear witness to his rejection by his own people, so very publicly.

But he was no coward. This was his duty, as much as any other.

He squared his shoulders.

"Am I to take that as a yes?" Jasper demanded. "Or are you fishing for a compliment on your fine shoulders? Be careful you do not burst the seams of that coat with all of that brawn. I will give you a quarter of an hour to stop brooding and get yourself downstairs to the courtyard. After that, if you have still not arrived—" He gestured out the window to the ice. "Do you see those children? I will tell them that you have treats for them and send them *all* up here to drag you down. All of them. Every last one. Do you understand?"

"Yes, Jasper," Linden said, half-listening, still distracted by his thoughts and the carefree figures below.

Then he took in what his friend had said.

"I will be down right away, yes," he agreed, hastily. "I will see you in the courtyard."

"Excellent." Jasper waggled a finger and gave a wicked grin. "A quarter of an hour, mind you. Or the children lay siege to the tower."

Gracie was winded, panting, and soaked through. She had been skating with the village children all morning and in- dulging their many demands to pull them to and fro over the ice, which she had done countless times.

Now, weary but happy, she trudged through the courtyard back towards the keep to change her clothes before returning for the start of the day's festivities.

The weather was auspicious. Bright and sunny, crisp and cool.

She took in the sight of the stalls set up in a semi-circle just outside the stables. They looked very pretty—all decorated with brightly-colored ribbons and greenery cut from the forest. There was a small stage where the puppet show and other performances would take place. Bales of hay had been set up as makeshift benches for the audience.

There were other decorative elements, of course. Jasper had carefully hung kissing boughs strategically around the festival site—cut evergreen, apples, oranges, and other embellishments all mounted on a round wire frame.

It was bad luck to refuse a kiss offered under the kissing bough, Jasper had warned her cheekily, thus prompting Gracie to avoid them carefully.

She had no wish to kiss anyone.

Anyone but one.

And that one would be disastrous.

"Ah, here you are," Jasper said, brightly, coming towards her. "I have just been threatening the recalcitrant master of the castle to come down or face the wrath of all of these angelic children. If I have to, I will tell those sweet little mites that

Linden has all of the gifts—which they have so set their tiny hearts on—hoarded away in his room."

"You wouldn't," Gracie said, laughing.

She could just imagine the look of panic on Linden's face as a swarm of screaming, giggling children scrambled up to his tower.

Linden liked children, of course. At least, she was fairly sure he did. But he did not seem exactly comfortable with them.

That was not his fault, of course. He had likely not had many opportunities. It was no wonder he was less gregarious than Jasper.

"Do you really think this will change their minds about him, Jasper?" she asked, suddenly. "Or was that simply a ploy to have Linden approve the festival?"

"I would never get Linden's hopes up about something like that if I did not believe it was possible," Jasper said, quietly. "If you had known him as long as I have, you would know..." He shook his head. "Linden may not realize it himself, but this is everything he yearns for."

Jasper gestured broadly about them to the stalls, the people, the children playing in the distance. "He longs to be a part of this. A true part of his community. Oh, I was born into it, of course. But even I have some idea of what it means to be cast outside the welcoming circle. Or, I can imagine."

"Because of Peter, you mean?" Gracie said, quietly.

"Because of Peter and I, yes," Jasper said, wryly. He shrugged. "There are a few judgemental souls in the village, but most have a live and let live approach. It helps that Peter and I do not flaunt our... connection." He grimaced. "Although I must say, sometimes I long to."

"It must be hard to hide," Gracie sympathized.

"Yes. You wouldn't know anything about that, would you?" Jasper said, with a wink.

"Now, enough chatter," he said, brusquely, turning away as Gracie's mouth fell open. "Here comes Linden."

Gracie followed Jasper's gaze.

Even after these weeks, she had not become accustomed to the sight of Linden Chevalier. She had adapted a strategy. Unless they were speaking—which they had not, since that day on the beach—she only looked at him sideways, from the corner of her eyes, never directly. As if he were the too bright sun and might blind her should she stare too long.

Which he would, in a sense. As he did now, as she permitted herself a rare lingering gaze.

He was gleamingly, smolderingly beautiful, like a pure medieval knight or a young King Arthur stepping off the pages of a painting.

Though it was always Lancelot who was shown with fair hair like Linden's, those long strands of dark gold and amber softening the hard planes of his warrior-strong face. Did

Lancelot have a mouth like Linden's? Full and strong and sensual? Suggesting unspeakable delights if one could only unlock the man who possessed it?

Was it a mouth like this which undid Guinevere?

He was wearing a dark grey cloak over a black coat and trousers. He looked tall and hard and lean, a young man in his absolute prime, broad chested, brawny shouldered, and moving with a powerful ease. In the short time since she had arrived, he had changed, she realized. There was a greater maturity in his eyes and he carried himself with authority in a way she had never noticed, like a man who was prepared to make difficult decisions for the sake of those under his care and would stand by them come what may.

Gracie swallowed and looked down at herself. She was clad in another old set of Jasper's clothes, well-made but hardly elegant or fashionable. She was damp with snow and sticky with sweat and there were strands of hair pasted to her forehead that had come loose from her braid. She quickly tucked them under the cap and pulled it down more firmly.

Lately, she felt as if she were wearing a cap even in her sleep. It seemed the most symbolic item of clothing to represent her disguised state.

And what had she gained for all her trouble, she thought ruefully? What had Mrs. Lennox gained? It was hardly as if she had discovered anything, helped anything. She was merely still there, and that was all that could be said.

If she had arrived as a girl, would Warburton truly have had her thrown out? Or asked her to leave much sooner?

The old knight seemed so bumbling and toothless of late, it was difficult to believe him holding that much sway.

Jasper slapped a hand to his head. "I've nearly forgotten. There are some more kissing boughs up in the stable loft. Peter and I left them there last night when we... Well, no matter." He grinned at Gracie. "Be a good lad and fetch them down for me? I'd best go and snag Linden so that he doesn't try to run back inside."

"Of course," Gracie said, feeling relieved. "I'll go now."

She walked past the stalls and into the stable. It was a large two-storey building. Gracie guessed there were at least fifty stalls, though not all were filled right now. A separate part of the stable held the castle's coaches. Various smaller rooms were set aside for tack and harnesses, washing up, and food storage. Above was the large hayloft with accommodations for the stablemaster or groom. Princewood's stablemaster lived in the village, so these were presently not in use.

As she walked between the stalls, she imagined them full in Princewood's prime.

Had Linden's father had siblings? She knew that Sir Guy was a distant relative, a cousin she believed, and that he stood to inherit after Linden or Linden's children. So presumably Linden's father had been an only child as well, or perhaps had only sisters.

What would it be to see this place full of life every day as it was today? With the laughter of children ringing through the air as a natural thing and not merely a holiday exception?

Perhaps Linden and Fleur's children would soon run through these halls, Gracie thought with a pang.

She crossed over to the stairs leading above and went up. It was darker up in the loft and she did not have a lantern.

There was one large window, open on the back wall of the loft and it let in the only light. Looking across and through it, she saw with surprise the battlements of the castle rising just a few feet outside. Almost close enough to jump to. The stable was built backing almost right up to the stone wall.

She paused a moment to give her eyes time to adjust to the shadows, then began to search for the kissing boughs. She wandered among the bales of hay, peeking about.

As she neared the back of the loft, she spotted a pile of dark items in the far corner that looked promising.

But when she walked over, she saw it was merely a heap of blankets atop a pile of straw that had been pulled together to shape a little bed. Someone had been sleeping up here, she thought, in alarm. And in that moment, all of her senses awakened.

She was not alone in the loft.

There was a scuffing noise coming from behind her and she heard the soft breathing of another person.

She was loathe to turn around and yet knew she must.

Clenching her hands into fists, she whirled around to face the   true   monster   of   Princewood.

"Where did Grayson run off to?" Linden asked, frowning a little.

"Oh, he went to fetch some more festival trappings we forgot in the stable loft," Jasper explained, waving a hand. "He'll be back in no time." He sounded amused. "He wasn't running away from you, if that's what you're worried about."

"Of course, I wasn't," Linden said, stiffly. Which was a lie. For the first time he wondered if Grayson had been working as hard to avoid him as he had been doing.

"He's only a few feet away, Linden," Jasper said, giving him a curious look. "And there are so many people about. What are you afraid of?"

Linden realized he had been staring at the stables.

"I'm not afraid. But I am also not at ease," he admitted. "How can I be?"

"You seem more worried about Grayson than anyone else," Jasper observed. "I should be offended. If I were to be murdered, I suppose you would just say 'Thank goodness, Jasper is gone. There won't be anymore of these dreadful festivals.'"

Linden smiled. "That's something that Warburton might say," he corrected.

Jasper continued studying him. "You know," he said, with an odd expression. "If one obsesses over someone and is possessed by an all-consuming wish to safeguard them from harm, then perhaps one should accept the situation and simply acknowledge it."

"What?" Linden said, sharply, narrowing his eyes. "What are you talking about, Jasper?"

"I'm talking about you, Linden. You are the 'one.' You are obsessed with Grayson. Anyone who knows you can see it. And since that number is really quite small, it's mostly me who can see it. Why don't you do something about it already?"

Linden stared. "Are you mad? What would you have me do?"

Jasper frowned. "Is it because Grayson is male? Is that the problem?"

"No," Linden said. And he knew it was the truth. "Though I admit I still cannot wrap my mind around... that. But it is not that." He shook his head. "It's Fleur, of course."

"Ah, of course, dear Fleur, your betrothed, your beloved," Jasper mused.

"She deserves my loyalty. I have sworn she will have it," Linden said, shortly.

"How noble. Although in truth, you have not sworn anything yet," Jasper countered.

"It is implied."

"Of course, of course," Jasper said, smoothly. "So very honorable. What does it matter that the lifetime happiness of three people is at stake."

Linden said nothing.

"Yes," Jasper went on, as if talking to himself. "You, Fleur, and... Grayson. What a love triangle."

Linden glared. "I would not describe it in such a way."

"Oh, no?" Jasper said, innocently. He studied his nails carefully, not looking at Linden. "And what if I were to tell you that things were not as complex as you might think. Even if I accept your very sophisticated claim that Grayson's—" He coughed into his hand delicately. "—manliness, were not a factor. Perhaps its absence would simplify things."

"What the devil are you talking about?" Linden said, starting to become annoyed. He looked around at the people walking by and lowered his voice. "This is not precisely the kind of conversation I wished to have today, Jasper. I thought we were trying to pave the way for me to be more accepted by people, not less."

"Aha, so you admit that it is a hinderance," Jasper murmured. "But never mind. I accept that. It is a simple truth of life. At least, of life right now."

Linden was looking towards the stables again. What could be taking the young man so bloody long? How much time did it take to fetch decorations? Unless Jasper had vastly underestimated the number of items and their weight, which would not be surprising.

"Oh, very well," Jasper said, abruptly. "I shall put you out of your misery. Enjoyable though it has been to watch." He leaned in close to Linden's ear, which meant he had to lift his head a little, Linden being a few inches taller. "Grayson is no boy."

"What the devil are you talking about?" Linden demanded.

"I believe you just said that. Please do try to keep up," Jasper complained. "I'm talking about Grayson. Grayson is a girl. A woman, rather, I suppose. Grayson is not a man. There. One impediment is now removed. Now that one illicit aspect has been eliminated, you may lust after them to your heart's content knowing there is a very easy solution for your dilemma.

You simply end this nonsensical engagement with Fleur and marry who you—"

They both heard the cry at the same time.

"We will discuss your insulting and farcical claim later," Linden declared. "I'm going to check on the boy."

"The boy is a girl and I'm sure they simply tripped on something and will be very embarrassed to see you, but as you wish. I shall stay here and keep watch on the rest of the festival," Jasper said, unconcernedly. "Oh, for heaven's sake, they're putting up the puppet theater all wrong. The curtain goes on the outside! The outside!"

Chapter 15

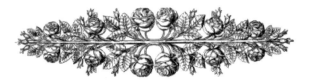

Love is not love

Which alters when it alteration finds

— Sonnet 116

It was Fleur, Gracie thought, stupidly, for a moment.

The woman coming across the loft towards her was Fleur.

Then she saw it was not Fleur. This woman was older, her hair long and streaked with grey, her clothes worn haphazardly as if she gave no care to her appearance.

There was a knife in her hand.

"It would have been better for you if you had not come up here, my dear," the woman said, almost sadly.

"I was looking for the kissing boughs," Gracie said, hearing how foolish she sounded.

The woman gave a short harsh laugh. "Kissing boughs?"

"Yes, for the festival," Gracie said, desperately. "Will you be coming to the festival?" She kept her eyes on the knife. It looked quite sharp.

"Oh, no, my dear, they would not like that at all, believe you me," the woman said, throwing her head back to laugh. "You are a funny lad, aren't you? And I'm sorry—"

She darted forward midsentence so unexpectedly that Gracie hadn't time to step back. She felt herself caught, like a fly in a web as the woman gripped her by the collar.

She twisted frantically, trying to slip free, and nearly did so, pulling out of the woman's grip, only to have her clutch at her head, grasping for anything to hold onto and finding the cap, digging her fingers in so tightly that Gracie let out a sharp cry of pain. She could feel the woman's nails, cutting into her scalp, through her coiled braid.

She threw her body away from the woman as hard as she could and cringed in pain, feeling the cap coming away and with it some strands of hair. Her braid was down, the heavy coil falling against her back, pieces of hair coming loose from its confines.

She was breathing hard and heavy, her fists clenched and raised across her chest. She had no weapon, but still, she would fight. She was not about to become another of this woman's victims.

"Why did you kill the coach driver?" she demanded. "Why did you hurt him? That night in the snow. He had done nothing to you."

But the woman was not even listening to her. There was something else on her mind as she looked at Gracie from behind narrowed furious eyes.

"You're a girl," she hissed. "Not a boy at all. A girl. Why? Why are you here?"

Gracie did not have a chance to respond before the woman answered for herself.

"You're here to take him. To steal him away," the woman concluded, her expression becoming more malicious.

"Who? Steal who?" Gracie demanded.

The woman advanced towards her slowly. Her knife was up.

"No, no, no," she muttered. "It won't do. I'm sorry, but he would be ever so angry. It simply won't do."

"Grayson!" Linden's voice rang out commandingly through the stables. "Where are you?"

The woman's head whipped towards the sound.

Linden was coming. Gracie could hear the sound of his feet on the stairs.

"I'm here," she shouted.

The woman hissed in annoyance, and lunged again towards her.

Gracie let out a cry and raised her arms across her face, then hurled herself against the charming woman with all her might, eyes closed.

The knife connected with the wool of her coat and could not break through. She felt the pressure as the woman pushed harder against the blade, but Gracie was pushing back as well, arm against knife, counting on her layers of winter clothing to stop the blade, forcing the woman back, loosening her control on the knife.

They had nearly reached the window. Gracie could see the stone parapet, and beyond, the sea.

Well, at least she would die with a view of the sea, she thought, foolishly. Then she clenched her jaw. She was not going to die.

"Grayson! I say, stop! Stop!" Linden roared. She could hear him racing across towards them and felt a surge of relief.

Abruptly, the woman shoved Gracie hard, causing her to tilt backwards.

Linden reached her as she fell, stretching his arms out and softening her landing.

"Are you all right?" he demanded. Then, "Who the devil was that?"

They both looked towards the window.

The woman had disappeared.

Linden let go of Grace and ran to the window. He looked between the stable and the wall, then back and forth across the battlement.

He turned back. "They're gone."

"Yes," Gracie agreed. "Well, thank goodness for that."

She looked at her arm. It felt bruised and the coat was slashed, but she did not think the woman's knife had broken through her second layer—a thick wool sweater—to the skin. She started to shrug out of her coat.

"Here. Let me help you," Linden said, coming back to her. Then he stopped.

"Your hair," he said, frozen in place, eyes wide.

Gracie flinched. "My hair." She touched her braid. One could hardly call it that now. It had come quite undone.

"Jasper was right," Linden said, incredulously. "You're a woman."

"I am," she agreed, unable to meet his eyes, readying herself for his anger. Would he throw her out that very day? "You must be wondering why I would do something so idiotic."

"No," he said, slowly. "Not really. At the moment, I don't really care."

She swallowed. "You don't?"

He shook his head. "What is your name? Your true name?"

"Gracie Gardner," she whispered.

"Gracie," he repeated.

"Are you... glad I'm a girl?" she asked, tentatively, watching his face. His eyes had not left her own.

He hesitated.

"I'm glad that you're you," he said, simply. He shook his head. "Jasper was right. I don't know what to do."

She was beautiful.

Yes, more beautiful than before—because there was something indescribable about the loveliness of a pretty woman with her hair tumbling softly down around her face. It could not be denied. He badly wanted to reach out and touch it, wrap his hands in it, feel the sandy tresses against his skin.

But what truly surprised him was that his desire was generally unchanged.

He had wanted her, whoever she was. As anything really.

All this had done was make the way seem slightly smoother, perhaps less taboo, and yet no less complicated. To Jasper it might appear that way, but appearances were deceptive.

She had taken a step towards him, her arm held in front of her. She was hurt. She had been attacked.

And here all he could do was foolishly gawk at her—her face, her hair, her form.

She was so close. Two feet away. She took another step. Inches now.

He watched her take a deep breath and blink slowly. Her eyes were dusky pools of brown, wide and intense.

"I'll be whatever you want me to be," she said, quietly but directly. "Anything. So long as you don't make me leave."

"Why would I make you leave?" he asked, wonderingly, before he remembered.

She was sunburned from skating all morning. Her nose was red and her freckles more pronounced. The rest of her face was tanned a healthy bronze. She was slender and gangly with no chest to speak of—like many a boy. Her hips were slim, almost indiscernible, and yet she had subtle curves and softness—she always had.

She had no ladylike pretensions that he had seen. She wore no bonnet. Demanded no lady's maid. Carried no parasol.

Rode like a boy. Spoke like a boy. But what did any of that mean?

She was herself. She was Gracie.

Her lips were rosy and wide, and when she smiled his heart pounded with a mixture of awe and delight.

She smiled. "You won't?"

He took a step closer towards her, nearly closing the gap, and saw her falter.

He tilted his head downwards, sensing her nervousness.

"Tell me not to kiss you," he instructed, wondering if she could see his desperation behind the stridency of his tone.

Her eyes widened.

"Don't... don't kiss me," she whispered, her voice breathy.

"You must say it as if you mean it," he begged, hoarsely, moving his head closer. Their foreheads were almost touching now. She lifted her face up to his.

He saw her shake her head, barely perceptibly.

"I can't," she whispered.

He would never know if she had actually said those words or if he had begun to kiss her as they were leaving her lips and imagined the rest.

He had wanted to kiss her since he first saw her, he knew.

Yet all along had known it would be dangerous to do so, too, but for all of the wrong reasons.

It *was* dangerous.

As they kissed, he felt something unlock inside that had been closed for a very long time.

The lock of his restraint had melted as if it were wax, and now all of his longings, his true dreams, his most secret hopes were coming alive.

Everything was exquisite. Everything was beautiful. Everything made sense.

Her mouth yielded to his so perfectly, opened to him so immediately that he was incredibly stirred. Her lips were soft and sweet. She smelled of snow and sunshine. He wound his hands into her hair, gently at first, then more firmly, holding her face closer to his own.

Her hands mimicked his, moving into his hair, curling it gently around her fingers, moving her palms slowly over his ears, his neck, caressing him there until he shivered.

He moved his lips against hers, exploring her mouth ever so gently, uncertainly. His tongue touched her lips, hesitantly at first, and she let out a soft moan and cupped her hands behind his neck, pulling him closer to her.

Heat flushed through him and he moved his tongue into her mouth, feeling his body coming alive with sensation as he entered her, then running his hands down the long stream of her hair and then lower still, holding her against himself so tightly he feared she would complain.

He was surprised he could still stand. His legs were braced hard against the floor, but the rest of him was reeling, breathless, hardly able to believe it was happening.

The one he desired was in his arms. And her touch was more incredible than he ever could have imagined.

He had yearned for her, been heartsick for her, and now they were here, together.

She did not cringe from his touch, but welcomed it. Somehow, he knew she craved even more, just as he did. He felt queasy with anticipation and lightheaded with longing at the thought of what might occur were he to lay her down now, there, upon the straw.

Would she touch him in turn? Where? Everywhere? What would it feel like? What pinnacles might they reach in one another's embrace?

He broke away, panting like a hungry man holding himself back from a feast. As he looked down at her, his hair fell forward to brush her cheeks in blonde waves and she touched a strand softly with one finger.

Her chest was rising and falling, her breaths coming as heavily as his own.

"That was my first kiss," he said, feeling young and shy and full of wonderment.

She touched his cheek, then raised her lips to his again.

She did not say that it was hers, he noticed. But he did not care.

She had her heart's desire.

She was enfolded in his arms.

His lips were on hers and she wanted them there, always—which was fanciful, she knew. But still, sometimes fancies came true. This was proof enough.

Her heart sank as loud voices reached them.

"Linden? Grayson?"

"Lord Chevalier?"

"Jasper," Linden breathed, pulling away.

"And Sir Guy," she whispered.

Still, she nuzzled against him, her lips to his neck, not wanting to give him up so quickly.

"We must go," he said, in a strained voice. "I must go."

"I know," she said, softly.

She touched her hair. "You had best go down first. Get Sir Guy away. I am not sure what to say about... this."

He touched her hair and smiled. "We will figure it out."

He moved towards the stairs. "Jasper already knows," he called back softly over his shoulder.

"Of course, he does," she said to herself, rolling her eyes.

Jasper came up nearly as soon as Linden went down.

"Did you find the kissing boughs?" he asked, innocently, looking all about.

Gracie put her hands on her hips. "Were there even any kissing boughs, Jasper?"

"Of course, there were," he said, brightly. "Ah, see here, by the stairs."

Gracie's eyes narrowed. "So, it was not just a ploy to send me off and then—" She hesitated, not sure she wanted to voice the accusation. It would be the same as suggesting Jasper had wished to matchmake.

"Send you off and what?" Jasper asked, grinning. He looked her up and down with satisfaction. "You finally took your hair down, I see. Had a bit of a scuffle, did we?"

"Oh, shush," Gracie said, impatiently. "It did not begin as that sort. You unwittingly might have sent me to my death, Jasper Lennox."

"That seems rather melodramatic," Jasper said. "I've never heard anyone describe kissing that way."

"Enough with the kissing," Gracie said, through gritted teeth. "Though how you know about that just by looking is beyond me. There was a strange woman up here. She attacked me."

She held up the slashed coat.

Jasper's eyes widened. He glanced about nervously.

"She is not here any longer. She ran off when Linden appeared. And it was fortunate he did," she admitted. She looked towards the loft window. "Perhaps jumped would be more accurate. I believe she threw herself out of that window. There was neither hide nor hair of her when we looked about."

"And you think..." Jasper said slowly. "That it was the same person who attacked Sir Guy? A woman?" He looked skeptical.

Gracie snorted. "That is the part you find most unbelievable?"

"Of course, a woman may be conniving, I suppose. But a murderess?" Jasper said, doubtfully.

"She seemed rather intent on murder to me," Gracie grumbled. "Have you forgotten your Macbeth?"

Jasper was looking dismayed. "I suppose then that the festival..."

"Oh, Jasper," Gracie sighed. "If Linden does not say otherwise, I suppose it will go ahead, uninterrupted. Whoever she was, she is gone. I don't see what good disrupting everything you have planned will do."

"I'll talk to Linden," Jasper said. "He'll want to do something, of course. Perhaps he can send a few men to search discreetly, without alarming the entire village."

"That sounds like a good idea," Gracie said, with relief. "When will this be over? They will find her, won't they Jasper? She as good as confessed to killing that poor coachman."

"Of course," Jasper said, slowly, looking as if his mind were elsewhere. He hesitated a moment, then added, "It is probably stupid of me, but that is not what concerns me the most." He shrugged forlornly. "I had such high hopes for the festival, for Linden's sake. I know it is foolish but I had hoped it would really change things. But now, with more bloodshed, more threats. I don't see how that will happen."

"But Linden is not to blame for any of these things," Gracie argued. "Surely people will understand that. And when he catches the culprit, they will be in his debt. They must be grateful."

"Must they? I certainly hope so," Jasper said. "Come, lets go down."

Warburton had been searching for Linden to consult with him on some of the details for the dance being held the following night.

Sir Guy was to be master-of-ceremonies and as expected he was taking the role with the utmost seriousness—despite it being a simple country dance which anyone in the village might attend, and nothing as stylish or elegant as a true ball.

Of course, thanks to Jasper there would be professional musicians and a hearty supper was to be provided at midnight. The great hall was also to undergo a decorative transformation. If Linden heard the words "kissing bough" one more time, he was ready to blacken an eye. Or at least toss one of the blasted kissing boughs into the fire.

Which was rather hypocritical of him, he thought, reddening.

"Are you quite well, my lord?" Sir Guy asked, peering at him from behind the quizzing glass he wore and clutching his pile of festival notes and memorandums to his chest.

"Very well indeed," Linden said, quickly, forcing a smile. "Jasper has done an excellent job of organizing the festival, has he not? From the looks of it, most of the village is already in attendance."

"Indeed, indeed," Sir Guy agreed, looking about them with less appreciation for the crowd. He sighed. "Villagers. Farmers and fisherfolk. If you had shown any interest in accepting invitations from your peers, or allowed me to make introductions in the proper circles—even in Edinburgh... Well, our guests tomorrow evening might be of a very different quality."

"Are you disappointed for Fleur's sake?" Linden asked, a trifle sympathetic.

He knew Sir Guy would always harbor pretensions of greatness. He suspected nothing would ever satisfy his ambitions, even if Linden did begin to take up a greater social role. To Linden, the most important part of holding a barony, however, was taking seriously the responsibility to care for the people who resided on his land. Not striving to impress others simply because they possessed grander titles or larger estates.

"Your peers would not have condemned you as these ignorant peasants you so treasure have done. Such a waste, such a waste," Sir Guy muttered, a little pathetically, reminding Linden of a small boy facing the disappointment of being told he could not have more sweets.

Then the older man's face brightened. "Well, at least you are fulfilling your parents wishes in one respect. By marrying my Fleur you are securing your lineage. Anchoring yourself to a respected family—one already connected to your own, of course. Your father would be proud of your choice of bride. You may be assured of that."

"I am sure he would be," Linden said, feeling his heart sink. "Though I am sure he would also be even more proud of the way we—" He made sure to include the faithful steward. "—have cared for Princewood's people."

"Hmph" was all Sir Guy said.

"Will you be staying to watch the puppet show?" Linden asked, politely. "I see a free seat on a hay bale just over there."

Just as expected, Sir Guy scurried back to the castle rather than remaining for the theater production.

Linden quickly had a word with a passing servant, then took a seat. The puppet show had already begun and within a quarter of an hour the tale of the brave knight Sir Yasper Flummox who was forced to fight the fire-breathing dragon Bortonbabble drew to a close.

He was not looking forward to the next item on the festival itinerary: the dispersal of gifts to the village children.

Jasper had insisted that Linden be the gift-giver and two large sacks were waiting behind the stage.

To Linden's relief, Mrs. Lennox appeared just as the puppet show ended to organize the distribution.

Clapping her hands together, she stood in front of the crowd of excited children. "Here now, Lord Chevalier has gifts for all of you. Form a line, if you please, boys and girls. Quickly now. There you go. No pushing. One at a time."

When a line had been formed to her liking, Mrs. Lennox began sending the children behind her, one at a time, to pull an item from the bag. One sack for girls, the other for boys.

Linden was not even quite sure what he would be giving out until packets of sweets and prettily wrapped dolls and new pairs of skates began to appear out of the sacks, to be pressed into eager hands, with a quick bow of the head from the boys or a curtsy from the girls, and a whispered "thank you, my lord."

A half hour later, the sacks were nearly empty and Linden found himself beaming from ear to ear.

There was something uplifting about being close to all of the children and seeing their happy and appreciative faces.

Furthermore, none had shied away or seemed frightened.

Linden found himself hoping that Jasper was right. Perhaps a sea change was coming.

As he was just about to put the sacks away, a little girl and her mother appeared. The little girl had evidently been crying. Her face was streaked and smeared, her nose red and shiny.

"Whatever is the matter?" Linden asked, in alarm. "Did you not receive a present?"

"She did, my lord," the girl's mother said, hesitantly. "But she dearly longed for a pair of skates like her brother's, you see..."

"And all I got was this stupid doll," the little girl said, holding up a small brunette figure, and beginning to bawl once more.

Linden bit his lip and tried not to smile. The little girl could not have been more than five or six. She had not grown used to disappointment. Nor should she have to, he decided.

"I'm sure there are another pair of skates in the sack," he said, solemnly. "And if there is not, I will have a pair found for you—even if we must send for them all the way to London."

The little girl's face brightened and the sniffling slowed as Linden fished in the boys' sack and finally pulled out a pair of shining skates.

The child's mother shot him a grateful smile as he passed them to her daughter.

"Thank you, my lord," the little girl whispered, holding the skates tightly.

"Yes, thank you very kindly, my lord," her mother added. "It was very good of you. Come now, Clara. We've bothered his lordship enough for one day."

When they were gone, Linden made a mental note to tell Jasper there must be ample skates in both the boys and the girls' sacks next year.

The time had passed so quickly since he had left the stables that he had not had a chance to handle the most pressing matter of all.

Fortunately, he saw Cam Lennox approaching.

"You wished to see me, my lord?" the grey-haired, burly man asked.

Linden quickly explained what had occurred in the stable loft, leaving out the detail of Grayson's transformation into Gracie. There would be time enough for that.

When Cam walked away, his mouth set in a grim line, Linden felt the weight of worry fall back upon him.

The hour with the children had been a welcome reprieve.

The minutes with Gracie...something else entirely.

But reality came crashing back.

His people were in danger.

Gracie was in danger.

And tomorrow a dance would be held in honor of his betrothal to a woman he did not nor could not love.

Chapter 16

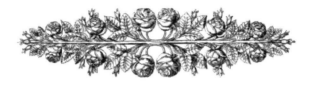

If thou remember'st not the slightest folly

That ever love did make thee run into,

Thou hast not loved.

— As You Like It

It was past midnight.

With the exception of her fright in the hayloft, Gracie had had a wonderful day.

The festival had been a tremendous success.

Jasper had been positively glowing as the last stragglers finished their ales and walked unevenly out of the courtyard and back down to the village.

Of course, for Gracie, the highlight of the day had not been the puppet show or the skating contest or the trick horsemanship. It had come before all of those things.

Funny how a kiss was enough to nearly make her forget the fear of what had happened just before. It was not her encounter with a potential murderer but the kiss she had thought of over and over again all day, until she had wrung the savor from it, only to go over it in her mind yet again.

Not the attack, not her unveiling, not the festival. Only Linden's lips on hers.

There was a knock at her door and for an instant her heart jumped. Could it be? Would he dare?

"My dear?" Mrs. Lennox creaked the door open and peeked around. "Ah, you are not abed yet then."

She stepped into the room and closed the door softly behind her.

"What a day this has been," she exclaimed, sinking into the closest chair. "And my Cam still out there, looking for... well, God knows what."

"You look tired," Gracie said, gently. She put down the brush she had been using on her hair and pulled the long length of it back over her shoulders. She did not have the energy to braid it tonight.

"I am, but I thought we should speak before tomorrow," Mrs. Lennox said, simply. "Linden knows then?"

"He does," Gracie said, blushing and then cursing herself for blushing and blushing deeper still.

"I see," Mrs. Lennox said, knowingly, and Gracie felt sure she did. "But Warburton does not?"

"No. At least, I don't think so." Gracie wrinkled her brow.

"Well, he will tomorrow," Mrs. Lennox said, with resignation. "There is no point in continuing this any longer. Especially with the dance to be held. Perhaps the timing is better than we realize. Regardless, you will need something to wear."

"Oh, yes," Gracie said, crestfallen. "I had forgotten." She brightened. "Perhaps Fleur...?"

"Ha!" Mrs. Lennox waved a hand. "I doubt she would be willing. No, I have a dress for you, my dear. Cam found your things, you know, that same awful day when he came upon your poor driver. They were crushed and wet, but there is at least one dress in there that's serviceable and I will make some alterations in the morning so that it is even more suitable."

Mrs. Lennox smiled at Gracie. "I must say, it is nice to have another young woman about the place. One who smiles once in a while and seems able to enjoy herself." Her smile became sly. "Do you love him then?"

Gracie stared. "I am not sure it matters. Tomorrow we will all be celebrating his betrothal."

"Pshaw! Still pushing on towards that foolishness," Mrs. Lennox said, shaking her head. "I can't believe it will happen in the end."

"What do you mean?" Gracie asked.

The older woman gave her a shrewd look. "It has always been hard to accept Warburton's claim, you know, that Gabriel and Hester—Linden's parents—wished for this match. Gabriel—Lord Chevalier—and Sir Guy... They were cousins. Yes, they were friendly, but it was always an imbalanced friendship. Gabriel tolerant and overly generous, Warburton grasping and greedy. Warburton has always had his eye on Princewood. His becoming steward was the next best thing to inheriting it himself. If Linden were to have no heirs, he would still inherit. How convenient, then, for his daughter to marry our lord," Mrs. Lennox said, pursing her lips in displeasure.

"You truly think it is simply greed which motivates him?" Gracie asked, tentatively. It did not align with what she had seen of Sir Guy. The man was pompous, certainly, but he seemed harmless and bumbling much of the time. Even his injury in the forest had not dispelled that impression. The old man had been embarrassed and trying to disguise what had really occurred, but that did not mean he had done so with any malevolent intent.

Mrs. Lennox shook her head. "I do not know. That is the trouble. If I knew for certain, oh, nothing would stop me. I would give Linden a piece of my mind, like it or not. But while there is still a chance that Warburton speaks true, that Linden's parents did wish this for him? My hands are tied. Even though we can all see this marriage is not right. Not for Linden or for Fleur. Only one person will be happy and it will not be the bride nor the groom."

She pulled herself up from the chair. "It would not be honorable," she said, carefully, looking back at Gracie. "For me to encourage you to become an impediment. Fortunately for me, I do not need to—for you already are. He is half in love with you already. I daresay much more than half." She shook her head. "Perhaps it will be enough."

Before Gracie could form a reply, she was gone from the room.

It was unfair, Gracie thought, frustratedly, to say such things and then walk away.

She paced the chamber, suddenly feeling trapped and restless.

If she were at home, she would go downstairs to the family's well-stocked bookcases and select something suitably distracting.

She looked down at herself, at her buckskin trousers and shirt. She had worn them all day. What would it matter if she did so a little longer?

She opened her door and went into the hall.

When she arrived at the library, she half-expected to see Fleur inside, reading by candlelight, though it was the middle of the night.

Instead, she saw flickering shadows dancing on the walls. A fire was going in the huge stone hearth, though it was fast dying out having been left untended by its maker who was staring absently into the flames, holding himself so still that at first Gracie thought he must be sleeping.

She stepped closer, her footsteps indiscernible on the soft lush rugs that covered the library floors in dark scarlets and purples.

There she lingered indecisively, in the dark, next to a row of high shelves, uncertain whether or not to make her presence known.

Wisdom said she should return to her room.

Temptation lured her with the opposite advice.

Linden was not asleep. He was sitting, if it could still be called that, sprawled as he was, in a deep armchair, his long lean legs stretched out in front of him, a half-full glass of what looked to be brandy clasped precariously in one hand. His face was in profile, angled towards the flames, his skin aglow in the firelight. His green eyes, framed by those ridiculously long, thick lashes, were pensive and intense as he stared in the fire.

He had taken off his tailcoat, undone his double-breasted waistcoat, and pulled off his cravat. Now the long strip of linen lay abandoned on the floor.

His shirt lay open, revealing warm masculine flesh and a tantalizing hint of curling golden hairs.

He looked unnervingly handsome, and Gracie felt a surge of raw need as she watched him.

He was as untouchable as fire and, suddenly, all she wanted to do was burn.

Linden was drunk.

At least, he was fairly certain he was. He had only drunk to intoxication on a few occasions—usually with Jasper. Typically, he preferred to keep his head level and sober.

Not tonight.

He felt entrenched in self-pity, grieving what could not be, mourning for what was to come.

Then there was the fear. Fear of losing Gracie. Fear she would be harmed.

And on top of it all was the guilt. That he should be thinking of her at all. That she should have become so foremost to him that her safety and her happiness were everything and the rest...nothing.

The more he drank, the more reasonable it seemed to feel the way he did... and the more terribly he wanted her.

But she was safe. Tucked away in her room. And he was here and here he would stay, becoming ever more drunk, until he fell asleep in the chair and the fire went out, and a servant found him in the morning.

How pathetic.

Then he heard a familiar little cough.

"Gracie?" he said, in a strangled voice, as if all the air in the room had gone out when she came in.

Yes, there she was, leaning against the stacks, still in her close-fitting trousers and one of Jasper's shirts.

"You're not wearing a cravat," she noted.

It seemed a strange thing to remark upon.

"Neither are you," he pointed out.

She blushed. Her hair was unbound and fell in soft waves behind her back.

The sight of her like that—all maidenly tresses and tightly-fitting clothing—was enough to break his will.

"Come here to me," he said, hoarsely. "Please."

She hesitated a moment, then came.

"You're so beautiful," he whispered, hearing the brandy.

And she was so, so close.

He reached out and took her hand, pulling her down and onto him.

That was his downfall.

He should have known better. Should have known that he could not see her without wanting to touch her. Could not feel her breath upon him without needing to kiss her. And from there...From there it could get very dark indeed.

He put his hands on her waist, slim and firm beneath the linen shirt and ran them over her, from the curve of her neck to the curve of her bottom, small and round, fitting perfectly in his hands. She gave a moan and shifted, moving more tightly against him, her hips cradling him.

He knew she must feel him, hard against her, but felt no embarrassment, no shame. Only pure, driven desire.

He clasped her neck with one hand and pulled her mouth down to his, closing his eyes as he felt her lips, warm and soft and just as hungry as he had hoped. He responded in turn, his fingers slipping along her neck, caressing lightly, while the other hand held her fast against him.

The kiss quickly consumed him. One kiss became two, then three, and then he gave up counting, surrendering himself to a long line of unending kisses, so that he hardly had time to breath in between. He could hear Gracie gasping, moaning, as he covered her with his mouth, touching his lips to her eyelids, her cheeks, the corner of her mouth, her neck, the pulse at the base of her throat—and then returned to cover her mouth once more, utterly shameless, thrusting his tongue inside her, biting and tugging gently on her lower lip with his teeth, running his teeth over her neck, feeling her shiver beneath him.

He wanted her. He wanted to claim her in any way he could, God help him.

His hands began working on her shirt. Tugging the tails up and out of her trousers, sliding his hands under and feeling naked skin beneath.

She let out a gasp as he ran his hands up her sides.

He felt daring, unstoppable, drunk with desire. His thumbs moved as if of their own volition to run themselves over her chest, searching instinctively until they found the hard nubs of her nipples, rubbing and pinching the puckered tips, and kneading her small shapely breasts until she was moaning and whispering things he could barely make out. Mostly "please" over and over again.

He took pity on her and pulled her shirt over her head, then sucked in his breath. All long and lithe, so slender, her breasts so perfect, softly curved and high, nipples like bright red berries, crying out to be sucked. He took one in his mouth and did just that. Then, feeling her writhe her hips against him, he bit a little harder than he'd intended and heard her gasp.

"Did I hurt you?" he said, immediately, guilt-stricken.

"No," she whispered. "It feels so good. Don't stop."

She ran her hands over his hair, filled her hands with his locks and gave a playful tug, tipping his head back and claiming his mouth with hers in a hot, greedy kiss.

He returned his hands to her breasts, playing with her nipples and caressing the small sensitive mounds. He could feel the tips of her breasts through his shirt and the touch drove him wild. Thoughtlessly, he gave a thrust against her, letting her feel his heat.

She pulled back from the kiss, her breathing labored, and looked down at him.

Her face was full of grief and longing.

"It's too late for me," she whispered. "But perhaps it's not for you..."

"I assure you it is," he whispered back, immediately understanding. He brushed his lips to hers. "Far too late. I loved you before today, you know. But you are most beautiful now that I know all of you. No more secrets. Don't hide from me, Gracie."

She touched his jaw, tracing his face lightly with her fingertips.

"This is unbearable," she whispered, and he could hear her misery.

She was so close to offering him everything, giving him all of herself.

She wanted simply to go on, to feel his skin bare against hers, to satisfy this ache burning deep inside her that only he could appease.

She wanted to offer him her heart, her body, her soul. She would ask nothing in return.

She would be his mistress, if not his wife. Was it not done all the time?

Then she would do it. For him.

Because this was love. And this was it for her. She did not wish to reach the end of her life, always regretting that she had left when she had it.

Nor did she wish it to be cheap and tawdry, a voice inside her said, as it would be if she did this.

Linden put a hand behind her neck and gently pulled her back towards him, his forehead resting lightly against hers.

"I love you, Gracie Gardner. No matter what or who you are, you are meant to be mine and I yours. If we were free, if this were a different time, another place, I swear to you, I would lay you down before this fire and run my hands and lips over you until no part of your body went untouched, until we were full of one another, spent on one another, too weary to move, and then, once we had slept, naked in each other's arms, we would begin anew, until we had learned every part of each other, here, and under the open sky, on the beach, in the woods. We would belong to each other, everywhere on earth, and the earth would know you were mine—" She heard his voice break. "—forever."

She touched his cheek, felt the wetness. "Oh, my love."

She pressed her lips to his, then to his cheeks, his eyelids, kissed his forehead tenderly, wrapped her arms around his shoulders.

"It is the brandy speaking, I suppose," he said, wearily. "Shall I apologize?"

"Never," she whispered beside his ear. "Never in a thousand years."

She moved her hands over his back, feeling the tightness in his muscles. She took in the strain in his face, his clenched jaw, the worry in his eyes.

"My love," she said again, tenderly. "Close your eyes. Let me touch you."

She ran her hands over his shoulders, then lightly across his chest, hearing the intake of breath as she brushed against his nipples through the linen of his shirt. She would allow him to leave it on, she decided.

She brought her lips back to his, hungry, wet, and desperate, her mouth devouring his with a passion she had not known she possessed, while her hands ran down his chest, searching and seeking. He was aflame and she was aflame and there was nothing but themselves. Only this heat, this spark, and her lips upon his.

Her hand brushed his trousers, found his cock, long and hard, and ran a hand lightly over it, feeling him gasp with shock and pleasure. She moved her hands to the buttons of his trouser flap and began undoing them nimbly, one by one, until she could slide her hand inside.

She had never touched a man like this before, but how often had she heard, if not seen, the sailors on the Witch do this? Countless.

He was trembling as she parted the flap. She lifted his cock out, letting it spring free, taking in his desire, the hard thick length of him, then making a fist around his shaft, running it up and over the wet swollen tip in a light teasing stroke. He let out a gasp and jerked against her.

There was a wild thrill moving through her. Helpless against their fate, she would take control for an instant and give him this pleasure.

It was mad, it was joyful, it was hers to surrender.

Stroke after stroke she ran her hand over him, lightly than gradually harder, while meanwhile her lips never strayed from his mouth, sucking, biting, never giving a reprieve—matching every stroke below with one above.

He thrust into her fist, his body arching, trembling with need. He wanted her. She knew this and it was a balm for her heart, if not her body. He couldn't have her. She couldn't have him. But she could give him this. Some satisfaction—and satiate herself in the process. She relished the feel of him, his cock filling her hand completely, taking pleasure from his low groans, allowing herself the pleasure of the sensation of his hands running, desperately, over her back, over her breasts, toying with her nipples as she worked.

When he was close to his climax, she broke the kiss, leaned her mouth down and took all of him inside her, letting him spill his seed, hot and wet, listening to his cries, feeling him shudder.

And then it was over.

He tugged her up, gently but urgently, and pulled her against him, wrapping his arms around her as her head fell against his chest.

They sat like that a while, until gradually his arms began to slip down, and his breathing slowed, and she knew he had fallen asleep.

Then she slid from his lap and slipped from the room.

She would go to bed and she would strive to dream—of a happy ending, if not for her then for him.

Linden woke, alone, and for a moment, groggy. Then his head cleared. The brandy had spent itself.

He recalled her touch, her hands on him, her mouth, with a hint of embarrassment. So intimate, but a half-measure. He had done nothing for her—nothing but talk of what he wished he might do.

Was he not a free man?

Love had bound them both in painful knots.

Perhaps it was not pure. It certainly was not uncomplicated. But it was love.

What had Jasper said? What was it he had suggested?

End his engagement with Fleur. Marry Gracie.

It sounded so simple.

Except that it would mean breaking his troth. With Fleur. And with his parents, in a sense.

For years, he had taken heart from knowing he would be living his life as they had dreamed he would, wedding the woman they had chosen for him.

But would they not wish for their only son to be happy?

He knew they certainly had been. Their marriage had been loving and close. Warburton had never said so, but Mrs. Lennox had told him many times. His parents were a delight to see together. Even a decade after they had wed, they took such pleasure in one another's company, always displaying small tender gestures, always making one another laugh.

He took such pleasure from Gracie's company. Not merely the kind they had taken tonight, but the kind of precious amity which could make for a lifetime partnership.

For the first time, he let himself dare to imagine what life at Princewood would be like with a true partner.

When he finally found his own bed and slept, his heart was lighter with the choice he had made.

Chapter 17

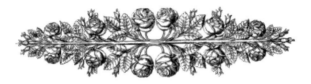

Well, God give them wisdom that have it;

and those that are fools, let them use their talents.

— Twelfth Night

Gracie was not sure what to expect Mrs. Lennox to come up with for her evening attire, but when she entered her room after an afternoon spent riding on the beach with Jasper, she let out a gasp of delight.

Mrs. Lennox had outdone herself. She had taken a rather plain robin's egg blue cotton day dress and transformed it with the addition of a semi-transparent black net overlay embroidered with azure flowers, and finished off with a thick gold velvet sash. White silk stockings lay beside the dress next to a pair of shimmering gold silk dancing slippers.

Where Mrs. Lennox had managed to find the slippers was at first the greatest mystery, for Gracie's feet were large for a woman.

But when she peeked at them more closely, she realized they were her own. They must have been severely water stained from the snow, but Mrs. Lennox had simply dried them out and re-covered them beautifully in new material.

Preparing the ensemble must have taken hours of work. And all this after the older woman had spent a long day and evening busy with festival activities.

She could never repay her for such a lovely gift—or for all of the kindness the Lennox family had shown since she had arrived. In each their own way, all three of them had enveloped her in their warm protection and she was immeasurably grateful.

The trouble was, Gracie had arrived at the conclusion that attending the dance that evening would be a disaster.

Not only for herself, but for Linden. How would the villagers take her queer transformation from boy to girl? She was likely to become a spectacle and embarrass not only herself but her host.

Moreover, if she were to be brutally honest with herself, by simply being there she would distract Linden from his duty. And she had already done so.

She could not regret what had passed between them the night before. But she could make an effort not to repeat it for both their sakes, not to mention the most wronged party in all of this.

It did not matter, Gracie bitterly scolded herself, that Fleur did not care for Linden or that the reverse was true. Fleur was his rightful betrothed and that was all that mattered.

Going forward, Gracie must respect that—or leave.

And after spending the day contemplating her meager choices, she had come to the conclusion that the latter was the option which would spare them all the most pain.

There was a tapping at the door.

"Gracie? Are you in there?"

It was Jasper. The door pushed open a smidgen. "Are you decent?" he asked, his voice muffled from behind the wood.

"I am, but..." Gracie began.

Jasper did not wait for her to finish.

"Excellent," he said, coming in and closing the door behind him. "I thought I should check on you before the dance. You know, to ensure you were not planning anything foolish." He wagged a finger at her.

"The entire idea of my attending the dance is foolish," Gracie retorted. "I should never have even considered it. And now look at this—" She gestured to the bed where the beautiful clothes lay. "—Your poor mother has spent hours making these..."

"Yes, so you really mustn't disappoint her after all her trouble," Jasper said, sweetly. "Besides, I helped. So, you would be disappointing both of us."

Gracie's brows went up. "You sew?"

"I do and proud of it. Rather a necessary skill in life. It's not as if I can do embroidery but I can hold fabric for Mother and do a basic stitch." Jasper shrugged his shoulders eloquently. "I am a man of many talents."

Gracie's lips twitched. "How impressive."

"Now," Jasper continued. "I suppose you fear your entrance this evening might cause a riot as the villagers assume you have been transformed as if through magic from male to female. However, I assure you, most of them care not a whit and have hardly noticed you at all. Except for the children, that is—they are all quite fond of you. Apparently, your time on the ice made quite the impression."

Gracie crossed her arms and narrowed her eyes. "Jasper. I have met some of the villagers. As Grayson. Even if I made only the slightest impression, a few people are bound to notice. I will be ridiculous and, worse, Linden will face further humiliation as well."

"I notice you don't worry about humiliating the rest of us, but no matter. I understand you are consumed by love. Tut tut! No interruptions," Jasper chided, seeing her open her mouth to protest. "This is not exactly high society, Gracie. We are not in London—or even Edinburgh. We shall simply tell anyone who bothers to inquire that I dared you to do it as a silly prank, that I wagered you, oh, say, twenty pounds. I don't have twenty pounds, of course, so please don't bother to ask for it. But you get the general idea. It was simply a silly lark. That's all it will have been, and quickly forgotten."

Gracie was not convinced.

"Oh, stop looking at me that way," Jasper complained. "You know very well you are fighting a losing battle and besides, if you are honest, you know you wish to come to the dance. Would Mother and I really urge you to go if we thought your doing so would shame Linden? Furthermore, I have saved the best for last." He smirked.

"What?" Gracie inquired.

"It seems our dear Linden is all in a lather about something," Jasper said, his eyes dancing with glee. "He has been on the hunt for his fiancée all day long. Rumor has it he wishes to tell her something of the greatest import. And by rumor, I mean all of the servants are speculating about it. Speaking of which, you haven't seen Fleur today, have you? It would spare us some time if we could push her in Linden's general direction."

"I have not," Gracie replied, utterly confused. "But I do not understand..."

"No, course you don't." Jasper was practically cackling. "But I *do*. And as I understand completely, even if you do not, that means, you must, must, must come to the dance."

He frowned petulantly. "You still don't look convinced. What more must I say?" he demanded, throwing up his hands.

Gracie covered her eyes and groaned. "Jasper... You are making little sense."

"What kind of little sense? No sense, nonsense, or good sense? Good sense is highly overrated, don't you think? Falling in love, for instance. It makes no sense at all. And yet we do it from time to time. 'Who ever loved that loved not at first sight?' and all that nonsense. Or is it?" Jasper gave an infuriatingly complacent grin.

"What have you done with that jester's cap?" Gracie said, crankily. "You should wear it this evening."

"Will you dance with me if I do?" Jasper teased. "If so, I'll fetch it straightaway."

He composed himself. "But in all honesty and with the utmost seriousness, I tell you, all shall be well. You must simply trust me." He bowed and backed towards the door. "I will see you in an hour downstairs."

Jasper took after his mother, Gracie decided. They both had an exasperating tendency to simply ignore opposition and overwhelm one with words.

With a sigh, she turned to the bed.

A nagging part of her whispered that Jasper had merely enabled her to do what she wanted to do in the first place.

She ignored it and started to dress.

It was only the seventh of December and it was a commonly held belief that decorating for Christmas too early was bad luck.

But, as is always the case, there were exceptions to the rule and Jasper Lennox was one of them.

Jasper, who adored all things royal, had been reading John Watkin's biography of Queen Charlotte and was inspired by the description of the monarch's decorative yew-tree to copy it with a version of his own.

Thus, a small Scots pine had been felled, decorated, and placed on a table in one corner.

As Gracie stood at the top of the stairs, looking down, she saw with amusement that the tree had already proven to be a draw to the guests, with many standing around it, chattering and pointing at the colorful assortment of fruit and sweets hanging from the branches alongside numerous small wax candles.

Her heart caught in her chest as she finished her glance about the room. There was Linden, standing alongside Sir Guy, with Jasper nearby. He seemed engrossed in conversation with Warburton, and was frowning as they spoke.

Although most of the village men wore their Sunday best—mostly homespun shirts with plain wool coats and trousers, Linden, Jasper, and Sir Guy had all donned more formal evening wear.

Gracie had never seen Linden in breeches before. They were black silk, fitting just below the knee where matching black silk stockings began, and displayed well-formed calves, lean and muscular. He wore a long dark blue tailcoat with black velvet lapels over a gold waistcoat, all topped off with a beautifully tied white cravat.

Jasper looked similarly dashing, though not as imposingly handsome, in a daringly-colored bright green tailcoat of wool broadcloth with a vest of brown silk satin decorated in a cut-velvet floral pattern beneath.

Gracie longed for Linden to break away from Sir Guy, look up, and notice her. Instead, Jasper's eyes were the ones which fell upon her, and he made his way across the room to meet her at the base of the stairs.

"Milady," he said. Then he dropped his voice. "May I remind you, Miss Gardner, that this is a simple country dance. We are simple people here. No one is looking at you—except some of the very simple young men, of course. Have I said simple enough times for you? Shall I trounce them until they dare not peer in your direction?"

Gracie did not even have opportunity to respond to this foolishness. They had reached the spot where Linden stood speaking to Sir Guy and the old knight appeared very put out. His normally florid face was redder than usual as he raised his voice shrilly.

"How can we have an engagement ball without both parties?" he demanded of Linden, as if the young baron had made off with his daughter.

"Where is Fleur?" Gracie whispered to Jasper. "I thought you were merely exaggerating when you said Linden could not find her."

"No one has seen her since this morning, but I'm sure she'll turn up," he said, unconcernedly. "When she wants to."

Gracie was struck with a horrid but well-deserved pang of guilt and the urge to flee the room. She had acted in love, yes, but what had seemed self-sacrificing in the dark of night seemed utterly selfish the next day.

How could she face Fleur?

She could do so with honesty, Gracie decided, and tell her everything—in private, but most certainly tonight.

"You do not think she wished to attend the dance? Being held in her honor?" Gracie murmured to Jasper.

"No," he replied. "I do not."

"Of course, she did," Sir Guy roared, overhearing him. "Fleur had her heart set on tonight. It was to be a grand occasion. She had a dress specially ordered from Edinburgh. Why wouldn't she wish to attend?"

"I'm sure I don't know," Jasper said, politely. "In that case, where is she?"

Sir Guy snorted in indignation, as if it were a ridiculous question. Then his eyes landed on Gracie.

If a man's jaw could be said to drop, then Sir Guy's did indeed.

Gracie watched as his expression turned from shock to fury.

"I believe my mother already mentioned, Sir Guy," said Jasper, quickly. "That my dear friend Miss Gardner arrived at Princewood wearing the only dry clothes she had been able to find when her coach was attacked on that awful night in the woods. I, foolish lad that I am—as you well know, convinced her to continue the masquerade as a lark. And now I am out twenty pounds."

Jasper pretended to pout. "Hardly worth the bet, but it was entertaining while it lasted. In any case, Sir Guy, please meet for the second occasion, Miss Gracie Gardner."

"I did not think your mother could possibly be serious," Sir Guy sputtered, looking as if fumes of smoke were about to come out of his ears. "What an asinine prank. What sort of a debauched young lady would ever agree to..."

"Yes, Sir Guy," Linden interrupted. "Thank you. Of course, Miss Gardner, you are welcome to Princewood, whatever your attire may be." He spoke distractedly, without looking at Gracie or Jasper. His eyes were continually roaming the room.

Sir Guy glared at Linden a moment, then stormed off.

"Our master of ceremonies is in fine form," Jasper quipped, looking at Linden.

"Yes," Linden murmured absently before finally focusing on them.

As he took in Gracie, his eyes bulged.

"Gracie... Miss Gardner," he choked. "That is... a lovely dress."

"The girl wearing it is lovely, too, isn't she?" Jasper prodded. "Slender as a willow tree and just as graceful."

Gracie stepped on his toe and ground her slipper a little, pretending not to notice when he let out a squeak.

"Of course," Linden murmured, coloring a little. "You look beautiful, Miss Gardner."

"Absolutely stunning, I should have said," Jasper chimed in, not put off by her warning attack in the slightest. "Of course, to some, trousers can be extremely attractive as well." He looked back and forth between them with a smirk.

"Jasper," Linden said, pleasantly. "Fetch Miss Gardner something to drink."

"I don't think she's thirsty," Jasper said.

"Jasper, I think Peter is looking for you," Linden said.

"Really? I did not think he planned to attend this evening." Jasper shrugged.

"Jasper—" Linden began. But he was cut off. A servant stepped up and whispered something urgently in his ear.

Linden frowned. "I apologize, but I must attend to something. My apologies, Miss Gardner." He shot a pleading look at Gracie.

"I forgive you, Linden," Jasper said, loyally. "Even though you said nothing complimentary about my appearance."

Linden rolled his eyes and turned his back, moving swiftly towards the stairs.

"I do believe the prey has been spotted," Jasper said, contentedly, watching him walk away.

A country dance had just begun. Apparently, the musicians had given up waiting for Sir Guy to officially open the festivities.

Gracie heard the familiar sounds of a lively reel.

"Shall we?" Jasper inquired, holding out his hand.

She took it and they stepped forward together.

Fleur was in the library.

She was always in the library.

Except that she had not been there each and every other time Linden had checked today. Nor had she been anywhere else that he could ascertain.

"Good evening, Fleur," he said, quietly, coming over to where she was sitting.

She seemed to have a favorite spot. Far at the back of the long room, under a large arched window, in a brocade-covered chair. Nearby an ancient tapestry hung over a wall, depicting a queen and her ladies strolling through a grove of trees.

Fleur looked up as he approached, but said nothing.

"Where have you been all day?" he asked, keeping his tone even. He took a seat in the alcove—near but not too near, like a hunter wary of startling his prey.

Except Linden did not want Fleur as his prey. He simply wanted to understand her a little. And be understood, in turn.

Was it too much to hope for?

"I don't want to marry you," Fleur announced, bluntly, snapping her book shut and setting it on the table next to her.

"I see," Linden said, evenly. "Could you not have told me that before this evening?"

"Could you not have done the same?" she asked, with false politeness.

"Touché," he admitted. He scratched his chin. "Where do we go from here? I take it you do not wish to come downstairs?"

Fleur snorted. "And waltz with you? Have Father wax poetic about how we were meant to be, while everyone stares and whispers about how ungrateful I look to be your bride? No thank you." Fleur shuddered and wrapped her arms around herself.

"They have spoken of me in much crueler terms. I doubt you would be their target. But I would never force you to do anything you did not wish, Fleur," Linden said, a little affronted.

Fleur ignored him and stood up. "Follow me. I want to show you something."

Chapter 18

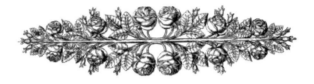

This above all: to thine own self be true,

And it must follow, as the night the day,

Thou canst not then be false to any man.

— Hamlet

Fleur had discovered the passages in the castle walls when she was eight-years-old.

The first entrance she found through sheer luck, one day in the library, when she had tripped and fallen against a hanging tapestry. Part of the wall had given away when she hit it and when she stood up and peered behind the hanging, she saw a space had appeared—narrow and dark.

Perhaps another child would never have ventured into the darkness. They would have called for an adult and shown someone what they had found.

Not Fleur. She dove right in, finding the latch to pull the panel closed behind her and walking through the darkness with her hands in front of her face until she came to the next opening where a small hole let in a narrow stream of light.

It was a small private chapel, built into one of the buttresses of the keep, accessible through the lord and lady of the keep's private apartments.

She found the latch, pushed, and tumbled out. It was a quiet space, though rather dusty. The chapel had not been in use for many years.

The next hidden panel she found was in the solar, right next to a small shuttered peephole. From there she walking along the dark passage until she found a flight of stairs—so unexpectedly she nearly fell down them and broke her neck.

There was an opening in nearly every room in the castle, and more than one hole to peek through in most.

Gradually, she memorized her way through the maze, explored every passage, mentally cataloged every panel, every latch, every swinging cover over every spy hole.

She took to bringing a lantern and a book, and would usually start her day in the kitchen house—snatching food when no one was around, then scurrying into the walls as quietly as a mouse.

No one ever caught her. No one ever really cared where she was.

She had thought she was the only one who had discovered Princewood's most well-hidden secret.

But she was wrong.

Now it was time to enlighten the master of the castle.

Let him have the knowledge, in case it was ever needed.

It was the least she could give him, for she could not give him herself and she could not give him the truth.

Linden watched in amazement as she pulled back the tapestry and opened the panel, then peered in as eagerly as a precocious child.

"This is incredible," he murmured. "How far does it go? Where does it lead? Are there more?" He looked at her closely. "How long have you known about this?"

When she said nothing, he grimaced. "That long."

"We might have played in them, together," he said, with a hint of sadness. "You and I and Jasper. Did you never wish for the companionship of other children at all Fleur?"

"You would have spoiled it," she whispered, not really feeling the guilt she knew she should. "You would have taken it and made it yours. Running and laughing, playing loudly. It wouldn't have stayed a secret for long. Soon, everyone would have known."

Linden looked at her consideringly. "I suppose that is true. And I suppose you needed a place that was truly yours, if you were so desperate to keep it secret." He ran a hand over his face and sighed. "Why show this to me now?"

She looked down at the floor. "With all that is going on... I thought you should know."

He was quiet a moment. She could feel his eyes on her. "I see," he said, quietly, and then she did feel guilt, knowing he did see. "Is there anything else you wish to tell me?"

"No," she said, quickly, pulling the panel shut again and tugging the tapestry back across.

"Tell him? Tell him what?"

She turned to see her father coming towards them. He did not look pleased.

"Tell you that our engagement is at an end," Fleur said, stepping forward.

"What?" Her father thundered. "What have you done, Chevalier? How do you dare? On this, of all nights! You are out to make me a laughing-stock. Asking for my assistance, my support, with this nonsensical endeavor and then throwing it all in my face as you disgrace my daughter."

"A broken engagement is no cause for Fleur's disgrace," Linden said, frowning at the older man. "Particularly not when it has not yet been formally announced to the wider world."

"Besides, it was my doing, Father," Fleur interjected. "Not Linden's. He had nothing to do with it. This is my decision."

Her father stared. "Yours? But... I do not understand."

For a moment he looked full of confusion and much older than his years. Then his face cleared and he shook his head. "Preposterous. You are betrothed. That cannot be dissolved so easily. Linden, I am ashamed at how easily you are willing to cast Fleur aside. After all of these years, knowing how your parents so dearly hoped to see you wed…"

"Enough, Father," Fleur said, loudly. "Do not begin telling that story yet again. Please."

Her father narrowed his eyes. "What are you saying?"

"I am saying," she said, levelly. "That you should not speak of what Linden's parents wished for him ever again."

She hoped he would understand. She was being as clear as she could.

"I think I should return and see to the entertainment of our guests," Linden said, looking back and forth between them. "Fleur, may I leave you to clear all this up with your father?"

Fleur nodded.

"Go to him," her father hissed, as soon as Linden was out of earshot. "Remedy this madness. This is stupidity, Fleur. Do not throw your future away. Our future! This match was everything."

"Everything to you, perhaps," she said. "Never to me. I have never wanted it. And now—" She gazed at him with incredulity. "After what I know, you truly expected me to marry him?"

"What do you mean?" Sir Guy's nostrils flared. "Nothing has changed."

"Everything has changed," Fleur exclaimed. "You—killed—his—father. And now you would perpetrate this... this... obscenity. Every time you mention what Linden's parents desired, I feel ill, Father. For it is a bold-faced lie, is it not?"

But his eyes had become cold and distant. He was shutting her out.

She had known him to bluster, to pontificate, to play the foolish old man. But she was unused to seeing him like this.

"You didn't have to kill him," she whispered. "Why did you do it?" She heard herself, near tears, and hated it. "Why did you not simply tell him the truth when you had the chance?"

She watched him swell with rage—not towards himself, but towards her—and knew he would never accept his guilt.

"And have been banished for it?" he roared. "Should I have seen your mother hang and all of us disgraced? Our name ruined? You would have preferred that, would you? To grow up in a workhouse, perhaps? Or out on the streets? Rather than living here? Here where you have had every advantage. We depend on the Chevaliers for everything. Every last farthing. We always have. And when I think of how close I came. How close I was—" He stopped, breathing hard.

"Close to what?" Fleur asked, quietly. "To having it all? Linden must have been such an inconvenience. But then, that is why you suggested he enter the water that day, isn't it?"

Linden remembered next to nothing of that day. But once Fleur had the largest missing piece in her hand, it was not difficult to find the others.

Should Linden ever find out, he would despise her—it was true. And she would have nothing—that was true as well.

But she would rather have nothing than something so terribly tainted and wrong.

"You will never know, Father," Fleur said, quietly. "How different it might have been. Linden's father might have been merciful. After all, he had allowed you to bring Mother to Princewood in the first place, to care for her here in private rather than have her placed in an asylum. That does not seem the act of a hardhearted tyrant to me. No, Linden's father was probably much like him. Too tenderhearted to see the truth."

She was tempted to say more. To lay out plainly just how parasitical her father's dependency had become. But what was the point?

She rubbed her forehead wearily. "Goodnight."

"Fleur," her father pleaded. "There must be more. What has prompted this? Was it the girl? Is there something between her and Linden? It was that which did it, was it not?"

Fleur's lips twisted in a hard smile. "She is welcome to him. Let him find some happiness if he is able. Certainly, he deserves some after what we have done to him."

She walked out of the library without a backwards glance.

Linden did not particularly wish to return to the great hall. It was noisy and full of people and he could not say that dancing held any great appeal at the moment.

But the great hall was where Gracie was—so there he would return.

As a free man.

He walked the corridor slowly, trying to convince himself it was true.

Since boyhood, he had been raised in the expectation that in time he would formally declare his engagement to Fleur Warburton.

That they would marry had been driven into his head by Sir Guy like a lesson in mathematics, and he had accepted it as, if not welcome, than at least inevitable and right.

All his life, his connection to Fleur had been his connection to his parents.

Now that was gone. What was left?

Some days he could hardly remember them. On rare nights, when he lay in bed, he was able to conjure up their faces clearly. They were smiling and warm. They looked at him with pride and with fondness.

There had been laughter in his father's eyes, and a smile always ready on his mother's lips. They had played together, romped the halls of the castle together, laughed together.

They had been a loving family once.

"I'm in love, Mother," he whispered to himself. "I'm in love, Father. I hope you will be happy for me."

He cleared his throat, feeling foolish, as a servant walked past carrying a tray.

Approaching the hall, he heard the strains of a waltz.

It was 11 o'clock, he realized in shock. Nearly time for the dinner and the fireworks.

The musicians had been told to play only one waltz that evening—in Fleur and Linden's honor.

A speech was to have preceded it, given by Sir Guy. But even in his absence, the musicians had rolled on, according to plan, oblivious to all that had been occurring upstairs.

No one was dancing. The floor had cleared and there was an uncomfortable silence.

Linden spotted Gracie, standing near Jasper who was looking grimly about the hall, clearly unimpressed with the turn things were taking. Linden would be in for a tongue-lashing later, he supposed.

By contrast, Gracie looked pale and solemn. Her eyes were downcast.

His heart constricted as he watched her. How awkward the night must have been. What strange looks and glances had she faced? Linden knew something about the judgement of others.

And yet there she stood. She had not fled. No, she was incapable of anything as cowardly as flight.

He felt a swell of guilt for leaving her, chasing after Fleur, without even a word of explanation.

He knew she would claim he did not owe her one.

But he did. He owed her everything. And he would tell her so. Now. This instant.

Seeing her in such feminine clothing tonight had caught him off guard. The dress she wore made her appear fragile and delicate, though he knew she was neither in truth.

With appreciation, he took in the curves of her wide mouth and her pointed chin, her sweetly snubbed nose, the dusting of freckles across her tanned cheeks. His love was not conventionally beautiful perhaps, but the epitome of an elfin maiden, glowing with a mysterious magic all her own.

His stomach knotted pleasantly as he recalled how she had come to him last night, her hair shaken loose from its braid, long tresses reaching to her waist, soft and undulating like warm sandy dunes in the summer. His fingers had wrapped around that narrow waist, now encircled in rich velvet. He had touched the luminous skin of her small swelling breasts, so soft and sensitive. What would she feel like elsewhere, beneath the skirts of that long dress, in her most secret of places?

He saw her smile at something Jasper had said. There was nothing on earth more splendid than her laugh, her voice, her smile. There was nothing more precious than her touch. She was the loveliest sight he had ever seen and, more than that, she was his home.

He went down the stairs quickly, and crossed the room, hearing the whispers of the crowd beginning as they watched him stride towards where she stood.

When he reached her, he simply took her hand and led her out onto the floor.

This was not the way it was supposed to happen, Gracie thought, dumbly, as the room spun around her.

She was no fairytale princess to be plucked from the crowd by the handsome prince.

The night was supposed to be Fleur's.

Yet here she was. And where was Fleur?

Linden's face was inscrutable as he waltzed her about the room, yet his eyes were lighter and his lips were slightly curved as if they longed to turn up in a full smile.

After a few minutes of silence, she could no longer stand it.

"What has happened?" she whispered.

"I am free," he said, simply, looking down at her—and this time the smile broke through, radiant as the sun, and just as warming.

She started to smile back, but a face in the crowd caught her eye.

Sir Guy stood on the stairs—his face like a glowering dark cloud. He watched her as they spun, never taking his eyes from her. Gracie tried to ignore him. She forced a smile and kept her eyes on Linden.

"I will tell you all," he murmured, as the song came to a close.

He guided her gently to the side with a hand on her waist. Her body hummed with sensation, yearning for more contact.

She noticed he had not brought them back to where Jasper stood, but towards a less populated corner. The few guests who stood there smiled at them both, then stepped away, leaving the nook blessedly quiet.

"I have you alone for a moment," Linden said, his voice low and husky.

"You do," Gracie said, not taking her eyes off him. She felt filled with nervous energy, her mouth dry, her palms sweating.

Linden pulled off his gloves and tucked them in his pocket, then reached for her hands and did the same to the pair she wore, sliding them gently down her forearms, to her wrists, his fingertips lightly skimming the skin and sending shivers through her, just like that day on the beach.

When she was bare, he took her hands in his and brought them to his lips.

"Fleur does not want me. She has no wish to marry me. Which is rather wonderful, I think, as I want you. Very, very badly. Marry me, Gracie." His sea-green eyes were steady and sure. "Be Gracie or Grayson, Gardner or Chevalier. Whoever you wish to be, whatever you wish to be known as, but stay. Stay with me, never leave me. Stay and be my true companion."

"But...your parents," she whispered.

He squeezed her hands gently. "I believe if they had had the opportunity to meet you, they would have understood. And I must believe they would wish for me to be happy—and to have a marriage like their own. That would never have been possible with Fleur, though I do care for her very much, in a brotherly way. That will not change."

She bit her lip, then gave a small nod.

"I shall take that as a yes," he said, softly. His lips twisted in a wry smile. "And while I am being so embarrassingly honest, I may as well say that I desire you so badly I fear I may die."

Her lips twitched. "Die?"

"I do Jasper credit, don't I? He has a talent for melodrama and I seem to have picked it up," Linden said, grinning foolishly and ever so sweetly.

Gracie longed to put her lips to his right there and then, but there were people close by. Rather a lot of them. And somewhere in the crowd, at least one person who would not be at all pleased by the unexpected development the night had taken.

So soon, she told herself, very soon. They would have one another fully, very soon.

Chapter 19

My bounty is as boundless as the sea,

My love as deep; the more I give to thee,

The more I have, for both are infinite.

— Romeo and Juliet

Linden's heart was pounding in his chest.

"Meet me in the solar," he had whispered to Gracie before the last reel was played, and she had nodded and slipped off through the crowd with a last squeeze of her hand as the fireworks display had begun.

Now he was there, waiting in the dark, a single candelabra lit on the table by the window. He could smoke while he waited. He could read. But no, he could do none of those things. He was too eager, too excited. Had he compared Gracie to an eager pup once before? Well, now he was the pup—desperate to pant at his mistress's feet.

There was a knock at the door. He was on his feet instantly, springing towards it.

"Jasper," he exclaimed, in disgust, as he saw who it was.

"Yes, tis I, your dear companion," Jasper said, raising his eyebrows. "I admit, I was not expecting such a disdainful reaction."

Linden coughed discreetly.

"Ah, I see," Jasper chirped. "Expecting another sort of visitor, are you? Well, I won't tarry long. I simply came to ask what on earth happened this evening. You were in, you were out, you were back in—and then looking as if you were hardly with the rest of us at all. As if your head was in the clouds, in fact."

"It was," Linden said. "It is still there now." He smiled.

"Oh, young love," Jasper sighed. "Well, tell me everything." He leaned against the stone wall with an easy nonchalance, and crossed his arms over his chest. "Or at least give me something I may bring home to Mother," he said, grinning widely.

"Simply tell her that Fleur and I no longer have any plans to wed," Linden suggested.

"She'll be elated. Thrilled. Delighted," Jasper said. "Shall we have more fireworks?"

"Then tell her I am still betrothed," Linden continued. "I suspect that's a riddle she'll figure out quickly."

"I have no doubt she will. I say, how speedy you are!" Jasper crowed. "Of course, when you whisked her away with you for that waltz... Oh, that waltz. Did you see the look on Sir Guy's face?"

"I did not," Linden said, guiltily. "Poor Warburton. I shall have to speak with him tomorrow and make amends. Fleur did not tell him in the most tactful of ways."

"Of course, she didn't," Jasper said, rolling his eyes. "It must have been highly entertaining."

"Not precisely," Linden said. "But Jasper, I must really ask you to..."

"Of course, of course," Jasper said, holding up his hands. "Say no more. Good evening to you. May it be a memorable one."

Linden closed the door and leaned against it with his eyes closed.

Who would arrive next? Perhaps Mrs. Lennox, just to make sure Jasper was telling her the truth.

And after that, Warburton to try to convince Linden that his daughter really did desperately want to be a bride.

He groaned.

"Are you well?" came a familiar voice, through the door. "Shall I leave you to sleep?"

"No," Linden cried, hoarsely, fumbling to pull the door open. "It's you," he said, looking at Gracie with relief.

"Were you expecting another lady?" she said, cheekily.

"I just finished getting rid of Jasper," Linden said, lamely, taking her in from head to toe. "Good God, did you walk through the castle wearing only that?"

"Ran, would be more accurate," Gracie said, letting her hands which had been clutched to her chest, fall to her sides.

"Come in, for God's sake, come in," Linden said, stepping aside so she could pass.

There was a pleased little smile on her face, which he found most provocative. But most provocative of all was simply her. She was wearing a loose white gown of some kind of brocade, untied and open. And beneath... A thin chemise of sorts that really left nothing to the imagination.

Which was quite all right, in Linden's view. He had imagined long enough and was ready for the reality.

"There is a murderer on the loose," he said, slowly, not taking his eyes off her. "And yet all I can think about is getting you out of that robe as quickly as possible."

"It doesn't seem right to be so very happy, does it?" Gracie said. "But here we are. We'll face whatever happens next together."

"Together," Linden agreed.

Had there ever been any other way? It was becoming hard to remember a time when she had not been in his life—this girl who was now so essential to him.

"But for now," he said, slowly, riveted by the sensual figure before him. "No more talking."

Their eyes met in undisguised raw desire. Two innocents, Linden thought wryly, inexperienced but hungry to learn, desperate with their need.

She stepped forward, hesitated, and that was all it took. His body moved to close the space between them as if of its own volition. His hand moved to the small of her back and pulled her tightly to him as the other cupped her face. His mouth settled on hers, forceful and possessive, knowing he would claim her that night in every way he could. Beginning with her lips, soft and sweet. He slid his tongue between them, teasing lightly until she moaned, then harder, thrusting with a hunger.

He lowered his hands to her waist, tugging the robe apart, and was already anticipating the freedom of running his hands over her when her hands covered his and stopped him.

"Linden," she said, and he could hear something like fear in her voice.

"What is it?" he said, immediately filled with concern. "Am I rushing you? Was the kiss too rough?"

"No, nothing like that," she said, quickly. "I must tell you something."

She sighed and rested her head against his shoulder.

"Anything, Gracie," he said, smoothing her hair gently and kissing the top of her head. "You may tell me anything."

"Truly? We shall see," she said, but her voice was muffled from his shoulder. He heard her draw a shaky breath. "Linden, I have done this before."

"This?" he said, with confusion. "Kissing? I know you said you had—"

"No, not only kissing," she interrupted. "Please, let me tell you."

He was silent.

"It was almost two summers ago. At a festival in the village. Friends were visiting from out of town. One of them was a boy, a little older than me. We had played together many times as small children, but had not seen one another in years."

Linden's chest felt constricted with jealousy anticipated, but he let her speak.

"We drank elderberry wine. Quite a lot of it. And then we snuck off together, and we... Well, we..." She paused.

"I see," Linden said, carefully. He thought of something. "Did he... force you, Gracie?"

"No, nothing like that. We were not ourselves, of course, but the blame was mine just as much as his. I do not... remember much of it. And when we woke, oh, I was so ashamed. He was sorry, too, of course." She took a deep quavering breath. "I was on my way, you see, to visit him and his family when the coach was attacked. I believe he has always thought us unofficially betrothed since that day—or at least, believed himself to be under obligation to me."

She stole a quick look up at him, then put her head back down. "But I was not going to marry him. Indeed, I regretted leaving home at all. It was a foolish mistake. And other than that, I have never felt anything but friendship for him."

"I see," Linden said, again.

"You did not know this," Gracie said, hurriedly. "And so, you must know you are not bound by what you said earlier."

"When I proposed marriage to you?" Linden said.

"Yes, that," she said. "I will not hold you to it."

She looked up at him, expectantly. "Perhaps you would like me to go now."

"Gracie," he said, gently cradling her face in his hands. "What you have told me—it changes nothing."

"It doesn't?"

"Of course not," he said. "Each of us has made mistakes in our past. Neither of us are perfect. This changes nothing about how I feel for you. Except, perhaps..."

"Yes?" she said.

"Well," he said, blushing. "Except perhaps—" He shifted on his feet awkwardly. "Perhaps it will be less uncomfortable...for you, I mean."

"Oh," she said, with understanding and blushed as well, very prettily. "Yes, I see."

"But you—" She met his eyes. "You have never...?"

"No, I have never," he said, wryly. "Does that change anything for you?"

"Of course not," she said, hotly, then smiled a little. "Oh, Linden."

"I love you, Gracie," he whispered, leaning to her ear and letting his breath tickle her skin, warm and soft.

"I love you as well," she whispered, wrapping her arms around his neck. "And want you so very much that it hurts."

His arms closed around her waist, pulling her tightly against him.

This time when they kissed, the touch of lips on lips ignited a firestorm. There was nothing to hold it back.

He could feel her along every inch of his body. Her heat and softness, her slender form. He kissed her harder, capturing her mouth until she was gasping for breath, her hands moving over him, stroking his neck, caressing his hair, his face.

This time when his hands moved to her robe, she made no protest, but dropped her hands to her sides as he slid it off.

"Your turn," she said, and began to tug his shirt out from his breeches. Her hands were small and warm and they skimmed his sides lightly, causing him to shiver in anticipation, as she made to lift his shirt up and over his head.

"I want to be close to you, Gracie," he said, his voice rough and raspy. "Skin against skin."

She nodded.

He ran his hands over her body first, lightly over her breasts, stroking her nipples until he felt them pucker and harden through the thin chemise, then sliding them down to her waist, over her buttocks, down to her thighs. Finally, he took the edges of the fabric and tugged them up, over her hips, letting his hands slide against her deliciously bare skin in the fabric's wake, feeling her break into goosebumps at his touch.

"Your turn again, I think," she said, a lovely smile on her wide curving mouth. She reached her hands into the waistband of his breeches and tugged him against her.

He was hard, unmistakably aroused, and she let out a little gasp of pleasure as he pressed against her.

"Off," she said, looking at him, hungrily. "Off now."

She fumbled with his buttons as she had not the night before, her haste impeding her progress until his hands came alongside hers, helping her undo the clasps until the breeches were loose enough to slide down. Down came the stockings as well, and he stepped out of the clothes, leaving them as a puddle on the floor.

They were naked, exposed, trembling with desire.

He knew what was to come and his body was telling him it could hardly wait, while his mind was hesitant, uncertain and admittedly even shy, afraid of any misstep he might make.

"Perhaps it might be better for you, if I was more experienced in this," he said, somewhat shyly.

"No," she said, firmly, and pressed her flesh against him, warm and hot. "Touch me. Anywhere. Everywhere. However, you wish. You can do no wrong." She drew a deep ragged breath. "Just put your hands on me. Please, Linden, please."

Her mouth met his again, hot and wet and desperate, as his hands roamed her body freely, caressing the fine curving lines of her back, the swells of her small, pert bottom.

"More," she whispered, against his mouth, sounding frantic. And then she took his hand and put it between her legs.

He gasped. She was wet, so very wet, hot and slick. His fingers slid between her folds, and she tightened her grip on him, shuddering at the contact as he stroked, gently at first, finding his way, then harder.

She was an unexplored land and he had no map, he thought wildly, as she gave another moan, and pushed against his hand.

He pulled his hand away and she let out a little cry of protest.

"Shhh," he said, and picked her up.

She was light and fit against him, but the feel of her sensitive flesh against his chest, warm and slick, was an exquisite torture. He longed to bury himself in her, but swore to himself he would wait until the last possible moment, until he was sure she was ready.

He carried her across the room and placed her carefully on the desk, then pushed her back so her breasts pointed upwards, nipples round red buds for his mouth to take and squeeze and nip as his hand slid back between her legs, pushing her thighs apart, opening her more fully to him.

He carefully thrust a finger inside, heard her moan of approval and inserted another as her fingers clenched his shoulders, then another. His thumb was circling above, having found a place he had only heard of. He stroke and circled the sensitive nub of flesh hard under the pad of his thumb as he thrust his fingers inside her, harder and faster, again and again, until she was leaning back, panting, her breasts heaving, chest slick with sweat, head tilted back, and then she was coming, crying out sharply, body shuddering, her tight cunny convulsing and squeezing around his fingers as she climaxed.

"Now," she said, hoarsely. "I want *you*. Don't make me wait."

He not have to be prompted twice. He slid his cock between her thighs and took her hard and fierce, filling her with a single stroke, unable to think of much besides his own burning need, his utter want to use her, take her, claim her, pound himself into her until they had both reached a place of beautiful oblivion.

She made no protest, only signs of encouragement. Leaning back on her elbows, she lifted her hips and took each stroke, each thrust, and met it head on, pushing herself against him each time with her own power.

It was not sweet, it was not gentle. It was fast and hard and oh, God, so very good. He could hear the slick sounds of their bodies moving together, smell the scent of her sex on his fingers and his cock, and it aroused him even more. He let out a deep groan and thrust hard, feeling his seed spill deep inside her. She moaned and arched and took it all, sweet and wild and willing.

He collapsed upon her, damp with sweat and their mixed scents, feeling her slender arms come up and around him, holding him in place while his breathing calmed and slowed.

"Did you...?" he asked, tentatively, and she shook her head, sending a sinking feeling deep into the pit of his stomach.

"But you did from...?" he asked, confused. He pulled away to look down at her.

She touched his face gently. "It is all right, Linden. It does not always happen that way for a woman, you know."

"Oh," he said, eyes widening. "But the other?"

She shivered at the memory. "That was very, very good." She hastened to add, "It was *all* incredible. I want you, again and again. You feel so right inside me. It's indescribable. But even if it doesn't happen, there is pleasure—a great deal of it, only of a different kind."

"I see," he said. Evidently, he had much to learn.

He coughed delicately. "And you learned all this from...?"

"Oh, no," she said, laughing at him. "I have three older sisters. They are all married, you know."

"Ah, of course," he said, smiling back with relief. He was not so ignorant then. Merely lacking in siblings. At least Jasper had shared that one valuable piece of knowledge with him, in spite of his overall disinterest in the feminine form.

Swift joy swept over him as quickly as the fear had and he picked her up again. She gave a little squeal of surprise and wrapped her legs around him.

"Where are we going?" she demanded.

"To my bed. And yours," he said, with a smile.

They awoke midway through the night in a blissful tangle of limbs. They embraced again, made love again, and then Gracie stole out quietly, bathed and robed once more, and made her way back to her room.

Soon, she thought with a quiver of delight, she would be beside him in the night always. She could burrow against his chest, feel his strong arms around her, nestle her head against his as they talked all night. Or made love all night. Did whatever they wished.

It was too much happiness to be true.

And it was all thanks to Fleur, Gracie remembered, with a pang.

Fleur, who was all alone. Fleur, who had no wish to be wed.

Fleur, who had set Linden free when she might have dug in sharp claws. Certainly, many other more ambitious young women would have, regardless of whether they cared for the baron at all.

But not Fleur. Sharp, fierce, candid Fleur.

Gracie determined then and there to win Fleur over. She would make amends, no matter how long it took. She would be honest with her about all that had come before—accept whatever harshness was dealt. She would accept rejection, over and over, if that was what it took, and would try again and again until she broke through Fleur's flinty exterior and was allowed to know the rest of the young woman who lay beneath it.

The keep was quiet as she padded through the hall, but it was a peaceful sort of silence. She did not feel afraid as she walked alone, in spite of the recency of the attack the day previous. It seemed impossible—as if it had happened a lifetime ago.

All that was real was Linden—and Linden was good. Thus, Gracie would dwell only on goodness and not the evil that had still not been found and rooted out.

That would wait for another day, she thought sleepily, as she opened the door to her room and slipped between the blankets.

Chapter 20

O time, thou must untangle this, not I.

It is too hard a knot for me t'untie.

— Twelfth Night

It was a cool and frosty morning as Cam readied his pack and prepared to make the trip to Sicilborough. The neighbouring village lay further down along the coast, about a two days ride.

"I've made up another packet of food for you and Jock," Mrs. Lennox said, coming out of the cottage carrying a large bundle tied up in a cloth.

"It's only two days on the road, Paulina," Cam said, eying the parcel with amusement. "Poor Sugar here won't be able to carry me if we put all that on her back."

"Oh, hush now," his wife chided. "You never know what might happen. You might be very grateful for the extra."

"Very well," Cam said, sighing the sigh of a long-suffering man but also one with a healthy appetite. "I'm sure it won't go to waste between Jock and I."

"Does Linden know where you two are headed?" his wife inquired.

Cam shook his head. "No. And no point in telling him anything yet. There is no use getting hopes up for naught. And naught is probably what it will come to."

"I daresay you're right," Mrs. Lennox said, twisting her apron. "But still, one cannot but hope."

Cam touched her cheek gently. "If there is anything to find out, we will find it. I promise you that. Jock was chomping at the bit when I told him what I had heard. I'd best go and meet him."

He leaned down to kiss her, then mounted the horse.

"I'll see you in a few days, my dear," he promised. "Be safe and look after that ruffian of ours."

She waved as he rode away.

Chapter 21

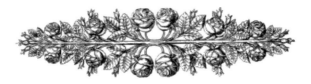

Love all, trust a few,

Do wrong to none.

— All's Well That Ends Well

When Linden awoke, there was a message waiting for him.

A meeting was to be held in the village that evening, to discuss recent events.

Word had gotten out, as it always did, of the coachman's murder and its gruesome details—which needed no exaggeration.

This had then been followed by tales of Warburton's injury in the forest—which, from the sounds of it, had been vividly speculated upon until they had reached the height of embellishment.

Taken together, the village was in a panic—and really, Linden thought, it was only a miracle that it had not happened already.

He would not downplay their concerns, for there was something to fear. He only wished he could come to his people with the comfort of knowing the culprit had been found.

He felt powerless. He had put everything he had into the searches, but in the end, they were no better off than the night Gracie had stumbled into the keep. Groping blindly in the darkness.

There was no need to tell Gracie of the meeting, he decided. She had been through enough.

Besides, the truth was that things could turn ugly. It would not be the first time.

Snow had begun to fall that morning and while it was melting as quick as it landed, the outside soon became a slick and slippery mess.

Linden and Gracie spent the day warm and snug indoors, completing small tasks. Gracie wrote letters to her family, telling them of her engagement and inviting them to journey to Princewood for the wedding, which she and Linden had decided would be held just before Christmas Day.

In between composing letters, Gracie told Linden tales of her family—of her rough-and-tumble happy childhood, of her family's idyllic-sounding home of Orchard Hill, of her three elder sisters (who sounded rather intimidating to Linden), and their husbands and families. One of whom even included a duke.

"Do you truly think they will toss all of their plans for Christmas at your home to the wind and come?" Linden asked, anxiously.

He was of two minds. On the one hand, he did not wish for Gracie to be disappointed. On the other, the idea of meeting such a large and boisterous group of relatives was daunting. Would they approve of him? Of the hasty marriage?

"What will your mother say?" he added. "Will she ask us to wait, do you think?"

Gracie smiled reassuringly. "All of my sisters married quite quickly once they had made up their minds who they wanted-ed. It is a Gardner family trait, at least among the women. And as I have most certainly made up my mind that I want you, I assure you nothing will stand in my way. I am the most stubborn of the four of us—" Linden had no trouble believ-ing that. "—and Mother will know better than to try to con-vince me otherwise. Please do not worry. They will be happy for us. Believe me. You will love them and they will love you."

Linden certainly hoped so. He planned to try very hard to win over Gracie's family, but social charisma had never been one of his fortes.

He tried to picture the castle full of family again, with Gra-cie's nieces and nephews running about. Apparently, her el-dest sister Gwendolen and her husband had a half a dozen youngsters.

Princewood had been quiet for so long. Even the dance had been such a brief interlude from its regular emptiness.

But it would be good to have it filled. Not only with Gracie's family, but with their own—someday.

"Do you wish for children?" he asked, suddenly worried that their minds might differ on the subject.

She scrunched her nose up in a way he found adorable. "I should probably make a horrid mother. I am impatient, too rough, and have never been particularly fond of babies."

As Linden's face fell, she quickly added, "But do not misunderstand. Horrid mother or not, I *do* want children with you. If we are blessed with them, I will be grateful. You would make a wonderful father. Perhaps you can be the one to take care of them while they are babies and I will be the one to teach them to fish and hunt and ride when they are older and much more interesting." She winked mischievously.

"I would not be averse to it," Linden said, loyally. "I know absolutely nothing, but suspect that Mrs. Lennox would find extreme enjoyment in enlightening us as to the care and feeding of infants."

Gracie laughed and turned back to her letters, while Linden sat back against the chaise and imagined holding a soft, sweet-smelling newborn in his arms.

Well, of course, it would not be sweet-smelling all of the time. But it would be theirs. A little boy or little girl, to raise and cherish. There was a lump in his throat as he sudden-ly imagined the horror his mother must have experienced as she died, knowing that her young son was quite close by. Had she believed he would be next?

He could not even imagine the awfulness of losing a child. Losing a parent was quite awful enough.

And as for his father... He had given his life to save his son. The ultimate sacrifice.

Linden could not imagine feeling a love that strong—at least, not for anyone but Gracie. But he looked forward to it—to having his heart open even wider with greater love of a different kind.

"Linden," Gracie said, softly, rising and coming over to him. "What is it? Your face is a picture of sadness."

He tried to smile, but instead felt his eyes becoming wet.

Horrified, he brushed the back of his hand over them. He was a grown man. He recalled how impatient Warburton had always been with his tears even when he was a child, grieving his parents. He had heard the tired old refrain that boys do not cry—or was it *should* not cry? –more times than he could count.

Gracie pulled his hand down. "Stop," she pleaded. "There is no need to hide from it. If the tears come, they come. Are you thinking of your own parents?"

He nodded, not trusting himself to speak. He looked at Gracie's face instead. Normally sharp and bold, now softened with concern.

She put her arms around him and drew him close, then moved back on the chaise and tugged his head gently down onto her lap. She ran her fingers through his hair. It was lovely and soothing. He closed his eyes.

"I love you very much, you know," she said, quietly. "There is no shame in crying or in showing your sadness. Trust me with your burdens and I will help you carry them."

He lifted a hand to touch her cheek. "I know. I know you will." He felt the tears coming again and closed his eyes.

"I don't think I realized how very lonely I have been," he managed, with effort.

"I cannot even imagine it," Gracie said, putting a finger to his lips and gently tracing them. "But you will never be lonely again, Linden. I promise you. I am here and I will never leave you."

"Never sounds like a wonderful dream," he whispered, and pulled her down for a sweet, slow kiss.

He walked down to the village that evening alone, enjoying the bright colors of a winter sunset—rich reds and pinks hovering over the tall ancient trees of the forest that skirted the village.

The snow was still coming down lightly. What had already fallen was fast turning to ice as night drew near.

As he approached the small wooden church that the village used for meetings, he caught the arm of an older lady just as she was about to slip and helped her up the stairs.

"Thank you, young man." She tilted her head up to smile up at him. He watched her eyes widen as she recognized him. "Pardon me. Thank you, my lord," she quickly corrected.

"Please, there is no need," he said, as he helped her to a seat.

The church was full. A few of the village leaders stood at the front, waiting to begin.

He groaned silently as he recognized one of the men. Donald Bryson was the hot-headed and frequently intoxicated owner of the village tavern, The White Hart. He was opinionated and brash and most certainly one of those who believed the worst of Linden.

Linden could only imagine what was to come if Donald was to help lead the meeting.

Sure enough, Donald spotted him in the crowd, gave an ugly scowl, and turned to whisper into the ears of the other men nearby. Soon they were looking in his direction as well—and then the whispers began to spread, until Linden soon felt as if everyone in the church was eying him with judgement and disapproval.

He sat up straighter, trying to ignore the rising feeling of panic welling in him. So many years of this. When would it end? The festival had been such a success, he had almost forgotten that this was the regular state of things. Perhaps it always would be.

The meeting began. There was a description of the recent attacks. Linden noticed that Warburton was not present and his account of what had occurred was given little weight. The noise level in the small church quickly began to increase as the villagers shared their fears that they were not safe, that their children were not safe.

Linden was waiting for the moment when he would be held to account but it did not come quite as he had expected.

Instead, a few minutes in, Donald Bryson rounded on him, silencing the crowd as he pointed a finger dramatically across the room at where Linden sat.

"It all began when the stranger arrived," he said loudly, his voice carrying across the church.

"Lord Chevalier harbored a stranger who claimed to have fled when the coach was attacked. But I ask you all—how do we know that the boy—who I might add, in a preposterous turnabout, we are now expected to believe is a girl—was not the one responsible for the driver's murder in the first place?"

He looked at Linden with disgust. "You brought the danger into our midst," Bryson accused, his finger still raised. "You gave the stranger shelter. Warburton's attack came after the stranger arrived. As did the slaughter of our animals. What more proof do you need that he is involved in all of this? That he is responsible?" Donald raised his voice louder as he ended with the question and the church burst into an uproar.

Linden stood slowly and waited for the noise to die down.

His panic had been replaced by a cold, hard rage. He kept his eyes fixed on Donald Bryson, who glowered and then averted his gaze.

"Donald Bryson has made an accusation and I will answer it," Linden said, calmly. His deep voice carried easily without his having to raise it to the shrill level Donald had adopted. "Miss Gracie Gardner arrived because of the coach attack, it is true. She was dressed as a boy from necessity, in clothes she had found belonging to the poor driver, God rest his soul. Miss Gardner had narrowly missed being attacked herself that night. It is a miracle she got away as she did—a young woman alone in the woods in a storm. When she arrived at the keep, she was exhausted and injured as the carriage she had been in had overturned. She was hardly in the condition one would expect an attacker to be in when taking on a strapping young coachman. Miss Gardner stayed and recovered at the keep. Many of you met her as Grayson. Yes, it was a foolish prank to continue in boy's clothing, but to accuse her of being responsible for a man's murder is nothing short of ludicrous."

Donald tried to intervene but it was Linden's turn to raise his hand.

"There is more," he said, gazing coldly at Donald. "I believe it is important to add that Miss Gardner was also the victim of a second attack—the same day the festival was held, in the Princewood stable. As soon as her attacker—who appeared to be a female, I should mention—discovered Miss Gardner was no boy, they resorted to violence and it was only the arrival of myself which prevented Miss Gardner from coming to injury."

Donald was sneering in a way Linden did not like.

"How convenient," Bryson countered, letting the words hover in the air for a moment before continuing. "How very convenient that it should be your word we should have to take on this. Once more acts of terrible violence are committed, and once more it is Lord Chevalier who must be relied upon for the truth of the matter—"

"That is not what I said," Linden interjected hotly, but there was no stopping Donald Bryson now.

"He demands that we trust him when he murdered his own mother as he murdered the coachman," Donald shouted, ignoring Linden. "He attacked Sir Guy, the only man to stand by him loyally all these years. That is gratitude for you! He is a monster and to think we have stood for it all these years—" Donald raised a fist in the air. "He is not fit to be our master. He is not fit to be our lord. I say we take him to London and make him face the king's justice."

It was all absurd playacting, Linden knew. Donald's bluff, if that was what it was, could easily be called. But the hate which drove his words—that could not be dismissed so easily.

"Listen to me," Linden said, a little more loudly this time, his voice carrying over the din. He waited for the church to quiet. "I have done everything in my power to find the perpetrator of these crimes. You speak of justice, and I am determined you shall have it. I have had the woods searched, as well as the keep and the grounds and the village. And I promise you, I will not rest until I have found who is responsible and Princewood is safe once more."

He would not mention what Cam had found in the keep's undercroft. Nor would he mention that Gracie had seen evidence that the woman who had attacked her had been sleeping in Princewood's very own hay loft.

Donald Bryson was right about one thing, in his way—and it was that Linden Chevalier had not protected his people.

He had failed them. That was the truth of it.

He could understand their fear. He could even accept their blame. But what he could not understand and what broke his heart, was their eagerness to turn on him with hate so quickly once again.

"Enough," an elderly woman's dry voice rang out.

Surprisingly the church immediately quieted.

Linden looked across the room at the speaker. It was the old woman he had helped up the stairs. She was standing up, rather shakily, her wrinkled hands resting on the pew in front of her. But there was nothing shaky about her words. She spoke with the confidence of a woman who knew she would be listened to.

"That's enough of that, Donald Bryson," she said, scornfully, looking up at the front where the man stood. "Every time some wrong is done, it is dropped on the head of our young lord. How many years will have to go by before that daft story dies? I was there fifteen years ago, working in the kitchens at Princewood—"

Linden stared in disbelief. He did not recall the old woman at the keep, but he had been no more than a child then. He did not recall many of the servants who worked in the keep at the time.

"—And I was there when Jock Robertson and Cam Lennox came in from the forest after Hester Chevalier's body was found," the woman continued. "I was there when, later that same dreadful day, they came in from searching the water for poor Gabriel Chevalier's body. I trust the words of those two good men. Two honest, honorable men—which is more than I can say for Donald Bryson—" There was a scatter of laughter. "—And those two good men made no accusations. Rather, they saw that little Lord Chevalier was nothing more than a terrified, heartbroken boy, who they had found clutching his mother's dead body as any child would have done in his place. The young lord had no recollection of what had happened, and it is little wonder. Few children in his place would have cared to recall the horrible sight he must have seen. All those who truly knew the family wept for them—and our hearts went out to that poor little boy. How this accursed nonsense began so quickly, I will never understand, but it is a foul and vicious lie."

"Sit down, you old crone! What kind of an innocent lad goes for a swim after seeing his mother slaughtered? He drowned his dear old Papa," Donald shouted, stubbornly. "Losing a mother was not enough for him. No, he hungered for more blood!"

There was a murmur in the crowd. Some were clearly shocked by what Donald had said. But it did not mean they would not agree with him in the end.

Linden curled his hands into fists, longing to plant one right between Donald Bryson's eyes.

"Hush now, all of you," the old woman commanded the crowd, paying no attention to Donald Bryson. "Stuff and nonsense. What child would have gone, knowingly, into that stretch of treacherous water? Someone encouraged the boy to go there—that is the truth of the matter. That is what I have always believed. Furthermore, it is what Jock Robertson has always believed and what Cam Lennox has always believed. The boy had no reason to go into the water that day. Someone encouraged him to, someone told him it was safe and put the idea in his mind while the poor boy was still half-dead with shock. And that same someone had a hand in poor Hester Chevalier's death, I guarantee it. Oh, it was no accident that they should both die the same day. But to blame their child? Hmph! Now that is truly monstrous." She waved a hand, dismissively, in Donald's direction.

Linden felt as if he had had the wind knocked out of him. This was the first time he had heard any of this. This was the first time he had heard that Cam believed he had been goaded into the water that day. Why had Cam never passed on his suspicions? Why had no one told him?

The sage old woman went on. "None of this has any bearing on what has happened. Lord Chevalier has told us what he has done to try to find the murderer—or murderess, if you will. What have you done, Donald Bryson? Besides spouting a lot of foolishness and stirring the village into a panic. Instead of gathering here like a flock of frightened chickens, you should be out looking for the person responsible—just as Lord Chevalier has been doing. This—" She stretched her arms out to gesture around the room. "—is the greatest waste of your time, all of you. And you should be ashamed of yourself, Donald Bryson. Drinking and stumbling down drunk most nights when you might have joined the search party and helped matters if you were so very concerned about our safety." She gave a derisive snort, and there were appreciative titters of laughter across the room.

Linden watched as Donald's face flushed red.

A grey-haired man, about the same age as the old woman, had been standing up at the front in silence all this time.

Linden recognized him as Ned Putney, the captain of a small fleet of fishing boats. He had a large family, including an impressive number of sons. Ten in all, if Linden recalled correctly. Most of the village was related to Ned in some way. He was a reasonable, well-respected man.

Now he stepped forward and raised his hands for silence.

"Emilia Shepherd has the right of it. Let's have less talk and more action. Who will come with me tomorrow to scour the woods? Perhaps Lord Chevalier would do us the honor of joining us himself," the man said, nodding respectfully in Linden's direction.

"Now, there will be no more of this talk of a child murdering his own family," Ned Putney continued, shaking his head solemnly. "It was a terrible business and we will speak no more of it. Lord Chevalier has opened his home to us. Perhaps Donald Bryson has forgotten how he enjoyed the festivities not to mention the free liquor provided by Lord Chevalier less than a day ago, but I hope the rest of you have not."

"And let us not forget Lord Chevalier's generosity with our school," a voice in the crowd shouted, and Linden saw Peter Carson stand up proudly.

"He has funded the school ever since he came of age and took charge of accounts at Princewood. He has helped numerous families among us, on many occasions—silently and without ever asking for thanks. When the Parsons lost their father, who sent food and funds to keep them through the winter? And that was not the first time nor the last." Peter sat down, blushing a little at having made himself the center of attention.

Linden could see many in the crowd nodding and murmuring their agreement.

He was just about to try to sneak out the door, embarrassed by the unexpected support, when the church doors opened with a bang and Jasper rushed in.

"Where is Lord Chevalier?" he demanded, breathing heavily.

His eyes landed on Linden. "Linden," he exclaimed, his voice panicked. "You must come back with me at once."

"Of course," Linden said, rising. Was it Gracie? His heart began to pound.

As he reached the doors, he paused for a moment to look back at the room. His eyes picked out the woman Ned had called Emilia.

"Thank you, Mistress Shepherd," he said, looking right at her and ignoring the crowd. "Thank you. I hope you know that all I have ever wanted—" His voice broke a little, but he pressed on. "—was to care for this village and my tenants as well as my father and mother did. I would never do anything to harm anyone in Princewood. The barony is a responsibility I do not take lightly."

"God bless you, Lord Chevalier," someone shouted from behind him and then another joined in and another.

Linden walked out and down the steps to where Jasper stood waiting. He was not even wearing a coat and his arms were wrapped around himself to stop his shivering.

"What has happened?" Linden asked. "Is someone hurt? Is it Gracie? Tell me, Jasper!"

"Not Gracie. My mother. She is gone, Linden," Jasper choked out. "The cottage is a mess and there is blood on the floor. Do you think...?" He broke off and covered his face with his hands, unable to complete the question.

"Come," Linden said, shortly. "Come with me and we will find her."

Chapter 22

Some Cupid kills with arrows, some with traps.

— Much Ado About Nothing

Gracie was drinking a warm cup of chocolate and finishing the last of her letters. She was just putting the seal on a letter to her dear friend Isabel Notley, who she had invited to attend her at the wedding, when Sir Guy burst into the room.

The older man face was troubled. "Miss Gardner," he began.

Gracie was on her feet instantly. "What is it? Has something happened to Linden?"

Did Sir Guy's face seem to sour slightly or was it her imagination?

"No," he said, impatiently. "It is not Lord Chevalier. It is Mrs. Lennox. She has taken a terrible fall. You must come with me, quickly."

"Of course, I will," Gracie exclaimed, rushing to the door.

They made their way down the corridor, with Sir Guy leading the way.

"Where is she?" Gracie asked. "How did she fall? And have you seen Lord Chevalier this evening? I have not seen him in some time."

"He went to the village for a meeting," Sir Guy said, rather shortly. "Come, quickly now, it is this way."

It seemed odd to Gracie that Sir Guy should say "it" rather than "she," but clearly, he was upset and in a great hurry to assist Mrs. Lennox. Gracie could easily empathize with that.

"I have never been in this part of the keep before," she commented, looking about.

"It is the oldest part of the keep," Sir Guy said. "Mostly unused now." He shot her a glance. "I do not understand why Mrs. Lennox was down here. Poking her nose about as always."

"She is a good, kind woman," Gracie said, loyally. "I am glad you found her so quickly. Is she very badly injured?"

"I am not sure," Sir Guy said, irritably. "You will see for yourself soon enough. Here, it is this way."

They had reached a dead end—or so it seemed to Gracie. The corridor stopped and in front of them was a stone wall covered by a tapestry. But to her surprise, Sir Guy approached the wall, pulled back the tapestry, and holding it to one side, gestured for Gracie to step forward.

When she did so, she saw a very narrow opening—one which Sir Guy must have passed through with some discomfort. She could see stairs in the dark, leading downwards.

It did not look to be a particularly appealing place.

"Did you not bring a lantern?" Gracie asked, turning back to Sir Guy.

"I do not need one," he said, curtly. "I know the way like the back of my hand. Go on now. I shall be right behind you."

Gracie felt herself wavering.

Of course, she wished to help Mrs. Lennox. But she wished Linden was about—at least so that she could tell him where she was going.

Did he know of this passage? Were there others? How strange to think of these secret places in the keep, but then it was very ancient.

"You are not scared of the dark, are you, Miss Gardner?" Sir Guy said, with what looked remarkably like a sneer.

"Of course not, but I am also not keen to take a fall like Mrs. Lennox," Gracie snapped. "How foolish not to have brought a lantern when you knew how dark it would be."

Muttering to herself, she started down the steps, keeping a hand on the stone wall as she went.

Sir Guy came behind, pulling the opening shut behind him with some kind of a latch or mechanism she could not see.

"Keep going," he instructed, as the light disappeared behind them.

And she did. Down the winding stairway, stone step by stone step, as slowly and carefully as she could.

"I saw you, you know," Sir Guy said, abruptly, from behind.

She could feel his breath on her neck. It was not a pleasant sensation.

"Oh, yes?" she replied, politely. "When was that?"

It seemed a strange way to begin a conversation, in the dark, while on such an errand.

"I saw you with him. After the dance," Sir Guy said, and Gracie felt an uneasy quiver in the pit of her stomach.

"I am not sure what you mean by that, Sir Guy," she said, calmly, taking another step.

"There are passages like this all throughout the keep. Did you know?" Sir Guy said, ignoring her comment. "Not only stairways, but passages behind the walls. Nearly every room has one or two peepholes where one might stand and see... oh, all sorts of things."

Gracie was disturbed by how different he seemed this evening—sly and crafty, rather than old and foolish.

"I suppose that is why they are so aptly named," Gracie said, trying to speak lightly. "I wonder which came first, the peephole or the Peeping Tom."

Sir Guy did not seem interested in the speculation.

"There is one in the solar," he noted, and Gracie almost stopped in her tracks.

"Oh, yes?" she said, vaguely, continuing down the stairs. She felt gripped by a feeling of dread. "How very interesting. I must have you show me sometime."

"I saw you there last night," Sir Guy continued. "Laying with him, like a harlot, under *my* roof."

Gracie did stop then. "I believe it is Lord Chevalier's roof, Sir Guy. And if you are truly saying what I believe you are saying, it may not be your roof for much long once Linden finds out what you have done."

She believed she could hear him sneering in the dark, if that was possible.

"You'd like that, wouldn't you? To see us thrown out?" he all but shouted from behind her.

She kept going down the stairs, hoping to get more space between them as quickly as possible.

"In fact, I would not. I have no desire to do so. None whatsoever. But I also find it despicable that you would do such a thing," she said. "Whatever could have possessed you to, Sir Guy?"

"I am possessed to do quite a number of things which might surprise you, Miss Gardner," she heard him say, just before she felt his hands press hard against her back.

And then she was falling, down, down, down, into the darkness.

Jasper did not walk but rather ran through the village. Linden followed, slipping and skidding on the slushy path, but managing to somehow keep his footing as they made their way back to the portcullis gate.

The forest encroached on the path that connected the keep to the village. Most of the trees were covered with the heavy sticky wet snow, their branches so laden down they were hardly moving in the breeze.

But the wind was picking up. If it grew stronger, there would be many trees knocked down that night, unable to bear up under the weight of their heavily iced branches.

Linden was thinking this while moving at the breakneck pace Jasper had set, when a flash of motion at the edge of the tree line caught his eye.

He came to a full stop, unable to believe what he was seeing.

"Jasper," he hissed, as loudly as he dared, and he saw his friend stop and turn.

"Look," he whispered, pointing to the forest.

Jasper walked back towards him a few steps, frowning in confusion. Then his eyes widened.

"The white stag," Jasper breathed. Even in his fear and panic, Linden could see the wonder on his face.

"I never thought I'd see it," Linden said, softly.

The stag was larger than life, majestic and beautiful. Truly, a king of the forest.

It stood as still as a statue, watching them for a moment, antlers raised high. Then the stag turned and slipped into the forest.

"What does it mean?" Jasper murmured.

"It's a sign," Linden responded. "A good sign. It must be. Such a noble animal could never be anything but good."

"I hope you are right," Jasper said. "It was beautiful. But Linden, my mother..." His face was pale.

Linden nodded and touched his shoulder. They were off again, and this time, they did not stop until they reached the castle.

The Lennoxes' cottage was situated in the lower bailey, close by the south portcullis gate.

The two men ran through the courtyard towards it, though Linden was not sure what the point was if they already knew Mrs. Lennox was not there.

Still, he supposed it would not hurt to check again.

As it was, the scene inside plainly told part of the tale.

Broken pottery littered the floor, a pot of soup had been spilled on the hearth, and pieces of furniture were tipped over. Linden saw the blood on the floor that Jasper had mentioned. Was it Mrs. Lennox's own or someone else's?

"There was a fight," Linden said, quietly. "Someone took her."

"Yes, but took her where?" Jasper said, tersely. Linden could see his hands curled into fists. "My father is away. I cannot..." He took a deep ragged breath. "I cannot lose her, Linden."

"We will find her," Linden promised. He had to say it. But as he said it, he vowed it would be the truth. He would not rest until they did—and he would make sure no one else rested either. "Come up to the keep. We'll alert the others and send out pairs to search. Most of the village is still awake. We can have one of the staff run down and ask there for help as well. I'm sure many will come."

Mrs. Lennox was well-liked by all. She had no enemies. Who would try to harm her?

None besides the one who had already killed senselessly at least once before, a voice in Linden's head reminded him.

They entered the keep. Flagging down a kitchen boy, Linden conveyed his instructions and emphasized the urgency.

The lad was young but bright, and excited at the prospect of helping to form a rescue party. He ran off back down towards the village as Jasper and Linden turned to the great hall.

"Shall we split up?" Linden asked. He wanted to find Gracie. She could help with the search, but even more importantly, he had to know she was all right. Once he knew that, his mind would be more at rest and he could put his full energies into finding Mrs. Lennox with no distraction.

But it was not as easy as that.

Splitting up to search the keep and locate Warburton and Gracie, the two young men met up just outside of the library—the one place they had left unsearched.

There had been no sign of Gracie, Sir Guy, or Fleur elsewhere.

"Let's hope they were all in the mood for a book," Linden said, grimly, pushing open the library doors, and crashing into Fleur who was just coming up to them with a pile of books in her arms.

The books went flying, Fleur was knocked backwards and landed rather gracelessly on the floor, looking very unimpressed.

"Watch where you're going," she complained, gathering up her books. "Why on earth would you need to rush into the library? The books aren't going anywhere. Well, other than these ones," she conceded, looking down at her precious stack.

"What?" she said, narrowing her eyes as she looked back and forth between them. "What is it? Why are you looking at me that way, Jasper?"

"My mother," Jasper said, hoarsely. "She's gone. She's been taken."

"Taken?" Fleur said, suspiciously. "What do you mean?"

"He's right, Fleur," Linden concurred. "The Lennox cottage is in disarray. There are signs she was injured before she was taken. We are looking for you—and your father—and Gracie. But you are the only one we have found. When did you last see them? Where could they be?"

"I have not seen them all evening," Fleur said, slowly, furrowing her brow. "I saw Father at dinner, but not Gracie. I supposed she was with you."

"She was, until about five o'clock," Linden said. "We took dinner, after which I left her, dressed, and walked down to the village alone."

It was now past eight. Three hours was not an alarming amount of time in normal circumstances. But these were not normal circumstances.

"No one we've talked to has seen either of them in at least two hours," Jasper said. "Where could they be? How could three people go missing all at once?"

Fleur's face was changing, Linden noticed. He watched her carefully.

"What is it, Fleur? Tell us." Part of him fully expected her to feign ignorance and abandon them to their own devices as she left with her books.

Instead, she met his gaze. "I have a dreadful feeling about this, Linden."

"That is not particularly reassuring," Jasper snapped. "What do you mean?"

"I will search the castle with you," Fleur said, quickly. "Why don't we split up? Linden will come with me and Jasper can go and... and..."

"And wander about alone, like a chicken with his head cut off?" Jasper snapped.

"Jasper, perhaps she is right," Linden said, understanding that Fleur wished to speak with him alone. "Perhaps you could go back to the great hall and see if the men from the village have come up to help. Then you could tell them where we have already searched and direct them."

"Yes, that makes sense," Jasper agreed, reluctantly. "Very well. Good luck." He was already off and running as Fleur turned back to the library.

"Where are you going?" Linden asked in surprise.

She looked at him. "Into the passage I showed you."

"You think that is where they have gone? All three of them?" Linden stared. "Why on earth for? I did not think anyone else knew of them."

"Neither did I," Fleur said, her face drawn and bleak. "But I think I was wrong."

"Fleur," Linden whispered. "What do you know? What do you think has happened?" He swallowed hard. "Do you think Gracie is in danger?"

She nodded slowly.

"Let's go," he demanded, gesturing for her to lead the way.

Half an hour later, Linden and Fleur were dusty and hot. They had made their way through the passages that lined the walls of many rooms in the keep but had found no sign of Gracie or Mrs. Lennox.

That neither of them believed Sir Guy was in any danger had gone without saying—and was very telling.

"There is one more place we could look," Fleur said, hesitantly, as they emerged from behind a hidden panel in a storage room of the kitchen.

"Show me," Linden said, shortly.

He was beginning to run out of patience. What was replacing it was a sickening feeling of panic—and exasperation with Fleur. She knew much more than she was saying. When she finally chose to share it, would it be too late?

"We'll need lanterns," Fleur announced.

A few minutes later they approached a tapestry at the end of a corridor. Linden was no longer surprised when Fleur pushed the tapestry aside to reveal a hidden entrance.

"These stairs lead down," he observed, peering into the dark staircase.

"We must go down to go up," Fleur said, cryptically. "Watch your footing. The stairs are very steep."

"As we go, perhaps you might enlighten me as to exactly what you think has happened, Fleur," Linden suggested, as he made to enter.

She nodded reluctantly.

For the first few minutes they descended in silence. Fleur had been right. The stone steps were shallow, narrow, and steep. In some places, time had taken its toll and the stairs were crumbling and treacherous.

Linden had reached his limit and was just opening his mouth to prod her again, when Fleur finally spoke.

"My mother killed the driver," Fleur said, from behind him.

Linden froze for a moment and Fleur nearly collided with him.

"I'm sorry," he said, automatically. Then, "I see."

"No, you do not see," she said, sounding as weary as an old woman. "But you will." He heard her draw a deep breath. "My mother was brought to Princewood when you were a child. Did you know that? I was living with an aunt in London then, but later, Father sent for me as well."

Linden frowned. "Your mother? I think I would remember that."

"You wouldn't," Fleur explained. "For you never saw her. At first, she was kept in a suite of rooms that were rarely used, near my father's. But after your parents died, Father moved her to... Well, it can only be described as a cell."

"The room in the undercroft," Linden said, slowly.

"That's right. You must have seen it when you searched the keep. I wondered what you must have thought then."

"Yet you said nothing," Linden observed.

"I said nothing," Fleur agreed. "It was wrong. And I know you will never forgive me. Especially when you know all."

"What do you mean?" Linden said, sharply.

"My mother did not only kill the coachmen," Fleur said, her voice low. "She killed your mother as well."

Linden felt as if his head were splitting. "That's not possible. Why? Why would she do such a thing?"

"She has not been right in the head since I was born," Fleur whispered. "Please, try to understand. Father would not accept it at first. He did not want to put her in asylum. I believe he blamed himself at first—and later, truly was to blame. Finally, he wrote to your parents. Your father was kind. Too kind. He urged Father to bring her to Princewood. He offered every aid. Father accepted. He had always longed to see the place, I think, knowing how close he had come to inheriting it all."

She took another quavering breath. "When he arrived, I think Princewood fast became his obsession. He knew you would have it eventually. Yet more and more, he began to dwell on the supposed unfairness—that was his word, not mine—that would have Princewood go to you and not to him. Eventually, I think his thoughts trickled into my mother. She saw his desires—and she acted on them."

"Dear God," Linden whispered.

"She started with your mother," Fleur continued, swiftly.

He knew she could not stop. That telling him this was taking something from her. He held back his questions and let her go on. "I think you would have been next. Except your father interrupted. He was walking to meet your mother. My father was with him. They came across your mother. You know some of what followed." She paused. "But not the whole."

He could hear her hesitation.

"My mother had fled when they found you and Hester—" It was strange to hear Fleur use his mother's full name. "—And you know that my father took you back to the keep, for you have been told that many times."

It was true. Sir Guy had told him the story over and over as a boy, when it gradually became clear that Linden would never remember it fully himself.

"But you do not remember why you went into the sea?"

It was a question, he understood.

"No," he said, shortly. "Why? Do you?"

"Yes," she said, starkly. "Father suggested it to you."

Linden paused. "What are you saying?"

"He encouraged you to go and play on the beach. Then he encouraged you to swim in the water. You knew how to swim even as a child then, I am told. You must have been overly confident, but still, you did not know of the undercurrent. Father did know.

"Why?" Linden whispered. His stomach felt knotted and tight.

Fleur ignored the question. "When you went in, he must have known you would soon be in distress. He ran back to the keep, calling for help. And the very person he most hoped to see was there. Your father. He ran down to the beach. He saw you in the water. And he went in after you."

"Yes," Linden whispered. "I know this part."

"Your father pulled you out of the water—" Fleur continued.

"I made my way out on my own somehow. He must have pushed me close to shore," Linden corrected. Or so he had been told.

"No, that is not what happened."

"No?"

"No, Linden. He pulled you out of the water, onto the beach. He was exhausted but alive. You ran to get help,"

No, no, no. This was not the way the story went.

"No, your father found me there, lying on the beach," Linden corrected, stubbornly.

"You were up and on your feet," Fleur contradicted. "You ran for help. You ran straight to my father."

"I do not understand," Linden said, slowly—while fearing he already did. "Why did he not help? Had the tide washed Father into the sea again?" That was possible.

"No, it was not the tide," Fleur said, her voice dropping to a weary whisper again. "You know that, Linden. Some part of you must know."

She sighed when he did not answer. "Father sent you back to the keep, telling you to bring more help. You collapsed somewhere between there and the village, while Father made his way down to the beach." Her voice broke. "He could have saved Gabriel. He could have saved your father. But he didn't. He dragged him back into the water."

"But Cam and Jock and the others..." Linden said.

"They arrived just in time to see father, soaked to the bone, standing there looking out to sea. He claimed he had tried to save Gabriel. That was why he was wet. But he was not a strong swimmer. Indeed, he could hardly swim at all. Everyone knew that. So they did not blame him."

They were nearing the bottom of the stairs.

"Hold the lantern up," Linden demanded, suddenly.

There was blood on the steps. First a little. Then, at the bottom, a pool of it.

"Whose blood?" he asked aloud.

"Mrs. Lennox's perhaps? Or Gracie's? But certainly one of them," Fleur said, wearily. "Come, follow me."

"Where did your mother go? Why did your father not kill me instead?" Linden demanded, as he trailed behind. He could hear the latent fury in his voice. There was no way to hide it.

Fleur seemed to understand.

"I believe he tried when he sent you into the sea. When it did not work, he had a new idea. It must have seemed like enough, for he did not try again."

A new idea. Of course.

"Arranging for us to wed," Linden said, bitterly. "It was not my parents wish."

"No," Fleur said. "Perhaps they would have approved of our marrying if they had lived, if none of this had happened. But we have no way of knowing. They had never even met me."

"All those lies." Linden clenched his jaw.

"He is a master of lies," Fleur agreed. "He told me many as well."

"When did you know the truth?" Linden demanded.

"The full truth?" Fleur shook her head. "Only a few days ago. After he was attacked in the forest. Mother had escaped again. He went to bring her back. She fought him off. I wanted to tell you then. Everything. That was when he told me about Gabriel."

"Why tell you?" Linden inquired. "Why tell you at all?"

"My mother knew the truth. She had watched him on the beach, you see. She was not always lucid, but at times she would seem so. And at those times, she would sometimes rage against him. He knew that if we went to you and told you the truth of what she had done, all of it was bound to come out in time," she said. "Here, up these stairs."

They had walked through a small, narrow corridor. Windowless and all stone, cool and damp, it must have been in the undercroft—and yet it was apart from it, with no doors leading into the main part of the keep's cellars at all.

Now they had reached an opening.

"Another staircase?" Linden exclaimed.

"Yes, but these go up," Fleur said, sounding weary. "You must go down to go up."

"Where do they lead?" he asked.

"The ramparts. It will take us a few minutes. Go carefully. These stairs are in even worse condition than the last."

He started up. "He told you, thinking you would protect him." It was a statement.

"Yes," Fleur said, quietly. "He counted on that. But when I broke our engagement instead... Well, I do not think he expected that. I have always done as I was told, before this. But I made things worse. Look at what I have done."

"What you have done?" Linden replied in surprise.

"If I had not broken the engagement, this would not have happened," Fleur insisted. "I drove him to do this."

"To do what, exactly? What do you think he has done?" Linden demanded.

Fleur was silent a moment. "He has taken Gracie. I am almost sure of it."

She did not speculate further, Linden noted.

"You knew who had killed the coachman, all this time," Linden observed, still trying to wrap his mind around it. "Yet you said nothing. You let us run around like fools. You put the village in danger. And Gracie! Gracie was attacked. Your mother attacked her in the stables, the day of the festival."

"I... did not know that," Fleur stammered. "No one told me."

"As you did not tell us," Linden shot back.

"I know I have done you a terrible wrong. My family has done you terrible wrong," Fleur accepted. "I can never correct it. I will accept whatever punishment you think just."

"Let's just find Mrs. Lennox and Gracie first," Linden said, tersely. "You really think they will be up here? And where is *here*?"

"The battlements," Fleur said. "Here. We are at the top."

They had reached the end of the stairs. There was nothing there but more stone.

"Push. Hard," Fleur instructed.

Linden threw himself against the wall, not sure what to expect.

The stone moved. Slowly at first, but when he pushed harder, it opened, revealing a gap large enough for them to squeeze through.

It was disorienting to come out into the snowy night after being so confined, but the cold air was refreshing.

"Go slowly," Fleur whispered. "My mother—I think she has been hiding up here. In a room in the guard tower at the end of the parapet, on the east battlement."

Linden nodded.

He started walking forward, slowly at first. The parapet was slick with melted snow and ice beneath.

Then he stopped and turned to Fleur. "You should wait here, Fleur."

"No, I want to come with you," she whispered. "You cannot face him alone."

"You will not be much help to me," he said, matter-of-factly. "If we both wind up trapped. But if you stay back a little way, you can go for help if something should happen to me."

She hesitated, then nodded slowly. "Very well."

He continued forward.

He reached the corner. The unbroken crenellated wall that had hidden him ended here.

He peered around. There were figures in the distance, at the end of the next parapet.

"I see them," he called back to Fleur softly, and saw her nod.

There was no cover. He would be completely exposed.

He carried no weapon, fool that he was. He had his body, his fists. That was all.

But there was no turning back now. If Fleur had told him sooner what he would be up against, it would have been different. But she had not.

He resisted the urge to run somehow, and walked carefully along.

It would not do to simply slip from the parapet and fall over the low battlement exterior wall, onto the cliff beneath, before he had even reached them.

He supposed he should be thankful it was a moonlit night. Fleur had the lantern, but he did not need one to see.

He drew to the midway point of the parapet and the figures began to take shape.

Yes. Warburton was there. He was holding someone in front of him. Gracie.

Behind, Linden could see a huddled figure on the ground. Mrs. Lennox.

He could make out the shape of a woman standing behind Warburton. Fleur's mother, he supposed. He did not even know her name.

She had killed his mother.

He clenched his fists. It would not help to think of that now. He must stay clear-headed. Gracie was still alive. Gracie could be saved.

God willing, Mrs. Lennox, too.

The figure on the ground was still, but that did not mean it was lifeless.

Hc said a silent prayer and took another step forward.

"Warburton," he shouted. "Let them go."

He took another step, then another.

He could see Sir Guy quite clearly now—and yet, he hardly recognized him.

The older man had undergone a transformation, Linden thought in amazement. The portly knight who could hardly catch his breath as he huffed and puffed his way through the castle was gone. He had been replaced by a man who seemed full of life and vigor, who looked taller and stronger than he had ever seemed before.

Instead of being cowed or afraid of Linden's arrival, Warburton had been waiting excitedly.

He was expecting him, Linden realized, his heart sinking. He had done exactly as Sir Guy had hoped.

And there was Gracie. Blood trickling from her brow, her face pale. Sir Guy had one arm clenched around her waist. His other hand held her arms back behind her.

Linden could see she was frightened. But she was hiding it well. Her chin was in the air. Her back was proud and straight.

"Linden," she cried. "Stop."

"Gracie," he shouted, before he could help himself. "Has he hurt you?" It was a stupid question. Of course, she was hurt.

There was a dull ringing in Linden's ears. He raised his fists and cracked his knuckles. He had never been a violent man. But now he longed to see Guy Warburton bleed.

"Good evening, Lord Chevalier," Warburton called, sounding bizarrely jolly. "Fleur brought you then? I knew I could count on her."

Best to hide Fleur's involvement, as much as he could, Linden thought.

"I found my own way," Linden said, keeping his voice level. "You did not really think you were the only one who knew the keep's secrets, did you?"

For a moment Warburton stared as if he believed him. Then he burst out laughing.

"Excellent bluff, my lord. You nearly had me, I must say." Sir Guy smiled.

Linden did not smile back. He took another step forward.

"Ah, ah. That's far enough, I think," Sir Guy cautioned. "No closer."

"Let the women go, Warburton," Linden said, calmly. "What do you want? What do you hope to gain from this? Is it me you want? Then let Gracie go."

"Your new betrothed," Warburton sneered. "You care for her then? More than you ever did my daughter?"

"I care for Fleur. Very much," Linden replied. "Especially now."

"What is that supposed to mean?" Warburton demanded.

"It means Fleur has told me the truth. All these years," Linden said. "You have held us both captives to your lies. That ends tonight."

"She told you all?" Warburton demanded. "Everything?"

Linden stayed silent.

"She covered her mother's crimes. She knew of her guilt. Yet she said nothing," Warburton declared. "Yet still you care for her, you say?"

Linden looked at him coldly. "You are her parents. She was torn in two directions. What child would not yearn to protect her parents?"

"Ah, yes," Warburton agreed. "As you protected your father?"

"You killed him," Linden spat. "He had helped you. Given you everything. Protected your wife. And you killed him."

"He had not given me *everything*," Warburton corrected. "I had hoped you would do that."

"Why did you not simply kill me that day on the beach?" Linden demanded.

Warburton shrugged. "I was sorely tempted. But while I was in the water—dealing with your father—you ran back to the keep to get more help. I had told you to stay put, but stupid child that you were, you did not listen. I lost my chance. And then, it seemed too much trouble. Too much risk. Far better to simply mold you myself. Prepare you for the future I would shape for you and for Fleur. It did not have to be this way, you know. You might have been very happy together."

Warburton frowned. "But it was a mistake. I was weak, too soft. I suppose I cared for you, in a way. Now I must correct my error."

"You lied to me all my life," Linden said in disbelief. "I trusted you like a father."

"Rather stupid of you, but then you were desperate for someone to love," Warburton said. "Everything would have been all right. If Fleur had not found her mother. That changed everything." He shook his head. "If she had only waited. I would have brought her back in time. Agnes was doing so well. She seemed so docile, so obedient."

Linden looked past Warburton to the woman standing behind. She looked like Fleur—but older. Her hair was wild and tangled, her clothing dirty. Linden could see how she might appear frightening.

But right now, she did not seem threatening at all—rather she stared at the back of her husband as if she were the terrified one.

"Why did she kill the coachman?" Linden asked, nodding towards the woman.

Warburton scowled. "Agnes has always believed she is capable of taking care of herself. Somehow, she came to believe I was the yoke breaking her back." Linden did not doubt this was true. He wondered how much Fleur suspected of her father's treatment of her mother.

"She broke free. Ran to the road. When she saw the coach, I take it she threw herself in its path and begged for passage. When the young man denied her, well—" Sir Guy shrugged eloquently. "She does not have much self-control, you see. I suppose she was disappointed."

"Disappointed," Linden repeated. That was rather an understatement—yet how desperate Agnes Warburton must have been.

How different things might be now if the young coach driver had been willing to give the woman passage. Or would things have been even worse? Would Gracie have been killed that night?

It was pointless speculation.

"She attacked you," Linden said, looking past Sir Guy to Agnes Warburton. "That day in the forest, when Jasper found you."

"Yes," Sir Guy acquiesced. "I almost had her then. But I slipped and she took advantage. But then, she did not go far even when she had the chance. And now she has returned to me." He looked over his shoulder fondly towards where his wife stood. "She will be rewarded for her years of patience soon."

Linden took a step forward, while Sir Guy was turned away.

"How is that?" Linden asked, quickly, as Warburton faced him again.

"She will be the new lady of Princewood now, of course," Warburton proclaimed. "Fleur has never wanted the position. And you—" He gave a short laugh. "You wanted it, but were never wanted. Were you? But Agnes—"

He turned to look at his wife again and this time Linden took the chance offered fully.

He ran, closing the distance as quickly as he could. He saw Gracie's eyes widen with hope.

Then Sir Guy turned back. Linden saw something akin to glee light up his face. He let go of Gracie, shoving her roughly down in front of him, reached into the pocket of his coat and pulled out an object which glinted in the moonlight.

A shot rang out and Linden fell.

Chapter 23

When sorrows come, they come not single spies,

But in battalions.

— Hamlet

Gracie heard the sound of her own scream as she ran forward as Linden fell.

She threw herself down next to him on the cold, wet stone.

His eyes were open and he was trying to smile reassuringly. But when he tried to raise himself up on one arm, he winced with pain.

She pushed open the grey wool greatcoat he was wearing and saw the stain of blood spreading across his chest.

Someone was flying towards them, running down the stone parapet.

Fleur did not stop when she reached them, but instead skirted around, and ran straight for her father.

When she reached him, she pummeled him with her fists.

"What have you done?" she raged.

Gracie saw Warburton grab his daughter by the wrist roughly.

"It's all part of the plan, I assure you." He spoke calmly, but Gracie could see he was struggling for composure. "Think of how grateful they will be."

"Grateful?" Fleur seethed. "Who will be grateful when you have murdered Lord Chevalier?"

"The people, of course," Warburton said, frowning impatiently. "When they find out that I have not only caught but stopped the monster in their midst. Oh, they all know that the young man has never been right in the head. Now they will have conclusive proof that he did indeed murder his poor mother, all those many years ago. Why he confessed in my very presence. Not to mention his senseless slaughter of that poor young driver. The tragedy is that these two poor women have fallen prey to his machinations." He shook his head. "And when Mrs. Lennox has always been so kind to Lord Chevalier, too."

"You're madder than Mother," Fleur spat. "Do you truly think I shall go along with this?"

"Help us, Fleur," Gracie cried. "Help me get him below."

Fleur began to move towards them but her father held her fast.

"Let me go," Fleur snarled, twisting and pulling to try to break free.

"I did not want it to come to this," her father said, looking at her sadly.

"Mother," Fleur cried, looking past him and finally engaging the attention of Agnes Warburton. "Tell him to let me go."

The woman behind shook her head and stayed where she was. "I cannot, my darling," Gracie heard her murmur. "But soon we will all be together. Listen to your father."

"Not like this!" Fleur seethed. "Mother, not like this. Not with more deaths. You can't do this. You have tried to escape him for years. Now we must stop him. He will surely hang for this." Gracie heard the girl's voice break. "He has done nothing but harm to you for years. You know it is true. Please, help me now."

"He loves us. He did it because he loves us. It will all be different now. You'll see," Agnes said, her voice shrill and desperate.

"It won't," Fleur whispered, tears streaming down her face. "This is not love."

"That's enough," Sir Guy roared, shoving his daughter down to the ground so hard her head smacked against the stone wall. She let out a cry with a hand to her head, and Gracie could hear her, weeping in the darkness.

Gracie's heart strained in two directions. Terror for Linden. Heartbreak for Fleur. Whatever happened now, at least Fleur had tried. No one could say she had not tried.

There was a rattling sound and a handful of pebbles flew onto the parapet, scattering around Warburton.

Gracie looked about wildly for their source.

"What's all this now?" a familiar voice said, laconically. "Strange place for a family gathering, Warburton, I must say."

"Jasper," Gracie cried, tilting her head up and straining to see him.

He had come from the other direction, and now stood across from them all on the west side of the battements. She could see his figure across the low wall where she sat, holding Linden.

"I should hate to have to use this," he said, raising a pistol in the air. "But it seems I may have to. What have you gone and done now, you doddering old fool?"

"He's a terrible shot," Linden whispered to Gracie, looking up. "Terrible. Truly awful."

Her heart pounded to hear his speak for the first time since he fell. At least he could speak. At least he could breathe. For now.

"That is not precisely reassuring," Gracie whispered back with a gulp.

Linden merely smiled faintly and closed his eyes. She was cradling his head in her lap, trying to wipe the snow from his face as fast as it fell.

When his eyes closed, she put a hand to his mouth. He was breathing, but slowly, and there was a rasping sound coming from his chest as it rose and fell which worried her.

Sir Guy was looking towards Jasper, facing the low stone wall that ran along the interior of the battlements.

"You picked an inopportune time to appear, Young Lennox," Warburton called.

"Jasper," Gracie shouted over him. "Sir Guy has shot Linden. Do you hear? We have to get him away."

Under the light of the moon, Gracie could see Jasper's face clearly as it twisted into an ugly scowl. He held the pistol level. He looked bold and confident. Perhaps he could truly pull this off, she thought, hopefully.

"Is that true, Sir Guy? Have you shot my best friend?" He shook his head. "You truly are stupider than even I gave you credit for."

Out of the corner of her eye, Gracie saw motion.

It was not Fleur nor Agnes.

Mrs. Lennox had sat up in the corner where she had been laying. She was not dead, Gracie thought in sheer relief.

"And what have you done with my mother, you sniveling bastard?" Jasper said softly. "Have you shot her as well?"

Sir Guy sneered. "This will be even more of a pleasure than shooting your friend was, Lennox," he said, raising his pistol. "Let us see who the best shot is, shall we? As I recall, you cannot hit the side of a stable wall if you were standing right across from it."

"My aim has vastly improved," Jasper snapped.

Gracie certainly hoped so. She looked down at Linden. He had not stirred since he last spoke.

When she glanced up again a moment later, everything began to happen at once.

Sir Guy had his pistol leveled at Jasper.

Jasper had returned the gesture—his face furious and bold.

And Mrs. Lennox... Mrs. Lennox was up on her feet.

Then she was running, shrieking as she came flying towards where Warburton stood.

She pushed Agnes Warburton out of her way.

"You leave my son alone," Gracie heard her scream. "You fiend! You mongrel! You cowardly cur!"

And then she was on him.

Sir Guy was a sturdy, heavyset man and Mrs. Lennox merely a petite, plump woman.

One would not think it an even match.

Sir Guy certainly seemed to assume he had the upper hand, for as he turned to face his assailant Gracie glimpsed an eager gleam in his eye.

But Sir Guy had underestimated the strength that righteous fury would lend the small woman.

Paulina Lennox was fueled with the ferocious power of motherhood.

She barreled into him shrieking all the while, like a runaway wagon knocking over a fence.

The momentum of her collision pushed Warburton across the parapet and into the exterior stone wall overlooking the seaside cliffs.

Mrs. Lennox caught herself before she fell against him, hanging onto the edge of the wall with one hand.

But Sir Guy was not so fortunate. He was tilting precariously.

For a split second it looked as if he might manage to right himself.

His hand touched the stone wall for balance and Gracie held her breath.

Then he toppled backwards and was over the low stone wall before anything could be said or done.

Mrs. Lennox rushed to the wall and looked over, an expression of horror on her face.

She turned back towards her son. "Jasper," she cried. "Jasper."

"It is all right," he said. "I'm here. I'm coming."

Gracie saw him running across the parapet, turning the corner, and then he was coming towards them.

But they had forgotten Agnes Warburton.

She had joined Mrs. Lennox in peering over the wall to the cliffs below and now her face was a terrible thing to see as she rounded on Mrs. Lennox. "You've killed him! You've killed my husband."

Gracie could only watch it all unfold.

Jasper still too far to do anything but raise his pistol.

Fleur struggling back up onto to her feet as her mother rushed forward.

Mrs. Lennox raising her hands to ward Agnes off.

"No, Mother," Fleur was shouting. "Stop."

And then Fleur had her. Grasping her mother by her coat, she struggled with all her might to pull her away from Mrs. Lennox who was backed up against the wall.

Jasper had raised his pistol, but now he lowered it again, seeing no way for a clean shot.

Instead, he sped up, reaching his mother's side, and taking her arm to pull her back along the walkway as Fleur struggled to hold Agnes Warburton back.

Fleur's mother was shrieking and flailing and scratching and it was all her daughter could do to hold her fast.

Finally, seeing that Mrs. Lennox had reached Jasper, Fleur abruptly released her mother's coat.

"Mother," she began. "Please..." But that was all she managed to get out.

Agnes Warburton had been straining hard to break free from her daughter and when suddenly she had nothing to strain against, the force of her efforts carried her across the narrow walkway to the opposite side.

The interior stone wall was even lower than the other and was not enough to stop her motion.

If the parapet had been less slick, less icy, perhaps Agnes would have prevailed. But as it was, she let out a long screech and plummeted down into the courtyard below.

Fleur screamed.

It was long, drawn out, agonizing scream that wrenched Gracie's heart to pieces.

Then Fleur was down on her knees, leaning over the stone wall, looking down below.

Mrs. Lennox broke free of Jasper and ran to Fleur like a mother to a hurt child.

"Oh, my poor darling," she murmured, gathering Fleur into her arms. "My poor Fleur. Oh, my darling girl. I am so sorry. So very sorry."

Fleur did not push her away or struggle to break free. She simply sobbed her heart out.

Meanwhile, Linden lay as if dead on Gracie's lap and the horror of their own situation was overtaking her.

She would never be a bride, she thought. He would never be a father. This could not be how it ended. Not for him. Not after all he had endured.

"Jasper," she cried, hearing her voice falter and break. "Help me."

Chapter 24

You have witchcraft in your lips.

— Henry V

Four Days Later

Linden was pretending to sleep.

The door to his room had just opened and he was sure it was Mrs. Lennox again.

The motherly woman had been up and down the stairs to his chamber countless times in the past four days, despite being bruised and battered herself.

Jasper said his mother had painful dark marks up and down her back from where she had been kicked and pushed, then dragged by Sir Guy, with a little help from his wife.

Keeping busy took her mind off her own troubles, Mrs. Lennox told Linden when he suggested she take more time to rest and send a younger servant up to check on him instead. Or, better yet, check on him less in general; but he was too cowardly to suggest this.

Then she had pinched him lightly for suggesting she was no longer young.

For the first two days, Linden had in fact been sleeping most of the time.

He slept so long and so deeply he felt as if he had lost those days.

When he awoke with more awareness, he was informed a surgeon had already come—first the one from the village, then another summoned from Edinburgh who had been a military surgeon and had more experience with bullet wounds. Linden's injuries had been cleaned, then sutured.

He was lucky.

Sir Guy's bullet had passed right through.

Right onto the parapet in fact.

Jasper had gone back up the next day and found it so that his mother would stop fretting about the surgeon being wrong and the bullet still being lodged in Linden's chest. He had then bestowed it upon Linden as a gruesome keepsake.

Linden had tossed it into a drawer.

The bullet had missed his heart and everything of importance.

But far luckier than any of this was that Gracie was alive and whole.

His betrothed was safe. Oh, how that word had taken on a completely different connotation for him than it had with Fleur. As had complementary words such as "bride" and "wife."

Just thinking of the words sent a little shiver of pleasant anticipation through him.

He was a happy man. Or, he would be, someday, if he were ever allowed to leave this room and see his beloved for more than a few minutes before Mrs. Lennox shooed her out again.

"Linden," a soft voice hissed. "Are you truly sleeping?"

His eyes popped open. "Gracie?"

She slipped into the room, closing the door quietly behind her, and came over to his bed.

"I swear, we should call Mrs. Lennox 'Mrs. Cerberus' henceforth," she grumbled. "Five minutes each day! That is the maximum amount of time she thinks you can tolerate of my company, lest you suffer a relapse."

She eyed him suspiciously. "*Will* you suffer a relapse if I stay more than five minutes?"

"I promise, I will not," he assured her, struggling to sit up in the bed. Gracie helped to place some pillows behind to prop him up. "I would not want you to have to face the wrath of Cerberus."

"Wonderful," Gracie said.

He drank in the sight of her eagerly.

Her hands had moved to her hips. She was wearing a pale green day dress of soft cotton which clung to her slender figure and complimented her sandy hair, which she had pinned up in a tousled bun.

They looked at one another for a moment, almost shyly, neither speaking.

"You look very pretty," Linden began, at the same time Gracie exclaimed, "Linden!"

"What?" he stammered, in a panicked voice, expecting to see Mrs. Lennox appear.

Gracie cleared her throat. "I do believe you are recovering *very* nicely," she said with a meaningful look. She was blushing wildly.

He followed the direction of her gaze to where the bedclothes had formed a tent just below his waist.

"Oh. That," he said, feeling his cheeks growing hot.

"How adorable," Gracie said, looking vastly amused by his discomfort.

"What is?" He shifted in the bed, trying to hide the evidence of his arousal, but it was no use.

Gracie snickered. "The delicate shade of pink your face has become," she said. "It is quite sweet."

"I'm glad I amuse you." He glared at her. "If you must know, I miss you greatly. Indeed, I think of little else, confined here as I am," he muttered.

"Oh, poor Linden," Gracie teased, in a faux-sympathetic voice, trying to hide her smile. "Poor, poor Lord Linden, trapped in his tower like a princess in a story. Although I am sure no princess ever suffered from such a condition."

"Not helpful, Gracie," he said, giving her a pained look.

She grinned and gave him a thoughtful look.

"No? What would help?" Before he could stop her, she had leaned forward and run her fingers lightly over the blanket. He groaned.

"Would that help?" she asked, blinking innocently.

"Gracie," he said, groaning again. "Stop torturing me."

"I know, I really shouldn't," she agreed. He saw her bite her lip. "Especially since..."

"Yes?" he prompted.

"Well, we cannot do anything just now," she mumbled, looking a little embarrassed.

"Because I am injured, you mean?" he asked, curiously.

"No," she said, carefully. "Because I should avoid it for a few days just now."

Seeing his confused expression, she came to sit on the edge of his bed.

"We are getting married very soon," she said.

"Yes, I know. I am looking forward to it very much," he said, grinning and taking her hand in his.

He brought it to his lips, plucked one finger up and putting it in his mouth, sucked very slowly, and watched her shudder.

"Linden!"

"What?" he said, smirking. "Go on. We are getting married."

"Yes, and... Well, I know you want children and I do as well, but not just yet," she blurted out. "I mean... Don't you think it would nice for it to be only the two of us for a while? At the start? Some time to simply enjoy one another?"

Linden grinned. "I plan to enjoy you very much."

She hit him lightly on the arm.

"But yes," he said. "Of course, I agree. That makes sense. Though I do not quite understand why that would prevent you today from..."

She hit him again, a little harder this time.

"Ouch," he said, in mock hurt.

"You really do not know much about women, do you?" Gracie said, sighing long-sufferingly.

"Why do you say that?" he said, rather stiffly. "I suppose I do not. Though Jasper did the best he could..."

"Jasper!" Gracie snorted. "It is a sad state of affairs when a man who prefers other men is your only teacher when it comes to female anatomy..."

"Jasper would resent that very much," Linden countered. "In fact, you might be surprised at how knowledgeable he is about the anatomy of both sexes, regardless of his lack of personal interest in one of them. Besides, he did pass on a few tidbits of wisdom... which I believe were accurate."

"I suppose he did," Gracie acknowledged. "I suppose he did not discuss women's courses with you in great detail, however?"

Linden reddened.

"Just as I thought." Gracie tilted her head consideringly. "For now, all you need to know is that if we do not wish for a child just yet, we should try to abstain at certain times. I will track my courses, you see, and there are times when it is... more likely to happen than others."

Linden was fascinated. "You will? And does this method of calculation work?"

"It has worked for my sister Claire for years. Gwendolen has six children now, so either it was dreadfully ineffective or she has merely not bothered. As for Rosalind, she and her husband have been away traveling so much that the topic has never come up between us." Gracie smiled wickedly. "But when she arrives, I will tell her you are interested in discussing it with her."

Linden's eyes widened. "You certainly will not. I cannot imagine a more awkward thing to discuss with one of your sisters."

Gracie waved a hand. "Oh, they are all very practical women. You need not be shy."

"In any case..." Linden cleared his throat. "I understand why we should not... today. And I thank you for explaining."

Gracie was looking at him in a funny way. "Of course, that is not all there is to it, you know."

"Of course, I know," Linden said, slightly crossly, not at all certain that he did. "What do you mean?"

He remembered the exquisite delight of touching her with his fingers.

However, to stand and do so would require a stamina he was not sure he possessed right now, if he were being honest with himself.

"I could pleasure you, for one," Gracie suggested, not meeting his eyes.

"You could," he said, entertained by her attempt to seem worldly-wise. "Except that it is not my turn."

"Your turn? What do you mean by that?" Her face broke into an amused grin. "Linden, do you mean to tell me that you are... keeping score?"

"Not precisely," he said, blushing. "But I have not forgotten that when we—" He cleared his throat.

"Madc love?" Gracie supplied.

"Yes, when we made love last time, it was not completely satisfactory for you," he said, feeling awkward.

"Oh, Linden," she said, softly. She leaned forward to kiss his lips. "It was very satisfactory."

"Yes, but you did not..." He trailed off.

"No, I did not that time," she accepted. "Very well. What would you like to do then?"

"You mean you think we have time to do anything before Mrs. Lennox storms in again?" he said, shuddering as he imagined her coming across them *in flagrante delicto*.

"Jasper has promised to distract her for at least two hours," Gracie explained. "So, we may do anything. Anything you like."

She leaned closer, smiling in a way he found utterly alluring. Funny how the more time they spent together, the younger and more naïve he felt in some ways, and the older and more sophisticated she seemed in others.

She had seen more of the world, he told himself, so it was natural. Henceforth, they would see more of it together.

He lifted a hand to her face and trailed his fingers lightly down her cheek, to her neck, down across her breastbone, until he reached the edge of the bodice of her dress.

"I have missed the sight of you," he confessed. He let himself look at her, really look at her, from head to toe—from her wide lovely lips, to the softness of her skin, to her narrow waist, and above that, the small swells of her breasts hidden beneath the dress.

"Oh God, Gracie, I have missed the sight of you," he said again, softly.

He met her eyes. "Anything?"

"I said anything," she replied. "Why? What do you have in mind?"

He smiled. "Take off your dress."

A strange expression crossed her face.

"What is it?" he said, quickly.

She swallowed. "I..." She took a deep breath and looked up at the ceiling. "I suppose it is still simply hard for me to really believe that you... desire me."

Linden stared. "Are you joking?"

"No, I am not joking," she complained. She sighed. "Look at me, Linden. I am skinny and plain. Not to mention freckled. I have no chest to speak of. I passed for a boy so easily that you believed it—"

"You made a beautiful boy," Linden protested. "So beautiful I was drawn to you then, boy or girl."

"Yes, well..." She looked down at the floor. "I do not think I am beautiful. But you certainly are. You glow like a marble sculpture."

"Like a sculpture?" he choked out, trying not to laugh.

She swatted him. "Do not laugh at me."

"Very well. You are right. I am sorry," he said, hastily. "I have simply never thought of myself in such a way. But Gracie... Oh, Gracie. How do I convince you that you are beautiful? You are so lovely to me." His voice became huskier. "And I desire you very much." He took her hand and guided it downwards. "Is this not evidence enough for you?"

"Men become aroused from many things," Gracie sniffed. "You might simply be overly warm. Or overly cold."

Linden rolled his eyes and kept her hand in his. "I assure you; it has nothing to do with the temperature and everything to do with you. The instant you entered the room, I was in a state of... well, desperate longing. I lust for you, Gracie."

All of this talk of how lovely she was and how much he wanted her was making him even more uncomfortably hard.

She had offered to do something about it, he knew, but he did not want that—at least, not yet. He wanted to do something for her. Something to make her feel she was the most beautiful woman in the world so that she would never doubt that he saw her as such again.

"Do girls touch themselves as boys do?" he said, suddenly curious.

"Of course," she said, surprised. "At least, the ones I know do. Not that it is a subject we speak of with regularity, but it has come up once or twice."

Linden decided the image of Gracie and her friends discussing how they touched themselves was not likely to help get rid of his erection.

"And will you? Now? Here? For me?" he asked, raising his eyebrows in what he hoped was a charming manner.

Gracie smirked. "You're serious?"

He put his hand to his heart. "Very."

"Fine," she said, abruptly. She looked flustered, but lifted her chin. "Where shall I begin?"

Linden scooted back in the bed a little more. Oh, God. Was this truly happening? Of course, Gracie did not seem particularly enthused, but hopefully that would soon change.

"You might begin with your dress," he suggested, helpfully.

"With taking it off you mean," she muttered. "You are fortunate it's one that buttons on the sides."

She nimbly undid herself and shrugged out of the frock.

Linden frowned. She was still very... well, covered up.

"How many layers do ladies wear?" he complained.

Gracie raised her eyebrows. "Oh, did Jasper not tell you that?" She lifted one hand and began ticking off fingers. "Day dress, petticoat, shift, stockings. Gloves, most of the time, but I hate them. Stays for some women, but I don't need them."

"Thank goodness for that," Linden said, impressed by the lengthy list. "How on earth do you find the time for it all."

"Men's clothing has layers as well," Gracie countered. "I should know. Though they are a little more practical."

"Very well, in any case, please... proceed," Linden said, loftily.

"Of course, my lord," Gracie replied with unconvincing meekness.

She was not getting into the spirit of things as much as he'd hoped, Linden thought, watching as she took off her petticoat.

That was much better. Her shift was loose but where it clung, it did not hide much, being of a very thin white muslin.

He could see the small buds of her breasts, nipples jutting through the fabric, and that oh so tantalizing triangular shadow between her legs.

She bent to tug her stockings off. Then, straightening and meeting his eyes, she raised her hands to her shoulders and pulled the fabric down.

It slid off her shoulders, down her arms, and then... It was just Gracie. Standing before him, slender, bare and beautiful. The flat planes of her firm stomach, her long shapely legs, and everything in between.

"Good Lord," Linden croaked.

"Is this what you wanted?" Gracie said, teasingly, still looking uncomfortable but clearly gratified by his reaction.

Linden nodded emphatically. "Most certainly."

"Very well. Instruct me, Lord Chevalier. What now?"

What now? Linden panicked. He would have to put it all into words.

He took a deep breath.

"Touch your breasts," he commanded.

"There is hardly much to touch," she protested, looking down at herself.

"Uh uh," he tutted, waving a finger. "None of that. No disparaging, my sweet."

She sighed, then raised her hands to her chest.

She was correct that her bust was small for a woman.

But she was wrong if she believed it nothing to lust over. Her breasts were high soft mounds, her nipples a lovely dusky red. They quickly puckered as she ran her hands over them. Linden saw her shiver.

"Lovely," he breathed. "Now the tips. Play with them."

She hesitated, then rubbed her thumbs over the puckered peaks, and let out a little gasp.

Linden clenched the bedsheets with both hands. Part of him wanted to tell her to bring herself over to him right now.

"More," he whispered, and watched as she cupped and squeezed her breasts, then took each nipple between thumb and forefinger and teased the puckering tips, rolling them gently. She moaned, and he let out a shuddering breath of his own, imagining the sensations she was feeling.

"Put a hand between your legs now," Linden whispered. "Spread your legs for me. Stroke yourself."

That was three commands and he expected her to complain or make a witty jibe. But instead, she ran her right hand down, seductively slow, over her sleek belly, down past her navel, and into the curling dark hairs below.

She took a shaky step towards him, then, let her fingers find their aim, and released a ragged breath.

"Does it feel good?" Linden asked, softly. "Touching yourself? Knowing I'm watching you and wanting you so badly? God, Gracie, you're hot and wet, aren't you? I want you so much."

She was too distracted to reply, fingers sliding between her legs and into the slick wetness. She was so close he could smell her sex, sweet and delicious.

She stroked her fingers back and forth, her thumb touching and teasing the sensitive crest above, then let out a moan of frustration. Desire denied.

"Linden," she implored. "This is all very well when I am alone, but you are right here and I want you."

She took in his rapt expression, his still-tented bedclothes.

"I want you," she insisted again, more urgently. "But you are... still too injured for this."

Damn if he didn't want to agree with her—but he knew she was right. If she mounted him, he could see his sutures coming loose as he lost control inside her.

That...would not be at all pleasant.

But there was another arrow in his quiver, thanks to Jasper.

"Come here," he instructed, holding out his hands to her. "Come up, onto the bed. Yes, that's it. Now shimmy up here, closer, closer."

"But..." Gracie whispered. "Linden, what are you..."

"Oh, your sisters did not tell you about this?" Linden teased. "Closer."

He reached up to hold her hips and tugged her down to him, breathing in the smell of her sex. That enticing smell alone could make him hard. He might come from that alone.

Gracie was twisting under his hands anxiously.

"Shhh," he said, reassuringly. "Please, let me do this."

And then he opened his mouth, tugged her down, and licked—a long, languid lick across that wet cleft, tasting her salty tartness. She moaned, tried to pull away, but he held her fast and licked again, more firmly this time, opening her folds gently with his mouth, then plunging his tongue inside.

"Oh, my God, Linden," Gracie breathed. "What are you doing to me?"

"Do you like it?" he murmured from beneath, as he licked again and again, sinuously stroking her with his tongue, rubbing his lips upon her heat.

He brought one hand between her legs to gently rub the sensitive bud just above, as he glided his tongue across her center, her thighs spreading wider as she became more and more overcome.

She was moaning, arching, murmuring words of praise and entreaty as he worked, and he loved it. He loved this. He loved her. He wanted her, all of her. He wanted to bring her to climax with his mouth, in his mouth, over him, all over, just like this. His cock was hard and heavy and throbbing. He ignored it, breathing in the scent of her arousal, relishing the sounds of her uninhibited enjoyment.

This was about Gracie. What she deserved. What she needed.

He paused a moment to move his thumb from her bud, replacing it with his lips, kissing it gently, then covering it with his tongue, flicking in quick strokes, before finally placing his mouth over it fully and sucking.

Gracie let out a long moan and reached a hand up to cover her mouth.

If Mrs. Lennox entered right now, Linden thought, recklessly, he would dismiss her on the spot. Fortunately, she did not appear.

He continued his work, making circles with his tongue against the tight hard bud that was so close to bringing her to ecstasy, while working his hand down between her thighs, sliding his fingers back and forth through the salty slickness of her quim. He stroked between her cleft, slowly at first, enjoying the soft wet silkiness of her, then thrust two fingers inside, spearing hard and fast, then hard and fast again, listening for her reaction as his cue. She cried out, arched and bucked against his hand, and he sucked again, thrust again, again, and again, knowing she was close, so close.

And then she came. Clenching around his fingers, wetness trickling down. Her body shuddering, then relaxing as the waves of warm bliss passed over her.

He slid his fingers out and moved his hands back to her waist, holding her gently as she finished trembling.

He wanted to pull her down against his chest, kiss her senseless, then push his cock inside her.

But that could wait. He could wait.

She sat drowsily a moment, shivering though the room was warm, then brought her hands to his face and lowered her lips to his, joining her fierce heat to his urgently, her tongue darting inside his mouth, quick and sweet, repaying him in kind.

He groaned and broke the kiss. "I beg you, Gracie. Have mercy upon me. No more for now. No more."

She looked highly entertained, her eyes sparkling. "As you wish, my sweet." She lay down beside him and snuggled up closer. He reached an arm out to pull her close, enjoying the simple delight of her warm bare body against him.

"We should have a little while longer," Gracie said, stifling a yawn. "That was lovely."

She ran a hand over his chest, very gently. "And to think you might never have touched me again," she said, very softly.

He hesitated, then spoke, "Were you frightened that night?"

This was the first extended period of time they had spent together alone since that awful night on the battlements.

They had needed to feel the closeness of one another's body before turning to words, he realized.

He felt reconnected to her now, as if nothing could tear them apart.

"You met death head-on and lived," Gracie said, frankly. "But at the time, I thought you were dying in my arms. Everything I had dreamt of seemed as if it were blowing away on the wind." She took a breath. "Which seems so selfish now, to only be thinking of myself. My dreams. When poor Fleur..."

"Have you seen her since?" Linden asked.

"No," Gracie replied. "She has not come to see you?"

"Mrs. Lennox may have turned her away for all I know. But no, I think not." His jaw tightened. "I do wish to see her soon though. To tell her she has nothing to fear. That she will always have a home here, for as long as she wants it."

"That is what I hoped you would say," Gracie said, softly. "You know her mother lives?"

"I did not," Linden answered, shocked. "No one told me."

"She is barely hanging on," Gracie said, hesitantly. "But there is a chance she will pull through. Her legs were badly damaged in the fall. She may never walk again."

"And Sir Guy?" Linden frowned. "Has he...?"

"No." He felt Gracie shake her head against his chest. "He was not so fortunate. Is it terribly wrong that I am so glad?"

"I don't think so," Linden said, slowly. "It is not wrong. But it does seem awful for Fleur to be left so alone in the world and to have had to deal with such terrible things by herself, with no guidance from anyone. It will sound strange to you, perhaps, but I will miss him. It is still hard to believe that 'faithful steward' was simply a role to him. One he played very well. I will miss the Warburton I thought I knew, the one I used to believe truly cared for me under all that bluster."

"I understand," Gracie said. "If you feel that way, it must be ten times harder for Fleur. If he had not fallen, if Mrs. Lennox had not stopped him..."

He knew what she meant. Would Warburton have eliminated his own daughter as easily as he planned to eliminate Mrs. Lennox and Gracie? Then blamed Linden for her murder?

Would Fleur's mother have stood for it? Her loyalty to her husband seemed so strong. She had been so deluded by his promises.

"Where is Fleur now?" Linden asked, abruptly. "Has she been all alone?" He pictured her sitting in the library, neglected and alone, and was sorely troubled.

"No, she has not," Gracie promised. "Do not trouble yourself on that account. You are not the only one Mrs. Lennox has been fretting over. She has taken Fleur under her wing. Or at least, as much under her wing as a mother hen could manage to do with such an entirely different creature."

"That is good," Linden said, relaxing. "Now if only Mrs. Lennox would devote all of her energies to Fleur instead of to me."

Gracie chuckled. "Don't count on that. Of her three 'children,' you are her favorite after Jasper, I think. But it has been heartwarming to see her put aside her dislike for Fleur and simply try to love her as best she can. Mrs. Lennox has a very large heart. She reminds me of my mother, in that way."

She stood up and started putting on her clothes. "I should go."

"Your mother," Linden mused. "Will she like me?" He blanched. "What will she say when she hears the full extent of all of your dangerous adventures? Of how close you came to…" He could not even finish.

"Oh, is that what we will be calling them going forward?" Gracie said, archly. "Adventures?"

"Escapades?" Linden suggested, with a small smile. "Travails?"

Gracie finished buttoning her dress and leaned over to kiss the tip of his nose. "The Noble Exploits of Gracie Gardner."

"Yes, I prefer noble to dangerous," Linden agreed. "In fact, perhaps you might leave out a few chapters when you retell all of this to your family."

"Perhaps," Grac
the room.

Jasper held up his hands. "I
your mysterious errand."

Mrs. Lennox smiled

Brushing the
and took
for co

"Has Fleur been like that all day?" Jasper whispered, as he came into the cottage carrying an armful of chopped wood.

Mrs. Lennox put a finger to her lips and nodded, then crossed the room to pull shut the door of the second bedroom.

"Well, at least she is putting my bed to good use," Jasper remarked. "Though I did not think she would be spending all of her time in it."

"I can hardly get her to eat," Mrs. Lennox said with a sigh. "Oh, I wish your father were back."

"Where has he gone off to, anyhow?" Jasper asked, curiously, putting the stack of wood down next to the hearth. "I don't recall you mentioning it."

"He went on an important errand," Mrs. Lennox said, cryptically. "Never you mind about what."

wouldn't dream of prying into

. "You silly boy."

flour off her hands, she stepped towards him
him by the shoulders. "Have I already thanked you
ning to save your mother?"

am fairly certain it was you who did the saving," Jasper observed. "All I did was nearly get myself shot."

Mrs. Lennox's face fell. "While I murdered a man."

Jasper took her gently by the arms. "Firstly, you did not know that would be the outcome. Secondly, you protected me, not to mention Fleur, Gracie, and Linden. That night was only ever going to end badly, Mother. You know that. This was the best outcome we could have hoped for. He died by accident, not intention."

"Yes, but..." Her brow was furrowed. "But that poor girl. What will become of her now? What will she do?"

"Does she have any other family? Any family that are not murderous or consumed by greed and envy, that is?" Jasper inquired.

"She has an aunt in London, I believe," Mrs. Lennox said, frowning thoughtfully. "But I do not know what kind of a woman she is, or if she has a family of her own."

"Perhaps Fleur should inquire and consider going to her," Jasper suggested, looking unusually serious. "A change of scenery. Some place where people won't know what happened. It could be good for her. Might be a chance to start afresh."

"Go all the way to London!" Mrs. Lennox exclaimed. "Away from everything that is familiar? And from the people who do care about her?"

Jasper gave a small smile. "Perhaps she would not be so far from all of them."

His mother studied him a moment. "You and Peter have ended things, then?"

Jasper nodded. "It's for the best. Well, it's best for Peter, in any case. He'll find a girl, marry, have a dull but safe country life. Most importantly, he'll never have to worry about not fitting in."

"I've quite enjoyed a dull country life," his mother mused. "It has been a fairly happy one. These past few days excepted. But I am sorry. Not for you, but for Peter. He does not realize what he has lost. But I hope he will be happy with his decision."

Her face softened. "Are you really thinking of London, Jasper? So far away from us?"

Jasper shrugged. "I don't know. For now, it is just a thought. But perhaps I could do some good. Kill two birds with one stone, as it were. I could squire Fleur about, make her feel less alone. And if her aunt turns out to be a tyrant, I'd be there to do something about it."

"I rather like the idea," his mother said. "We would miss you, terribly, of course. But I rather like the idea of you and Fleur together. She could write to tell me of all the mischief you will surely get up to."

Jasper waggled his eyebrows. "How do you know it won't be Fleur getting into hijinks?"

His mother let out a snort just as the bedroom door opened.

"Fleur," Mrs. Lennox exclaimed in delight. "Come out, come out. Jasper has just stopped in for a visit."

"I thought perhaps Mr. Lennox had come back," Fleur said, walking slowly out of the room like a sleepwalker. She was thinner than she had been before, and paler, too. The black crepe dress she wore was wrinkled, as if it had been slept in. "I can leave you two alone to your visit."

"Nonsense," Mrs. Lennox scoffed. "You are one of the family now, Fleur. Take a seat by the fire. Here—take this chair. It's very comfortable. Can I bring you something to eat? Try to manage something, dear, won't you please?"

"Perhaps some tea..." Fleur said, trying to smile and failing miserably.

Mrs. Lennox nodded and bustled about the room. "Mr. Lennox will be back soon. And when he returns, he might have a piece of news that will brighten us all up. You mark my words."

She perked up. "Oh, and of course, there is the wedding to plan! That will be a happy occasion."

"But first a burial," Fleur said, quietly.

"Yes, of course," Mrs. Lennox said, looking distressed. "Of course, that must come first."

"Linden has said that—" Jasper cleared his throat. "If you wish it, your father may be buried in the Princewood plot. Or there is the village one, of course."

"The village would be best, I think," Fleur said. "I do not think it would be right to..." She shook her head and trailed off, gazing into the fire.

Jasper exchanged a look with his mother. "Well, I'll be off. If you need anything, you know where to find me."

He had been staying in the keep, having given up his room to Fleur. Mrs. Lennox had insisted staying in the keep would not be good for Fleur right now—not to mention the constant presence of her father's body laid out for burial.

"Jasper has suggested you might go with him to London," Mrs. Lennox said, once the door had closed and the tea had been made. "Should you like that, do you think, my dear?"

"To London?" Fleur looked at her blankly.

"Yes, a change of scenery might be good for you," Mrs. Lennox said, tentatively. "You have an aunt in London, I believe?"

"Yes, but I have not seen her since I was a small child," Fleur murmured. "London," she said again. "So far away."

She met Mrs. Lennox's eyes. "Does Linden want me to leave? Should I pack now, do you think? Is Mother able to be moved?"

"Linden wish you to leave?" Mrs. Lennox exclaimed. "No, of course he does not expect you to go. Quite the opposite. From what I understand, he wishes for Princewood to remain your home, as long as you would like. No, London was not Lord Chevalier's idea, my dear. That scheme was all Jasper. Perhaps a foolish idea. So far for you to go, and if your aunt is all but a stranger."

Mrs. Lennox rose up to refill her teacup. "As for your poor mother, if she recovers, you will have to decide what you wish done."

"If her actions become public knowledge, there will be a trial, I suppose," Fleur said, miserably.

"I am sure the poor coachman's family would appreciate knowing the truth of what happened," Mrs. Lennox said. "But they may not wish for a trial either." She cleared her throat. "I know that Lord Chevalier has suggested some kind of compensation for their loss if they would agree to avoid a trial. In turn, he would ensure that your mother…"

"Will not hurt anyone again?" Fleur finished. She looked down at her teacup. "She was not always like this. Part of it was father, of course. But also, the terrible time she had."

"Yes, I understand she experienced awful loss which may have contributed to it. That is sometimes the way, with women, after a confinement. A terrible dark cloud comes down on them. I myself had a melancholic spell after I was brought to bed with Jasper. Of course, that is not to imply that all women who suffer from that become... Well." Mrs. Lennox stopped abruptly.

"Violent murderers," Fleur supplied, dully, stirring her tea.

"Yes, quite." Mrs. Lennox pursed her lips. "I know that Lord Chevalier is also making inquiries into the possibility of Lady Warburton being sent to Ticehurst."

"Ticehurst? The asylum in Sussex?" Fleur exclaimed. "So far."

"It is far," Mrs. Lennox agreed. "But it is a private asylum. And I am given to understand, a far better place than most."

"It must be very expensive," Fleur said, slowly.

"Now, you must not worry about that," Mrs. Lennox said, briskly. "Linden will speak with you about it when he has an opportunity. He wishes to do everything in his power to help."

"You've spoken with him about it all," Fleur observed.

"Well, my dear, we did not have much choice but to speak of it without you," Mrs. Lennox said, gently.

"No, that is not what I mean," Fleur said. She closed her eyes briefly, then leaned forward to grasp the older woman's hand. "Thank you. For your kindness. I am sorry I have not been... much help... with everything."

"All any of us wish for you is that you rest and recover. Small steps," Mrs. Lennox chided gently, standing and going over to the table. "And now, some bread and cheese for you, I think. You must try to eat, my dear. And perhaps you will think on that idea of Jasper's, wild though it seems. A fresh start might be just what you need."

Chapter 25

O, grief hath changed me since you saw me last,

[...] But tell me yet, dost thou not know my voice?

— The Comedy of Errors

Early one morning, a few days later, Linden woke to the sound of singing. It was a familiar tune. An old hunting song that he remembered hearing in his childhood.

A man's voice sang of a stag being hunted in the woods...

The Hart Royal sped where the old oak stood,

Dark were his flanks and his lips ran blood.

King John has sent after me companies three,

But none of them shall bring death to me.

They hunted me high and they hunted me low,

With horse and hound and fine crossbow.

All through the land up to Nottingham town,

But never a one could drag me down.

It was a beautiful melody, though haunting at the best of times. Hearing it now brought back a flood of memories.

Jumping out of bed, he crossed over to the window to see who was singing.

A man was in the courtyard below, standing near the stables, brushing down a horse. He was singing as he worked, his deep mellow voice echoing off the stone walls.

Neither the man nor the horse was familiar.

Gracie's family was set to arrive any day, but Linden doubted any of that large party would arrive alone.

Before he quite knew what he was doing, he had dressed and was making his way downstairs and out of the keep.

It had been raining all that long December week, but today the clouds had cleared and the sun shone down.

The strange man stood in a patch of light next to the horse, a beautiful dark bay, still singing.

When he heard Linden approach, he broke off and looked up.

"Good day," he said, with a broad smile. "It seemed too beautiful outside for sleep. Robin and I only arrived last night, but he's longing for a good gallop along that beach of yours. Aren't you Robin?" He ran a gentle hand along the animal's gleaming flank and the horse whinnied its appreciation.

"Who are you?" Linden asked, speaking more bluntly than he meant to. "Where have you come from?"

The man seemed surprised. "Do you work in the keep? I would have thought they'd have told you. I was summoned by the baron himself." He shook his head as if in disbelief. "Ah, a baron. Don't get many of those around Sicilborough."

"Sicilborough? Is that where you've come from? Cam Lennox and our stablemaster just returned from there," Linden noted, furrowing his brow.

"Aye, it's they who brought me the message," the man confirmed.

He was a handsome man, Linden observed. Tall with broad shoulders, but lean in the legs. His hair was a dark gold, streaked with grey. He looked to be about forty or fifty. With that sun-darkened face, it was hard to say. Although the man was dressed plainly, in homespun clothes that had clearly been hard worn, there was still something almost patrician about his bearing.

"They say I have been here before," the man remarked, suddenly, laughing a little. The words sent a shiver down Linden's spine. "I cannot say I recall this place, though there is something about it which makes me feel as if I should."

"I say," the man said, with concern, seeing Linden's expression. "Are you well? You look as if you've seen a ghost, lad. Come. Here, sit down."

He led Lindon over to a hay bale and pushed him down onto it gently.

"Thank you," Linden said, distractedly. "You say you were told you have been here? Who told you that?"

"Oh, the two men you mentioned—Cam and Jock." The man shook his head with a puzzled smile. "At first, they claimed they had come to see my carvings—I carve wood, you see. My wife runs a shop in the village and I sell my wares. Simple things, mind you. Nothing to boast of. But they seemed more interested in asking questions than in the wood. Though they did buy a few gifts for Christmas," he allowed.

"What sort of questions did they ask?" Linden inquired, doing his best to keep the urgency from his voice.

"Oh, you know, questions about the past. I have an odd history, one might say, you see." The man shifted awkwardly. "Most everyone in Sicilborough knows it by now. I was a stranger at first, but now I've lived there nearly fifteen years. I'm not sure what a baron would want with the tale. But they paid me handsomely to come so here I am."

"Tell me the tale," Linden asked. "Please. Would you tell me?"

The man shrugged. "There is not much to tell. They might have told their baron themselves. It is not a long one. I'm a foundling, you see."

Linden furrowed his brow. "A foundling?"

"Aye, a foundling from the sea," the man said, with a twinkle in his eyes. "I was fished out of the water, half-drowned, by a woman from the village fifteen years ago. Remembered nothing and no one. Not even my own name. She renamed me, in fact. Taught me almost from scratch. I was that muddled. Oh, in time some things came back again. Small things—like the song I was singing just now. But nothing that might tell me where I was from, who I was."

"Or what you were doing in the water that day," Linden said, quietly.

"Or that," the man agreed. "It didn't turn out too badly, as it stands. Made the woman my wife in time. We have a good life together. Some days I think the not knowing bothered her more than it ever did me. You can't miss what you don't remember."

Linden's eyes had widened. "You have a wife?"

"She journeyed with me, in fact. Hermione is her name," the man said, cheerfully. "Here she comes now."

A woman had just emerged from the keep, and was tying a red scarf over her hair to keep the breeze from blowing it into tangles. She was a petite dark-skinned woman with a sweet smile, pretty glowing cheeks, and curling grey hair that must once have been nearly black.

She waved when she saw them and made her way over.

"Good morning, my lovely," the man said, pecking her on the cheek before picking her up by the waist and swinging her about as if he were a man of twenty.

The pretty woman giggled like a girl and tugged his arm playfully. "Sebastian! Put me down."

The man set her carefully on the ground again, his eyes shining.

There was love between them, Linden saw, his heart clenching. Anyone could see that.

The woman was watching him as well. Her face changed as she took him in and she glanced back to her husband, then at Linden again, her smile beginning to slip away.

"My lord," the woman said, dropping into a curtsey.

"There is no need for that," Linden said, swiftly, just as the man said, "What do you mean, Hermione?"

"This is Lord Chevalier," his wife explained, before Linden could say anything further. "At least, if I am not mistaken," she added, looking at Linden questioningly.

He nodded.

"The baron himself," the man said, eyes wide. "And here I've been talking to him all this while."

"Do you... recognize him, Sebastian?" she asked her husband, very gently, looking back and forth between the two men again.

"Recognize him?" The man frowned. "I cannot say that I do. Should I recognize him, Hermione?"

Sebastian's wife met Linden's eyes. She was a kind woman. That was plain enough.

"It's all right, my love," she said, hastily. "Are you taking Robin out for a ride?"

"I was trying to," the man said, cheerful once more. "Will you be all right with this gentleman, Hermione?"

"She will be safe with me, I assure you," Linden said, stiffly, bowing his head.

The man did not need telling twice. He mounted the horse and trotted towards the south gate.

It was the route Linden preferred to take, when going for a ride on the beach. But that meant nothing. There were only two gates, after all.

He looked back at Hermione. "Is it possible?"

The woman seemed as shaken as he felt. He felt a twinge of pity. This could change everything for her. Was she afraid of how greatly?

"There is an undeniable likeness between you," she murmured. Almost sadly, Linden thought.

"Yet he remembers nothing at all?" Linden asked.

She shook her head. "Nothing." She hesitated. "I called him Sebastian. Sebastian Mariner. I thought he must be a sailor who had been shipwrecked. Though we never found any pieces of a wreckage on our beaches."

"So, you are Mrs. Mariner then?" Linden remarked.

He could not deny he felt like weeping.

This stranger had had his father these fifteen years. Fifteen years that he and Linden might have spent, together, here at Princewood.

Sicilborough was only a two days journey. All this time. It was unthinkable. Unimaginable. Unspeakably wonderful—a miracle. Yet unspeakably tragic as well, to have been denied a father all these years.

"He does not remember me," Linden said, miserably.

"Perhaps he will in time," Mrs. Mariner said, softly. She took a deep breath. "He remembers more than he may have let on. He has... nightmares. Not so often as he once did, but he gets them."

"What kind of nightmares?" Linden inquired.

"Of your mother, I believe," she said. "Of the day she died. Of you. In his dreams, he is powerless, helpless to save either of you."

"But he did save me. He saved me that day." Linden shook his head. "All this time. For neither of us to have known. It is cruel."

"I know, it is awful," Hermione said, quickly. "How you must hate me." She bit her lip. "I made many inquiries, you know, when he was found. But we all assumed him a sailor. And so, we searched for a ship he might have sailed on, expecting to learn he had fallen overboard or been in a wreck. Never did I expect to find that he was—" She took a breath. "Well, the master of... all of this."

"Though I suppose you are the master now," she said, quickly, blushing. "I'm sorry. I do not know what I am saying."

"Everything feels upside down," Linden said.

"Yes, exactly." She shot him a look of relief.

He made her uncomfortable, he understood. She was afraid he would blame her. She was afraid he would take her husband away.

How frightening that must be for her.

"You have no children together?" he asked, shortly.

"Not precisely, no. I had a daughter. I was a widow, you see. But she is grown now, with children of her own. Three little ones." She smiled at the thought.

"A daughter," Linden said, slowly.

He had a stepsister. His father had another child of a sort. How much time had she spent with her stepfather? He felt terribly jealous of this young woman whose name he did not even know.

"Your friends have told me some of what passed here not so long ago," Hermione said, hesitantly. "Such terrible events."

"Yes," Linden said, curtly.

She pressed on. "The man that was killed—he was a kind of guardian to you, after your parents died. After you... believed they had both died, I mean. His betrayal must have been dreadful, after so many years. At least Sebastian had myself and my daughter. But you—you were all alone, without mother or father. It must have been very lonely."

"I had friends," Linden replied. He felt the need to make this known. He was not a pathetic child for her to feel sympathy for. Though part of him insisted that he was—and that her sympathy was nothing to scorn. "I had... companionship."

"I'm so glad," she said, blushing once more. "I'm sorry. I do not know quite where to go from here." She looked at her feet. "I suppose you will wish to tell Sebastian? Who he really is, I mean?"

Linden stared. Did he wish to? How would he do it? What would the result be? Would his father grieve as if the events had happened only recently? Would he be able to recall anything from that time at all?

It would upset their lives, that much was clear. But his father's much more than his own, not to mention Hermione's.

"No," Linden said, abruptly. "I do not wish to tell him. Not now." He met his stepmother's gaze. "But I do wish to get to know him. And perhaps, someday, you might tell him—when you think he is ready."

He shut his eyes a moment, willing the tears back. She was not his mother. She would never be his mother. But she was his father's wife. She had brought his father happiness when he might have been all alone and desolate. He might have died on that beach, if not for her.

"You rescued him," he said, steadily, opening his eyes gaze back at Hermione Mariner. "You have my gratitude for that. Always. And you will always be welcome here. Not only the two of you, but your daughter and her family as well."

He looked away again, scuffing his feet on the ground. "I am not sure if Cam told you but I am getting married. In a few days, in fact."

He paused. Was it too much? Would she refuse? "I wonder if you might be willing to stay. For the wedding, I mean. I know he does not remember but... I would like my bride to meet my father, even so."

When he looked back up, the tears were coursing down her cheeks.

"Of course," she said. "Of course, we will stay."

Chapter 26

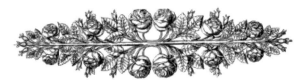

He says he loves my daughter:

I think so too.

— The Winter's Tale

Everywhere Linden went, it seemed there was a Gardner to run into.

Or, if not a Gardner than a relation of a Gardner. Three of whom were, frankly, rather intimidating men—one a sailor, one a squire, and one a duke.

So far, Linden liked the duke the best.

Lord Englefield—or, Angel as he had been instructed to call him—seemed the most lighthearted of his three future brothers in law, despite being at least ten years Linden's senior.

He was certainly the one who smiled the most. Perhaps that was because he had so many children, Linden pondered. Certainly, one had to smile when six young children were constantly chasing after you and begging for "horse rides" on one's back or tickles or stories or playtime.

Of course, not all of the six children belonging to Gracie's sister Gwendolen were so young.

Henry Gibson, Gwendolen's son by her first husband (an earl, no less—she had simply married up and up), was only two years younger than Gracie and certainly past the age of demanding tickles. He was a serious, fine-looking young man. Gracie said her nephew wished to become a physician and was looking forward to attending Oxford the next year.

Of Gracie's three sisters, Rosalind seemed the merriest.

She had put Linden at ease straightaway.

Gwendolen seemed perpetually distracted—as was to be expected from a mother with such a busy brood, while Claire was rather aloof and sarcastic, though Gracie told him not to be put off by this as her bark was worse than her bite. It had not reassured him.

But Rosalind had made every effort to get to know Linden—and best of all, she had regaled him with tales of Gracie's childhood (pockets full of frogs and constantly-muddy petticoats) and their time spent together on the high seas (in which her younger sister had managed to stay hidden in plain sight for more than a month). They commiserated over Gracie's uncanny talent of disguise and had spent a full evening tramping along the beach together.

Only with Rosalind had Linden shared details of all that had occurred since the time Gracie had arrived at the castle.

Gracie herself had told her family an abbreviated version—although Linden was sure that most of them were able to read between the lines quite well.

Particularly Claire and Gracie's mother, Caroline, who seemed wise and astute.

In fact, he was hiding from Caroline Gardner right now.

Well, not precisely hiding—that would be cowardly. But *avoiding* would not be an inaccurate description.

He was currently avoiding her by taking up residence in the library, seated in an armchair across from where Fleur was reading.

Every once in a while, Fleur would glance up, smirk, and then go back to her book.

Linden's book lay before him, sadly neglected. What he really wished to do was go and find his bride.

But every time he sought Gracie out, she was surrounded by relatives—boisterous children or chattering sisters. Or she was cloistered away in conversation with her friend, Isabel Notley, Claire's husband's daughter.

The rest of the time she seemed to always be with her mother or Mrs. Lennox—or both—being fitted for her wedding dress and trousseau.

At least Linden's father and his wife seemed very comfortable with the commotion. Sebastian had hit it off very well with Captain John Merriweather, who had come to Orchard Hill as a guest for Christmas and, when the rest of the family uprooted themselves for the holidays, had come along at the insistence of Rosalind and her husband Philip.

Philip's sister, Cherry, and her daughter Philippa Rose, were there, too. Yesterday, Cam had just narrowly caught Philippa Rose from jumping out of the hayloft and down into a pile of hay nearly two storeys below. The child had grown up in London and seemed blissfully happy to be enjoying country life for a spell—but also blissfully unaware of the different dangers.

Come to think of it, perhaps Philip Calvert was not half so bad for a brother-in-law.

Last night he had taken Linden aside and suggested that he and Gracie consider a wedding trip on one of the ships he owned—the Witch of the Waves. Linden was impressed when Philip suggested surprising Gracie with the idea after the wedding. Linden could think of nothing he would like more than to leave Princewood behind for a time and see some of the world with his new wife.

He must have dozed off, for when he next opened his eyes, the library was nearly dark.

Fleur was still there. She was looking at him with a smirk which was much more pronounced.

"I suppose preparing for a wedding can be quite exhausting," a woman's amused voice said from beside him.

He jolted upright to see Caroline Gardner sitting in the armchair beside him. She was smiling and composed—while he was busily wiping a spot of drool from the corner of his mouth like a child.

"I think I'll leave the two of you alone so you may get to know one another a little better," Fleur said, smiling sweetly and completely out of character.

"How gracious of you, Fleur," he muttered, as she walked past.

"Thank you, Miss Warburton," Mrs. Gardner said, pleasantly.

As Fleur closed the library door behind her, Caroline Gardner looked at him.

"I think you've been avoiding me, Lord Chevalier," she said.

"No. Of course not," Linden protested, stupidly. "I am delighted to have this opportunity. To get to know you better. Just as Fleur said."

"Excellent," Mrs. Gardner said, covering a small smile with her hand. She was a very pretty woman. Perhaps fifty or so. Her dark hair was smoothed back into a stylish chignon. There were strands of silver in it, of course—but these only added to her air of mature beauty.

Linden had seen Captain Merriweather looking at Caroline Gardner more than once with appreciation during dinner. He wondered if she had noticed as well.

"Gracie's father died before she was born," Mrs. Gardner was saying. "She never knew him. I have been father and mother to her, all her life."

"She was fortunate to have you," Linden said, and he meant it. He would have been immeasurably grateful to have his mother or his father beside him all these years.

"Yes, especially considering your own circumstances, I suppose," Caroline Gardner said, softly. "It must have been very difficult."

Linden prayed she was not about to give a sympathetic speech. He appreciated her understanding, but did not wish to be pitied by his bride's mother. He wanted to be seen as strong and competent—especially when it came to caring for her youngest daughter.

"But you have become a fine young man, even without the guidance of parents. It is not only Gracie who says so," she continued. "All of your servants speak nothing but good of you—and I must say, Lord Chevalier, that one may judge a man quite accurately by the way he treats those in his employ."

Linden stared. Had she been speaking with everyone around him? The villagers as well? He cringed as he considered what might have been said.

"Cam and Paulina Lennox are such fine people. They say you are like a son to them. Despite your different stations, they love you very much," she went on.

"I love them as well," Linden interrupted, surprising himself with his fervency.

Mrs. Gardner smiled. "Jasper Lennox sings your praises, of course. As your closest friend, that was no surprise." She paused. "But what did surprise me was what your former fiancée had to say."

Oh, Good Lord. He would strangle Fleur. No, on second thought. He could not strangle her. Not when all of the Gardners were here.

He sank lower in his chair. His former fiancée. He supposed that was an accurate description, although the engagement had never been formalized. What had she said? It could be nothing good. But whatever she had said would have been fair. And true. That was Fleur for you.

"She cares for you very much," Mrs. Gardner said, gently, touching him on the arm.

Linden's eyes must have widened in shock, for Caroline Gardner looked amused again.

"As a dear brother," she clarified. "And a trusted friend. She does not believe you would have suited as anything more and she was very quick to reassure me that she was not in any way opposed to the breaking of your betrothal or to your rather hasty marriage to another woman."

"Gracie said all of the Gardner women married rather hastily," Linden said, weakly.

Caroline Gardner laughed aloud. "That is true. Although, perhaps not in my own case. One might say Henry and I waited for years. Though when it came down to it, we wed quickly once we were able."

"In Gretna Green, I believe. Gracie was telling me," Linden said, leaning forward with interest.

"Yes, it is quite the tale. I will share it with you another time, perhaps," Mrs. Gardner said. "But for now, we are speaking of you and Gracie."

"Of course," Linden said, understanding he had been put in his place and must be patient a little longer.

"The people of your village," Mrs. Gardner went on. "They have quite mixed feelings towards you."

Linden groaned silently. That was an understatement. Mrs. Gardner was being very kind to phrase it that way.

"Some view you with compassion, knowing your past. I spoke with a Mrs. Shepherd who spoke very highly of you. Others view you with appreciation—it seems you have done all you can to help those in need, usually without any expectation of thanks or recognition. A few foolish souls still fear you and see you as a monster, holding you responsible for the events fifteen years ago." Mrs. Gardner stopped and looked at him closely.

"Even though recent revelations may have exonerated you in every way," she said, carefully. "People in the village seem not to have been made fully aware of all of the details of what occurred that night. They do not seem to realize, for instance, that Fleur's mother was the one responsible for your mother, Hester's death. Nor do they know that your father, Gabriel Chevalier, still lives, under the name Sebastian Mariner, though Gracie shared that knowledge with me."

"I did not wish to have Fleur's reputation become as besmirched as my own," Linden said, quietly. "She has already been through enough."

He gave a rueful laugh. "Whereas what does it matter to me if people continue to think me the monster they have always believed me to be? I am used to it. Fleur is not. She should not have to... go through that. I would not wish it on her."

"That is extremely generous-hearted of you," Mrs. Gardner said.

Linden blushed. "I... I do not think it is. Just..." He took a breath and it all came out in a rush. "I have known Fleur so long. And in all that time, she has never been happy. She deserves some happiness. It doesn't seem fair that I should be so happy while she should be so miserable."

"No, it doesn't," Mrs. Gardner agreed. "Life can be horribly cruel and unfair, to those who deserve so much better. And then, it can be so overly generous to those who have done nothing to deserve it at all."

She was silent a moment, looking off into space. Then she shook her head. "Lastly, I spoke with Gracie. Of course, she is brimming over to praise you. Even though she has only known you for a few short weeks, and even though she admits that she fell head over heels for you before really knowing your character at all."

Linden shifted uncomfortably. If he was someone's mother, that would probably not seem like a good thing.

"I was not sure Gracie would ever marry," Mrs. Gardner said. "I certainly did not want her to settle for marrying John Crawford, just because of a foolish mistake. I know she has already spoken to you of this."

"She has. And I could not care less about that. I love her. Neither of us is perfect. No one is," Linden said, emphatically.

"That is very true," she agreed, smiling. "And it is a wise thing to keep in mind when beginning as husband and wife."

A husband. Would Linden truly be one soon? It was like putting on a strange new set of clothes and being uncertain of whether they would fit.

"Lord Chevalier," Mrs. Gardner said. "I am very glad that my daughter has found a man she loves so passionately and so deeply that she wishes to become a wife. None of my daughters had to marry. I would never have pressured them to do so unless it was for love. I am very fortunate that each of my four children have found someone worthy to bestow their love upon. I can already see what my daughter sees in you, and I wish to welcome you to our family."

Linden couldn't speak. He *wanted* to speak. But his throat had closed up entirely. He didn't trust himself to blink either. He was fairly sure water had accumulated there.

He held himself very, very still and waited for the sensations to pass.

Mrs. Gardner was watching him, not with amusement, but with immense compassion.

She leaned forward and took one of his hands in her own smaller ones. They were Gracie's hands, he realized, looking down belatedly. They had the same hands.

"I look forward to knowing you better, Linden, and to coming to love you just as Gracie has," she finished.

That was it. That had done it. He could feel a drop running down his cheek. He was humiliating himself.

Mrs. Gardner reached forward and touched his cheek with one finger, brushing the tear away. "It takes a brave man to let himself feel, Linden. Do not be ashamed of feeling. But it is true that there have been enough tears in this place, haven't there? It is time Princewood experienced some joy."

She rose from her seat and left him alone.

Linden sat in the library until he had quite lost track of time.

A family. He was joining a family.

The prospect made his heart race with unspeakable happiness.

Chapter 27

Kiss me, Kate, we shall be married o'Sunday.

— The Taming of the Shrew

"Gracie, you make a lovely bride," her mother whispered, touching her cheek.

"She is right," Claire agreed, leaning forward to kiss Gracie's cheek. "And it is nice to finally have an opportunity to attend one of my own sisters' weddings." She elbowed Gwendolen in the side, as her older sister stepped up beside her.

"Beautiful," Gwendolen said, ignoring Claire and smiling as she bounced two-year-old Caro on her hip.

Rosalind simply stood there and beamed, tears glistening in her eyes.

"Well, I think you're ready," Caroline Gardner proclaimed. "Come and look at yourself."

She pulled Gracie gently towards the mirror.

Gracie was generally not one to fuss over clothes, but even she had to admit it was a beautiful dress and that, perhaps, she even looked a little beautiful in it.

Her gown was of a fine pale violet silk with a silver gauze overskirt embroidered with seashells and flowers. The neckline was low and scallop-edged, with long-sleeves trimmed with flounces of lace at the wrists. The sash was thick silver satin, with a diamond broach pinned in the center. It had belonged to Linden's mother.

Gracie's hair had been left long and loose, with just a few pieces pulled off her face, held back by pearl-covered clips.

On her head was a crown of greenery—a garland of laurel and ivy.

"You look very, very young and very, very pretty and very, very happy," her mother said, with a hand on her shoulder. "Now let us go to church."

"Perhaps she's changed her mind," Jasper whispered. "It's not too late, you know. Better late than never."

"Hush, Jasper," Mrs. Lennox hissed from the front pew where she sat. "Don't make me come up there and kick you in the shins."

"But Mother," Jasper said, looking offended. "I was merely trying to be—"

"A terrible pest," Linden provided. "She hasn't changed her mind."

But he could not help peering towards the arched stone doorframe again, waiting for it to darken with Gracie's shadow.

Waiting was torture. Especially when the ancient little church was packed to the brim with villagers and Gracie's family—all of whom seemed to be staring at him at the same time.

"There she is," Jasper exclaimed, at the same time Linden saw her.

God, she was beautiful. She fairly shone like a star in her wedding gown.

But she was more than merely beautiful—she was full of love, mirth, wit, and heart. She was his and he was hers. He hoped she was as pleased by the sight of him as he was with her.

"She looks very pretty," Jasper whispered in his ear. "You look very pretty, too."

"Shut up," Linden whispered through clenched teeth. "Enough commentary. From here on in, silence please."

Jasper was quiet for a moment as Gracie walked up the aisle.

"It's too bad she doesn't have any brothers," Jasper hissed, just as Gracie reached them.

Linden rolled his eyes, turned his back, and took his bride's hands in his.

Things went by very quickly after that.

Later, Linden would wonder whether any grooms ever really heard their own wedding service. All he could do was stare at his bride and contemplate how different his existence might have been if he had never met her. It was horrid to think murder had brought them together. He was not sure how that would fit into the stories they would tell their children someday.

Little had he known that night when a boy named Grayson stumbled into the keep, that he had found the missing other half of himself.

He had tried to convey that in the vows that Gracie and he had written for one another.

The vicar had been shockingly lenient about allowing them to tack their own words onto the end of the service. Perhaps it had something to do with the fact that Linden was a baron and paid his salary, but regardless, they were grateful.

"Gracie Gardner," Linden began. "I will love you the rest of my days and beyond. You are the missing piece of me I never knew would make me whole again. You've unlocked a love I never knew I could feel. A happiness I never dreamed I would experience. I vow to treasure you, protect you, honor you, and to stand by you today and tomorrow and every day thereafter until the end of time itself. Please be my wife for I yearn to be your husband."

"Linden Chevalier, you grew to love me when you didn't even know my true name," Gracie began.

Oh, that would be an interesting one for the vicar to figure out, Linden thought, wryly, as he grinned.

"You loved me for me, no matter who that was. You fought for me. You almost died for me. My heart was yours from the moment I met you. I gave it, freely, never expecting to receive yours in return. Now I ask you to be my husband, for I am desperate to be your beloved wife—" There was a scatter of laughter there, and Linden caught Mrs. Lennox wiping away tears.

"With the two of us bound together as one, we will never lack for joy. We will take on any sorrow, any challenge, and face it together. I love you, Linden Chevalier. Have I said that already?" Gracie asked, turning to their guests with a shy grin.

Then there was real laughter and Linden joined in, laughing and crying at the same time, until he was not sure if he was crying from laughing or crying from her words.

He saw his father there at the back, beside Hermione. Her head rested on his shoulder as she looked up at him with tender eyes. Sebastian Mariner, formerly Lord Gabriel Chevalier, was beaming with happiness as he looked towards the front of the church and clapped heartily.

He did not know he was attending the wedding of his own son.

But Linden knew and that was enough.

His heart was full of love and hope—and it was more than enough.

THE END

Need another Gardner Girls fix? Wondering if Caroline will get a second, second chance at love? Curious about what will become of the child John Merriweather has become responsible for?

Sign-up for my newsletter at www.fennaedgewood.com to receive an extended epilogue exclusive to subscribers in late 2021!

P.S. If you enjoyed Hugh Cavendish, the witty rogue from To All the Earls I've Loved Before, be sure check out his story in How to Get Away with Marriage when it releases Christmas 2021!

Thank You!

Dear Readers,

I hope you've enjoyed Gracie's story.

If you enjoy following author newsletters, you can sign up for mine at www.fennaedgewood.com

You'll receive the latest book updates, opportunities for ARC (advance reader copies), giveaways, special promotions, sneak peeks, and other bookish treats, including a FREE special extended epilogue for the Gardner Girls series coming in late 2021, exclusively for subscribers.

If your time spent in the pages of this book was pleasant, I hope you'll consider leaving a quick rating or even a review—as an indie author, your feedback is extremely valuable to me and will help other readers decide whether to read my books as well. (Yes, there is a real person back here!)

I wish you continued happy reading! May your TBR list be never ending.

Fenna

How to Get Away with Marriage: Must Love Scandal, Book 1

How to Get Away with Marriage:

A Fake Engagement Regency Romance

(The Gardner Girls Book 6 / Must Love Scandal Book 1)

The most wanted rogue in London...

Hugh Cavendish—mischievous rogue extraordinaire—has been named one of society's most eligible bachelors. The new title does not sit well with him...nor does the clamoring of debutantes at his door. Adding insult to injury, his father has demanded he marry within the year or risk being cut off.

Determined to buy himself a temporary reprieve, Hugh conscripts a simple school miss into playing the role of his fiancée. What a lark!

This was not the kind of solution she had in mind...

Beatrice "Triss" Weston is a simple, practical young woman, who does not believe in putting up with nonsensical games—like the one proposed by this smooth-talking rogue. No respectable young lady would agree to such an offer, but desperate times call for desperate measures. As Beatrice is forced to give up her position and leave her home behind, accepting employ as Hugh's fake fiancée becomes her only option.

Courting more than scandal...

But their ruse becomes a more dangerous adventure than either of them could ever have anticipated. As Triss's past catches up with her, Hugh not only finds himself at risk of losing his heart, but his head in the bargain.

The Duke Report: Must Love Scandal, Book 2

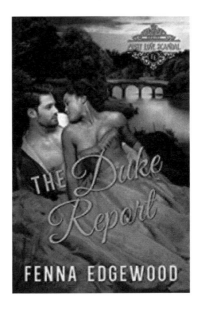

A lady should never pursue a gentleman... nor write scathing exposés about him.

Just because Charlotte "Cherry" Lambe understands the rules of decorum doesn't mean she believes in following them. Enjoying the freedom offered by widowhood, she has dedicated herself to promoting the cause of vulnerable servant women in England, determined to set an example in courage for her young daughter. When she receives a tip from an anonymous source, one of the greatest perpetrators in London seems to have fallen right into her hands and she holds nothing back in putting his evil deeds into print.

Breaking News: The duke is a blackguard!

Ewan Orkney, the Duke of Crossley, is indisputably every-thing a duke should be—handsome, courteous, well-bred, and above-all, a man of honor. At least, Cross holds this rep-utation until a scandalous column is published decrying him as a cruel employer and the leader of an exploitive ring of powerful men. Humiliated and enraged, he resolves to seek out his opponent and issues a public challenge—inviting the anonymous newspaper writer to his estate to conduct their very own private investigation.

Challenge Accepted

Shocked to discover his adversary's identity, the duke soon finds himself intrigued beyond measure. Mrs. Lambe is the opposite of what the duke has been brought up to believe a lady should be. Unconventional, intelligent, and outspo-ken, her outlandish qualities put together with an admitted-ly lovely exterior make for an entrancing combination.

Sinister Plots and Sizzling Seduction

Stirred by the intrepid reporter's wit and passion, the duke is horrified to realize the scandal of the year may be playing out in his very own heart. Yet it soon becomes clear that some-one wishes to silence Mrs. Lambe and her pen for good. As the lady of letters becomes embroiled in a sinister plot, Cross quickly finds himself committed to keeping his erstwhile en-emy safe no matter what the cost.

About Fenna

Fenna is an award-winning retired academic who has studied English literature for most of her life. After a twenty-five-year hiatus from writing romance as a twelve-year-old, she has returned to the genre with a bang. Fenna has lived and traveled across North America, most notably above the Arctic Circle. She resides in Canada with her husband and two tiny tots (who are adorable but generally terrible research assistants).

She loves to connect with other readers and writers. If you'd like to get in touch, receive the latest news on her releases, and get access to free bonus material, please sign up for her newsletter at www.fennaedgewood.com[1] or shoot her an email at "info@fennaedgewood.com"

---

1. http://www.fennaedgewood.com

Printed in Great Britain
by Amazon